STEALING THE SELKIE'S HEART

ELLA ROSE

Published by Lightning Platypus Press

Print ISBN 979-8-9856038-1-1

Cover art by Deranged Doctor Design
(http://www.derangeddoctordesign.com)

ALSO BY ELLA ROSE

THE SELKIE SEAS SERIES

Novels

Losing the Selkie's Skin, a Selkie Seas prequel novella
(https://books2read.com/losingtheselkiesskin)

Stealing the Selkie's Heart, Book 1

Saving the Selkie's Heart, Book 2 (coming December 2022)

Short Stories

"Watched" in *Worlds Apart*,
A M/F selkie flash fiction story (forthcoming)

"The King's Anchor" in *Beyond Atlantis*,
(http://books2read.com/DSPBA)
A M/M selkie short story

CONTENTS

1. Chapter 1   1
2. Chapter 2   6
3. Chapter 3   15
4. Chapter 4   20
5. Chapter 5   25
6. Chapter 6   36
7. Chapter 7   42
8. Chapter 8   52
9. Chapter 9   66
10. Chapter 10   77
11. Chapter 11   84
12. Chapter 12   91
13. Chapter 13   99
14. Chapter 14   110
15. Chapter 15   118
16. Chapter 16   127
17. Chapter 17   143
18. Chapter 18   149

19. Chapter 19   159

20. Chapter 20   165

21. Chapter 21   176

22. Chapter 22   183

23. Chapter 23   190

24. Chapter 24   204

25. Chapter 25   212

26. Chapter 26   218

27. Chapter 27   231

28. Chapter 28   240

29. Chapter 29   245

30. Chapter 30   249

31. Epilogue   261

32. Free Preview of Saving the Selkie's Heart   267

Afterword   276

Acknowledgments   278

About the Author   279

CHAPTER 1

1861, ISLE OF SELBANE, in the Hebrides off the west coast of Scotland

Ronan rose from the water in his seal form, letting his body acclimate to the change in air pressure. The late summer air of the afternoon was cool against his fur, though that didn't bother him. He had enough insulating blubber built up that he didn't feel the cold anymore. His black eyes gazed across the tiny tan pebbles dotting the white sand of the cave.

Deserted, as usual.

He beached himself on the sandy shore, set down the necklace held carefully between his teeth, and reached down with his head. Using his teeth to grasp the small fasteners under his belly, he unhooked the first catch, then the second. Minutes later, the sealskin fell from his naked body like a furry towel sliding off his back.

He stood in his human form and looked down at the sealskin. Selkies rarely came to shore, but he had a different need than just moving about—the meeting with the siren emissary. The war between Ronan's selkie clan, Liath Clann, and the sirens had been long, almost two decades, and now news of the latest siren civil war had changed everything. He had to inform his Prince, Lord Prion, who lived in a small home on the western edge of the island.

Reaching down, he took the silky mass of his sealskin in his large hands, marveling as he always did at the oily, glossy texture of the fur. It was a rich gray-brown and dotted with thick lines of scars around the neck from the decades of battle. He folded the sopping, heavy mass of it with care, tucking the flippers and tail flaps underneath the bottom of the pile. He set it on a rock, out of harm's way, so it wouldn't get stepped on or washed out with the tide.

This cave was his go-to for changing. Secluded and often empty, he had found it by accident when a storm waylaid his clan years ago. Though they seldom stopped in this area, he felt it was good to have safe harbors dotted along the migratory route between their typical breeding grounds in the south and their cooler grounds north of Scotland.

He moved to the far side of the cave, wincing as his tender feet crunched over the small pebbles in the sand. He didn't use them much, and the skin was soft. Dodging the large boulders that sat like sentries along the water's edge, he found the one he was looking for. It was smaller than the rest and sitting close to the rocky wall of the cave.

Behind it, wrapped in oilskin to protect them from the weather, he found his stashed bundle of clothes: a thin cotton shirt and drawstring pants. He slipped them over his body, flinching away from the discomforting feeling of the cloth clinging to his wet body. It was different from the feel of his sealskin, more alien. He couldn't wait to get this meeting over with so he could shuck out of them again and return to the blissful chill of the water.

Despite the tense nature of the siren's emissary meeting, it had gone better than expected. The newest reigning sirens seemed eager to end the war that had lasted between them and Ronan's clan for nearly a decade. Though Ronan knew the sirens often fought amongst themselves, the civil war that had brought about the new ruling class came as a surprise to him. The last siren king and queen had mitigated some of that, uniting the unruly siren clans together under one rule. But a week ago, there had been a new uprising and now the siren clan had fresh rulers, rulers who weren't interested in continuing the war of their predecessors.

But damned if he didn't distrust the sirens. They were a wily bunch, always haggling for more shares of any deal they'd tried previously to negotiate. They loved words and were known for being silver-tongued, often trying to use language to gain more advantages than the opposing group. He would have to be careful with them, for sure, and keep them from adding any small loopholes to the new treaties they had requested.

As Anchor for his clan, Ronan took his responsibility seriously, excluding all other things. Having taken the Anchors' Vow, he eschewed all things that might divert his attention from protecting his clan—no mate, no entanglements, no distractions. He'd been an Anchor ever since he was slightly older than a pup; it was his life. And this peace treaty would help secure the safety of his clan for centuries, long after he'd passed on.

He returned to the necklace and picked it up, weighing the feel against his palm. It was a small necklace, made of the thinnest sea grass twined through thin, grey bones bleached by the sun. At the end was a small dark shell, whose cone ridges diminished to a tip the diameter of an eyelash, impossibly small, and symmetrical the whole way around. A flyspeck cerith and a rare one. It was a gift, brought by the siren emissary, a good-faith gesture to show the sirens wanted peace and not war.

He walked to the mouth of the cave and peeked out. One hand reached up to tousle the long hair that fell to his shoulders in wet tangles, another strange feeling for it not to be smooth fur. He felt an itching across his skin, as if unseen eyes were watching him. Yet, when he scanned the tall sea grass for movement, he saw nothing. He turned and glanced behind him, taking in the cave with a critical eye, searching for any sign of disturbance. But the sand lining the cave was too pebbled, and he couldn't tell if nature or an intruder had disheveled the ground. He cocked his head, preternaturally still as he listened to the surrounding sounds: the whoosh of the sea as the waves spilled over the shoreline, the small tap of water dripping from the roof of the cave ceiling on the boulders, his own heartbeat.

For a moment, it seemed as if there were two heartbeats, an echo that followed his. But it wasn't an external sound. It was something inside his body, a beat, then an answering reply, a call-and-response. For a few beats he felt the repetition and marveled at the new sensation, the same strong rhythm he'd always known, followed by its ghost. Then the moment passed and all he felt was his own again.

It was a strangeness, something of significance, and he marked it to his memory. It was a portent, an omen, he was sure of it, but of what, he couldn't decide. He shrugged to himself, feeling the damp hair cling to his shoulders with the movement.

Time would tell, he supposed. He scanned the grassy area outside the cave again, just to be sure, but saw no one about.

Pocketing the necklace, he set out, stepping over the sandy dunes. He headed toward the westernmost tip of the island, which was the farthest from the sea town that lay along the northern shore. As he walked, he felt the tug at the base of his stomach, just behind his navel, of his sealskin. All selkies had a magical tie that allowed them to return to their skins when in human form. It was possession-magic, which all selkies felt as long as their skins were secluded and safe. The feeling only went away when a non-selkie touched the skin, transferring the magical bond of ownership to themselves. But that had never happened to him, and as long as he kept his skin safe, it never would.

He set his jaw grimly, running through the speech he'd rehearsed for Lord Prion on the way to the cave. It would be enough, he told himself. The gift, the treaty. This was good. It would all turn out okay.

If he told himself enough, maybe he'd believe it.

CHAPTER 2

Una MacCallan was not just a smart woman; she was what her husband used to call "wily." Too wily, he'd said, but that was neither here nor there now. She didn't see it as a negative, though he said it that way—to her, it meant she knew how to survive once he was gone, lost to sea only three years into their marriage.

She remembered the morning she'd found out, having arrived at her fish store on the edge of the harbor to find Walter Brown, deckhand on *The Harvester*, waiting for her. Behind him was a small group of people who had the watchful look of people who are trying not to be noticed but who want to be close enough to hear the conversation. They were too busy doing absolutely nothing, and she didn't like the look of it. People meddling in others' business was a sure way to tick her off.

So she'd met Walter with more aggression than she'd meant to. "Walter Brown, what are you doing hanging around my stand at this hour? You know I'm not open until mid-day." Her voice came out sharp, hard enough that he flinched and glanced uneasily over his shoulder at the group behind him. Una thought she saw several women lean surreptitiously closer.

"Mrs. MacCallan, I... I was sent..." He stammered to a halt, blushing and wringing his hands at his belt. "I mean to say—"

"Well then, say it!" she'd spat, and his blush deepened. Immediately she felt bad for making the young man upset, but she was in a hurry to get her fish supply from the docks, and she didn't have time for this fellow.

"There's been an accident."

Una's scowl slipped from her face in her surprise. There were accidents all the time on the open waters; it was the occupational hazard of being a fishing town. But nobody had ever bothered to inform her of them before; she always heard from them from local gossip from the women who came to her stand to buy fish.

"Blair." The word slipped from her lips, and even before the word was all the way out, Walter was nodding, looking grateful he didn't have to say anything further. Behind him, the crowd was staring, wearing equal expressions of shock and greed.

"His ship hit a reef a few hundred miles out, and... none of the men made it. Captain Campbell was the one who came across the wreckage late last night."

"How did they know it was the *Laguna*?"

"Pieces from the boat, ma'am. From the, you know..."

"The wreckage." Her voice sounded like it was coming from very far away. Dimly she registered the hushed whispers from the crowd, but inside her was a low hum.

What was she going to do without Blair's income? Would she be able to survive? And then, on the tail end of that thought, *I should feel more than this.* It was true that their marriage was not one of love. Blair had been her sea captain father's beloved second-mate, and he'd been around their family since she was young. It had been natural to assume they'd be married someday—the entire town knew he was a good man, and his father couldn't imagine her with anyone else. So she'd said yes when he asked for her hand. She'd been happy with Blair, content even. But love? There was never room for that in their marriage. They'd both known it.

Una brushed her hair back from her face from where the cool wind of late afternoon had blown it into her eyes. So much had changed that day. How would her life have been different if Blair had returned to her? Would she still be selling fish for a meager profit down on the docks? Would the town have turned around for the better, or would the hard times that had come on when she was young still be continuing, as they were today? There was no way to know.

All she knew was that the mussels she was looking for would carry a good price at the fish market, if she could find enough of them. The town's big import was fish, and fishing was what the town was good at—catching them, processing them, feeding their families off it. The sea gave them everything. But not so many of them took the time for the smaller catches, the mussels, the codling and wrasse, the peeler crabs used for bait. That was where she cornered the market, hunting the hard-to-find locales to find the specialties enjoyed by some of the more successful of the islanders in Selbane. The mayor, in fact, had a weakness for mussels, and she expected to sell several pounds to the house servant who bought for him.

She made a mental note to herself to look back through her father's old journals again—though she'd pored over them after his death, she may have missed mention of some of his honey holes, the places where good catches always happened. They might help her later if this mussel adventure didn't play out the way she hoped.

She rubbed her palms together, noting how the rough edges scraped against each other. *This haul better be good*, she thought. Her month depended on it, given the lean times the town was going through.

She had found the cave a few weeks ago, back when she was scouting the shorelines in her small fishing boat for likely harbors for peeling crabs. It was secluded and close enough to the island's saltwater inlet that she bet she'd find plenty of mussels inside. But the water entrance had seemed too small, so she now beached her boat just outside the cave, amid a clump of sea grass to hide it from passing fishermen, and walked a short way past the cave to a rocky outcropping nearby. She'd found the small rocky area after she'd first found the cave and used the natural camouflage of the rocks to hide her mussel-gathering supplies, so she didn't have to haul them with her every time she visited.

Once she grabbed a bucket, she walked back to the cave, stepping around the sandy ground near the wall until she found the mouth entrance.

Inside was a wonder, with a high-arching ceiling of chipped gray stone. A small sandy beach dotted with tan and black pebbles lay at the mouth's edge, surrounded by large boulders that stood like a barrier against the water. She guessed she'd timed it perfectly, arriving during low tide—otherwise, she bet water would mostly fill the cave.

"I couldn't have docked my boat here anyway," she mused as she walked in, stepping carefully to avoid turning her ankle on the shifting sand. She moved to the far side of the cave, where the boulders were closest to the water's edge. Then, crouching down, she dipped her bucket in the water so she'd be able to keep the mussels alive during her trip back, and began hunting for the small black mussel shells she hoped she'd find dug into the side of the boulders. It was important to look for the right kinds: ones that looked clean, not too covered in barnacles, and of a medium size. Too small and they weren't worth the effort it took to prize the meat from inside.

She was in luck! Along the side of several of the boulders, she saw the black mussels sticking up like small mouths where the rocks were still wet. She set to work prying the mussels off with a sharp, twisting motion, grateful for her rough hands that worked better than any set of gloves she knew other fishermen sometimes wore.

She was busy ripping away the mussels when she heard a disturbance in the water, a live-sounding splashing noise. Peeking around the boulder, she hoped not to disturb whatever it was. She knew seals sometimes passed through here and knew they could be dangerous if a human encountered one up close. Still, the lovely creatures were a fascination for her, and she couldn't help but hope to see one up close.

And again, luck was on her side. A large gray seal, a male from the size of him, lumbered out of the water with a loud splash. She marveled at its size and the glossy head that looked left and right as it emerged, scanning the cave for enemies. Or food. She scooted the bucket of mussels further away from the water's edge. The last thing she needed was to lose her catch to some hungry animal.

As she watched, the seal dipped his head towards his belly, she assumed to scratch an itch. But then she saw the skin open, like a coat, revealing pink skin underneath. The seal's head slipped to one side to show a man's head, with gorgeously tousled red hair. His green eyes scanned the cave again, then one hand came up and swept the sealskin from his head as if brushing off a hat. Hands and knees appeared from underneath the sealskin, and then he was rising, naked and glorious, from the sand. The sealskin fell from his back as he stood and sighed.

Una froze in amazement. She knew the lore, probably better than most on the island having learned it all from her father, but to see a selkie in real life... It was incredible. She was watching her childhood stories come true, of men who wore sealcoats and swam in the ocean as an animal, only to come to shore as a human. Yes, she knew her history well, and even as her brain screamed at her that she was seeing magic in the flesh—and what tantalizing flesh it was—another part of her mind was plotting.

She remembered sitting at her father's feet, could still smell his pipe smoke as he talked, telling of the magical tale of how the selkie woman saved the town centuries ago, when the divide between humans and supernatural creatures wasn't so far apart. She remembered how her father described her, as fair as milk and with hair as dark as the sea, as she came forward and brought prosperity to the town. How she took a human husband and gave up the honey holes where fishermen caught boatfuls more than ever before. She had saved the town from ruin, back then, and wasn't it so unlikely that the town would need a savior now if it were to ever flourish again?

She watched the muscles in his fair skin flex, his abdominals contracting as he bent and gathered the sealskin from the water's edge and carefully folded it, placing it ever so gently on a rock to keep it safe.

Yes, she knew her lore. So she kept quiet, appreciating the view as the lean man turned and retrieved a bundle from the far wall. She watched him dress—with some disappointment—and stuff something into his pocket. Then he strode with purpose from the cave, off to whatever business he had on land.

She stayed where she was for a long time, wondering if she had the courage to do what she had planned. Could he be the key to saving the town? Could she tame him, bind him the way the lore said? She'd heard of selkie wives, how the men found the abandoned sealskin and kept it, binding the selkie women to them until they bore children, fey and bountiful, for them. Then they returned the skin and kept the children, letting the women fade back into the water whence they came.

She had no need of a selkie husband, that much was clear. But the town needed help. And if this selkie could tell them where to fish, the town could turn around, could prosper once more.

Rising, mussels momentarily forgotten, she stepped to the rock where the sealskin lay bundled on top of it. With gentle hands, she reached out, caressing the skin, feeling the silky, oily texture of the still-wet fur. It was like a fur coat, she told herself. There was no harm in touching it.

She picked it up, expecting to feel the heavy weight of it. But instead she felt a jolt, like lightning, run up her arms. Her fingers clenched in the skin, bunching the material in her fists. Something had happened. Something magical. Her fingertips still tingled from the electric jolt that had now faded to a slight prickle.

As if jolted into action, she moved quickly, folding the sealskin into a bundle. She looked around the cave for an alcove, an indentation, *somewhere* to hide the skin. She didn't know how long the selkie would be gone, and she needed the skin hidden when he returned. Without that leverage, he would have no reason to help her.

Then she remembered that she already had a hiding hole! Holding the wet sealskin to her chest, sopping the front of her dress, she ran out of the cave to the rocky outcropping where she hid her mussel-gathering buckets. She pulled the buckets out of the hole and carefully placed the sealskin in. Then, using her dress as an apron, she gathered some small stones to cover over the top of the skin.

When she was done, she stepped back and evaluated her work. It would hold. At a quick glance, the area appeared to be nothing more than a rocky outcropping, a natural rock formation in the ground itself. But if the selkie got closer, he would see through the holes that there was something underneath them.

Let's not give him a reason to look around then, she thought.

She ran back to the cave, remembering her mussels. She collected the meager fare, promising herself that if this scheme worked, she wouldn't have to collect another mussel for the rest of her life.

But as she turned, she collided with a hard wall. It knocked her back a step, and she peered at what she'd hit.

Her eyes met the smoldering green gaze of the selkie man, whose anger radiated off his body like a heat wave.

"What have you done?" he growled. His voice carried a dark promise of a threat.

CHAPTER 3

SHE RECOILED, ONE HAND going protectively over her bucket of mussels. Then the rational part of her brain spoke up. *He can't risk hurting you*, it said. *Not until he knows his skin is safe.*

She cocked an eyebrow at him. "Don't worry, it's safe." She hoped he couldn't detect the slight quaver in her voice or notice how her hands trembled around the handle of the bucket. She forced her hands into fists at her side and straightened her back, looking him in the eyes. "But I need your help."

"My help." Barely more than a growl, it wasn't a question. This close, she could see amber flecks in the green irises of his eyes. The pupils themselves weren't round, like a normal person's, but contracted to a slit in the light. The effect was striking and feral. A pink flush reddened the hollows of his cheeks. "Why would I help you?"

She raised her chin. "Because you'll never get your skin back if you don't."

It was a bold statement, one she immediately regretted as his body jerked, nostrils flaring. She recalled stories of fishermen who'd caught wild seals in their nets, how men had gotten mauled trying to cut them free. She had very much ensnared this one in a net of her own, and she prayed she wouldn't get bitten while trying to tame it to her will.

He smoldered in silence, considering her words. His eyes searched hers as if he could read the location of his sealskin off them. She felt an answering flush rise in her cheeks as he stared at her. This close, she felt the primal energy coming off him in waves, and it sparked an answering energy deep inside her. This was a desperate man. And he'd just met an even more desperate woman. She just had to contain how desperate if she wanted any possibility of getting him to capitulate.

He looked away, out toward the sea. She could see the muscles in his jaw flexing in vexation. His nose was very straight in profile, and his close-cropped beard wafted in the wind. "What do you want?"

"Your help. Your knowledge," she amended. "Our town has fallen on hard times of late, and—"

"It's cursed."

"What?" She stared at him in shock.

"Everyone knows these waters are cursed." He turned his vibrant gaze back on her. "I can't help you."

"What do you mean, cursed? It's just a lean time, is all. We're just—"

"It's a curse." He leaned towards her, letting his upper body invade her space. She took a step back to keep distance between them. "Started about twenty-four years ago. We pass through here but never stop. At least, not when we can help it. The water is fouled, the fish dying. The reefs are crumbling to ash, and nothing breeds in these waters anymore. It's dead. Your town is finished." He turned away.

"That's not true!" Una exclaimed, stung. "It's not finished. We just need a few good hauls to find some new fishing grounds." Her voice became low and urgent. "I need your help. Centuries ago, a selkie saved this town by helping it find new areas to fish. That's what I need from you now."

He turned back to her with a scowl. "You think 'a few good hauls' will save this place? You're mistaken. What part of 'cursed' don't you understand?"

And she realized she did understand. "A curse? Really?"

He nodded, jaw flexing. "Now, where is my skin?"

She looked down at her hands, thinking quickly. If the town was cursed, there was no way she could save it herself. She needed help. Someone who knew about magic.

"What do you know about this curse?"

He sighed, and it was an explosive sound of frustration. He ran a hand through his hair, tousling it. "I don't know, lady. It wasn't a natural event. There was no lava seepage or earthquake or natural rift. It wasn't some natural disaster that happened in the water. All I know is that twenty-four years ago, we were making our normal migration through here and..." He shuddered, and the sight made her body feel cold. "It wasn't natural. It was just... wrong. And we all could feel it, even the pups. There was an imbalance to the magic here, something dark and nasty about the waters. It felt like poison. We've avoided it when we can, but it's getting harder and harder to find a safe passageway to our breeding grounds. And now that we're trying to settle a peace treaty with—" He stopped, scowling.

She wondered what he'd been about to say.

"It doesn't matter," he said. "It's just cursed, OK? End of story. Now *where's my skin?*"

But she shook her head. "No, you are a magical creature. And you recognized a curse when it happened. You must help me get rid of it. I can't do it by myself. I don't have any magic."

"That's for sure," he muttered, looking away.

She scowled at him. "What's it going to be? You can leave me here and my town and go back to the water. But you're not getting your skin back until I lift that curse. With or without your help. And there's no telling how long a simple *human*—" she made the word sound like the insult he obviously felt it to be "—might take to figure it out. Can you wait that long?" She crossed her arms in front of her, holding the wrist of the hand holding the bucket, and glared at him, waiting.

He flung an arm out to the side in exasperation. "I've told you everything I know about it! I'm not some shaman that goes around fixing magical maladies. I'm a warrior. I don't deal in magic, and I don't solve human problems. It doesn't do you any good to keep me captive."

"Shaman or not, you're the closest thing I have," she said in a firm voice. "Now what's it going to be?"

He looked out to the sea for a long time, clenching and unclenching his jaw. He was a fine man to look at, if a bit angry and high-minded. He clearly wasn't used to someone else calling the shots.

She watched him, feeling a pull to move closer, to touch and see what his skin felt like. Would it feel like anything she'd ever touched before? Without realizing she was doing it, she reached out a hand and touched his forearm. When her fingers brushed his skin, she felt a jolt, a small electrical spark like when she held his sealskin in her hands. She gasped as he jerked away, but the look in his eyes changed. He looked down at her with a speculative gaze that wasn't there before, a slight wondering in his eyes as he appraised her, as if he couldn't believe she'd had the audacity.

Like a wild animal, she thought, *never touched by human hands.* It had been a mistake to touch him like she would another human, but she hadn't been able to resist. It was a curious thing, this pull she felt towards him, and she supposed it had to do with being so near something so wild.

That had to be it, she told herself with a small mental shake. *Just the newness.*

He gave her a calculating gaze. "All you want from me is to help you lift a curse? And I get my skin back when we do?"

She nodded warily. She didn't know what brought about the sudden acquiescence, but she didn't trust it.

He sighed. "Fine." He spat the word out. "I'll help you." His dark eyes held a mean promise when he looked at her. "But you're going to regret this." He turned and walked towards her boat.

"I already do," she muttered to herself.

CHAPTER 4

RONAN SMOLDERED THE ENTIRE boat ride back to the dock. How could he let himself get caught like this? How could he have made such a simple mistake? It was one thing to lose your skin in the heat of battle, for an enemy to rip it or ruin it while you defended yourself or your clan. But to lose it to a human? It was a horror story told to pups, a cautionary tale to always know where your sealskin was. While it was in your possession, the magic bound you to it, but once another held it, that bond broke, leaving you vulnerable and alone and... human. This was worse than death—it was the loss of the sea, of the clan, of his other half. He didn't know what he would do.

No, that wasn't quite right.

He glared at the back of the woman rowing the boat. Her strong arms pumped the oars with effort on the choppy ocean water, but he didn't offer to help. He would find out what she needed most, other than rescuing her pathetic town. A woman willing to meddle with magic needed something; he just had to figure out what.

Besides, how smart could she be? She didn't know the first thing about magic, other than some fairy story she'd heard as a child. And she certainly didn't know how to help herself, from the threadbare look of the shawl around her shoulders. This was a desperate woman. He just had to find the right button to push, the right key to turn the tables and get her to release him. His clan needed him.

He could have overpowered her, hurt her to make her tell where his skin was. As a soldier, he'd had to do many distasteful things to protect his clan; he wasn't above such actions, if it got him back to them faster. Yet, there was one very uncomfortable truth that made him refrain: she was his True Mate. The other half of their souls, True Mates were the only ones for whom fate paused. And that gave him pause. He could feel the pull to her, like warm water rushing over his skin, drawing him closer, inviting him to touch. She was attractive for a human, that was for sure. That hair, bound in a tight bun at the nape of her slender neck, was shiny and thick from the looks of it, with the sunlight gleaming off it like brushed copper. Her lips, despite being pressed into a thin line, had seemed shapely and a tantalizing shade of pink, cracked though they were from the sea life she obviously led.

It had to be tied to his skin, this desire. Nothing else could explain the spark he'd felt when she'd touched his arm or the exhilaration he felt at the thought of doing it again. This attraction, so similar to the pull of his sealskin, had to be linked somehow. There was no other explanation for it.

But he couldn't give in to it. Fascination or no, he couldn't give in to the pull of her. He'd sworn the Anchor's Vow, had given his life to protecting his clan above all else. He had sworn to eschew love and to never be tied to a mate, regardless of the circumstances. There was too much at stake in his own clan for him to be so selfish and take a mate, to father children—too much distraction from his duties.

He had long ago decided it wasn't part of fate for him, anyway. He'd lived decades without taking a mate. And while, when he'd been younger, the fantastical concept of True Mates, those mates rumored to be the other halves of your soul, had been alluring, he'd grown up to realize it was just a story adults liked to tell. If they even existed, how did one even find their True Mates? They could be dead or in another clan far away or have lived in a time gone past. He'd rather hoped that would be the case for himself, so he'd never face the temptation of choosing a life of love over his sworn duty. He knew that only the strong survived, and he'd made himself as strong as he could be, both physically and emotionally.

And now here he was, captive to a woman he felt a supernatural attraction towards, a *human* of all creatures. It wasn't right. But though he was a soldier, he couldn't bring himself to harm her to get his skin back. No, he'd find some other way to manipulate her. Everyone had their price. He just had to find hers.

As she rowed, Una thought about the selkie she'd captured. She figured it was best to think of him as a selkie instead of a man. Her attraction to him was too strong to ignore, but there were more important things than lust, as she'd well learned.

Strangely enough, the whole experience reminded her of how different things had been with Blair, her lost husband. Being married to him had been convenient, safe, amicable. All the things that were important in life, all the things necessary for two people to survive together. They had made a nice living and enjoyed each other's company. But the physical attraction she felt for the selkie had never been there with Blair. Maybe in the beginning, perhaps, but as time went on and Blair had never approached her in that way, had made no overt loving gestures towards her other than that of a friend and companion, she had learned to let go of the foolish notions of what marriage *should* be like. What she had envisioned as a child was never fully realized, and she learned, as a woman, that love wasn't anything worth pursuing. Not when survival was on the line. The world was not safe, and fanciful notions like love just impeded actual life.

She'd realized that perhaps love just wasn't possible for her. And that was fine—she'd come to terms with it. Though she'd longed for love, for the bright blush of a first kiss to the secret glances her aunt and uncle shared when they thought no one was looking, she knew there were priorities in life, and that fate had not made that a priority in hers. Still, there was some part of her that wished it could have been different. That life wasn't as hard and ruthless. In a better situation, perhaps there would have been time for love. Perhaps there would be room for something other than basic survival. But that wasn't her life, and she was fine with it.

If she told herself that enough, perhaps she'd believe it.

CHAPTER 5

RONAN HESITATED ON THE threshold to her home. Una bustled past him, gathering clothing from the backs of chairs, tidying her simple dish from breakfast that she'd left on the kitchen table.

"Come in," she said, motioning him in with one hand. "I don't bite."

Ronan cast a doubtful look around the inside of the home, taking in the shabby, pock-marked carpet on the floor; the faded couch; the scratched, worn top of the kitchen table. Everything about the place screamed *alone*. The door led straight into a simple living room, which bled into a kitchen nook, and just beyond the stove, he could see a bed with rumpled white sheets and a few pillows. A fireplace sat to the left of the living room and on top of the thick wooden mantle, he saw a wooden box with a strange metal contraption sticking out. It was more of a shack than a home, and he felt cramped inside it.

He stepped over the threshold, instinctively feeling inside himself for the magical pull of his sealskin. Then he shook himself. Of course, he wouldn't feel it, not if it was still in her possession. The lack of it made him feel vulnerable, naked in a way that had nothing to do with clothes. He didn't enjoy feeling so bare in front of a human.

Humans and selkies weren't exactly enemies, but they often steered clear of each other. Selkies had worked for centuries to seed the myth that hunting seals was bad luck, and for just as long, fishermen had respected that. It was a black mark to catch a seal in a fishing net, and while it was a massive inconvenience for the fishermen, they usually tried to free the seals without harming them. And since humans couldn't tell the difference between regular seals and selkies, it made their working relationship easier to bear. They each tried to stay away from the other and let them live their own lives.

And now here he was, planted inside a human town, forced to live in a human hovel.

If Ceannas could see me now, Ronan thought. His second-in-command Anchor would have laughed himself to death.

"So this is where you live?" Ronan tried to keep his voice neutral, but Una paused with an armful of clothing and scowled at him.

"Yes, it is," she said defensively. "And I happen to like it very much."

Ronan raised his eyebrows and put up his hands in a *sorry* gesture. "I was just asking."

"Yeah, well, I didn't ask you to ask, now did I?" She dropped the clothing in a heap on the far side of her bed, near the wall, and blew her hair off her forehead with a gusty sigh. "You can stay here for a bit while we... we... figure all this out."

Ronan bristled. "I didn't ask to come here, remember?" He passed a hand through his hair angrily. "We need to get some things straight. First, I'm not your friend or your pet. If you want to live in a... place... like *this*, feel free. But I'm going to find somewhere hospitable to stay while I'm held captive."

In a flash, the animosity drained from Una's face. "You don't find my home hospitable?" she asked. There was a plaintive note to her voice that struck a chord in him, as if he'd hurt her feelings on purpose. He knew he did nothing wrong, but he suddenly felt ashamed.

"No, I just... it's not..." He sighed, feeling drained of energy, weary beyond measure. "Look, it's been a long and rather disappointing day. I missed a very important meeting that could have far-reaching consequences for my clan. And I missed it because you have a foolhardy mission that's impossible to complete."

"It's not impossible," she breathed. "I know it. I can save this town."

"What has this town ever done for you?" he asked in a nonchalant tone. He was genuinely curious for the first time, but he wondered if she was as fickle as most humans he'd encountered—when pushed, it took little to shake them from their morals. If he could get her to realize how foolish her attempts would be...

"You obviously live a tough life. This place can't be easy to bear. Why haven't you moved on to somewhere easier to live, migrated to better waters?"

"This is my home," she said, putting a hand across her stomach, as if the mere thought of leaving sickened her. "This is the place I grew up in, the place I love."

He shook his head, frowning. "But somewhere *else* could be your home. You could even come to love it. How do you know you wouldn't unless you tried?"

"I could never leave here. My heart is here." She moved to one of the side windows and pointed. From his vantage point, he could only see the ocean stretching out a few yards away. "Because that view has been my life for so long, I can't imagine not seeing it. To live inland, away from the sea life? Do you know that I've mapped that horizon with my eyes for twenty-two years? I know every tree, every outcropping, every wave swell that crosses that two-by-two square of landscape.

"I walk out my front door and I'm greeted by the sight of boats, of ships, of the men and women who man them, who've ridden the ocean for longer than I've been alive. And the people on those boats bring me my livelihood every morning. They help me survive. They took me in when Blair..." She paused and looked down at her hands, which were twisted in her dress front. "When I needed someone the most, they took me in. This town. Those people. And if I don't do something, they will perish. They will lose their livelihoods, and the town will dry up. And then they will lose their homes. I cannot let that happen. Not while I'm still alive and able to stop it."

The passion in her voice captivated him. He saw her face come alive as she looked out the window to her small ocean view, and he understood. He understood completely. It was as if someone had asked him why he never left his clan to go out on his own. To find an easier job or less demanding family. Because it was about family and love and commitment. She had committed to her clan the same way he had committed to his. It was written all over her face as she spoke.

He felt a stirring in his body as he looked at her. She had a flush in her cheeks from her speech that he found remarkably tantalizing. Her hair had come loose from the boat ride, and dark tendrils curled around her cheeks, framing her face. She was not conventionally pretty—her nose was too small, and her face was a little too long for that description. But she captivated him.

He mentally shook himself. *We are nothing alike*, he told himself. *Get a grip on yourself.*

"I just think it would be better if you left off this misguided attempt at saviorhood. It won't bring you anything but grief. It's how curses work."

"How do they work?" she asked, moving around to sit on the armchair. "And please, sit." She indicated the couch across from her.

Reluctantly, he moved forward and sat. The couch was lumpy and sank low underneath him, like a rotted sponge. He re-situated himself further forward so that he perched on the edge of the frame instead. "What do you want to know about them?"

"Everything." Her voice was hungry, her eyes dark pools that he could drown in if he let himself.

He tore his eyes from hers with a mental shake. What was it about her that drew him so completely, made him forget his mission and what he was trying to do?

"I don't know what you did—pissed off someone, killed something sacred... it doesn't matter. Curses work like this: someone or something gets angry, and they lay down hateful magic on you or your clan. It's usually designed to hurt the person who offended the curser. Sometimes there's a certain amount of time that's supposed to pass before the curse is lifted. Sometimes the curse isn't lifted until the transgressor is dead."

Una sat straighter in her chair but made no other motion. Ronan figured it was to her credit she didn't seem shocked or scared by this information. Rather, she seemed to take it in stride, as if news like this was nothing new to her. Then again, he supposed, perhaps it wasn't. He knew nothing about the life she lived here. Perhaps the curse had affected her more than he knew.

"If a creature attached it to somebody, would that person know it?"

"Not necessarily. Maybe the person doesn't understand magic or doesn't let themselves believe in it. Or the curse could be a quiet kind, insidious, that creeps into someone's life like a string of bad luck."

Una gasped. "That's exactly what people have been saying about the town for the last twenty-four years. That we're in a string of bad luck."

"Two decades of bad luck?" Ronan asked. "Are you people really that stupid?"

Una bristled. "Not stupid. We just don't have time for magic. We are simple people. We fish the waters, we feed our families, and we go about our daily lives. There's nothing magical about it or us." Her voice took on a derisive tone. "We don't see lightning and wonder if we angered some elder gods or something. Our ships don't crash because mermaids enticed the sea captain."

Something in Ronan's face must have changed, because she cocked her head. "Don't tell me those creatures are real?"

"I'm not sure about elder gods. Those are beyond me. But mermaids?" He shuddered. "Vile creatures. Like lampreys in the vague shape of human women. We kill them when we can."

Una's mouth pressed into a thin line. "I did not expect to hear that," she said in a prim tone. Then she shook her head. "But unless mermaids caused this curse, they're irrelevant to us."

Ronan smirked. That she could just dismiss fantastical creatures after she'd learned of their existence... it told him a lot about her. That she was the kind of person for whom frivolity and magic didn't exist, or worse, didn't matter. He wondered what she made of him the first time she saw him.

"What do I call you?" she asked suddenly.

He stared at her.

"Really," she insisted. "I'm Una. What do I call you?"

"Your captive?" Ronan said in a derisive tone. Una scowled and waited. "Ronan," he ground out through clenched teeth. "You can call me Ronan."

"Strong name," Una murmured. "And what do you do, Ronan the selkie? In your clan? You seem very concerned about their safety. Are you some kind of warrior there?"

"What do you know about our kind?" he asked instead, trying to keep the urgency from his voice. If she knew about his clan, others might, and that may pose a very real threat.

She shrugged, and a lock of hair fell from her bun to slide down over her shoulder. It caught his attention immediately, and he stared at the thick strands of it. He wondered if it was as silky as it looked. If it would shine when it cascaded across a pillow. He licked his lips at the thought. How delicious would it feel bunched in his fist?

He shook himself, aware that she was staring at him staring at her. A faint blush crept across her cheeks, and he smiled inwardly. It was nice to know he affected her at least a little of the way she affected him.

She broke eye contact and looked toward the window. "Not much. Just what my father told me of the lore growing up."

"The lore?"

"The myths, the legends. The stories of the magical creatures that supposedly lived in our waters." She smiled, and he saw the nostalgia in it. She must have loved her father dearly for such an expression to come across her hard face. "When I was little, he told me the story of the selkie wife, the woman caught from the sea by a fisherman. He saw her change when she came to shore, saw her unfasten the sealskin from her naked body, and when he saw the woman she became, he fell instantly in love with her, such was her beauty and ripeness of body. So much so that he had to have her.

"So he waited until she had left, then he stole her sealskin and hid it away. She was bound to him, body and soul, and she became his wife. She bore him many children, who all sailed away to find their fortunes elsewhere. And then, when he was old and gray, and she hadn't aged but a few years herself, he gave her back her sealskin. She took it to the shore and put it on and slipped into the water, never to be seen again. They say she sought out her children, who sailed far and wide, and looked after them while they were on the water."

She fell silent, staring toward the window without seeing it. Her mind was on her father, of his low, soft voice as he told her the story. She'd mimicked his intonation unconsciously, falling into the rhythm of the storytelling the same way he always had.

"Is that it?"

"Hmm?" Una looked at him as if only just remembering he was there. "Oh, no. There was one other story, of a man who caught a selkie woman and made her his wife. But instead of children, for she could not have them, she bartered her freedom for information. She told him the places to go to catch the most fish and where the prized ones were that would bring in the most money. She gave him the location of honey holes, and he sent his fleet out to bring in the catches."

"And then he gave her freedom in exchange?" Ronan found he was interested, despite himself.

"No," Una said in a regretful tone. "The town prospered under this information, but the man realized it would never be enough. He couldn't let her go—what if the town fell into disrepair again? She was his golden goose, and he could never let her go. It's said he kept her as his wife until he died. Only when he died, it was with the knowledge of where her sealskin was, so that it left her as a human, never to shift into her seal form ever again."

Ronan was horrified. To lose the best part of yourself, the other half of your soul. It was a terrifying prospect. "And how do I know you won't do the same to me?" he asked.

"I swear it," she said. At his skeptical expression, she looked around her room, as if looking for something. Then she rose and crossed to the bookshelf. She withdrew a leather-bound book with fishing line holding the spine together and brought it over to him. She knelt in front of him and set the book on his lap.

"This was my father's journal. It's the most sacred item I possess." She placed her hand palm-down on the cover. "I swear on my father's name I will release you once we lift the curse."

He eyed her. What trust could he put in the promises of humans? Especially after the stories she'd told him. But he had little choice, he figured, and those were children's stories. Lore of things that never happened, however truth-tinged they might be.

When he placed his palm on top of hers, his large hand covered hers. Immediately, her neck tensed, and he saw the flush work its way up the hollows of her cheeks again, saw her breast rise and fall a little more quickly. He smiled. She wasn't so immune to him as he first thought.

"I accept your vow," he said. While he didn't know how much stock he could take in human promises, he knew the importance of them among his people. For his kind, his vow was his soul. He looked into her eyes. "I will help you try to lift this curse," he said in a solemn voice. But silently, in his mind, he added, "... *if I don't get my sealskin back first.*" The faster he got back to his clan to plan the treaty with the sirens, the better.

She nodded once, then stood and put the book away. Her face was still flushed.

Maybe that was the key, he thought as he watched her lean body move beneath the dress she wore. Perhaps he could use her attraction to him to his advantage. She had to be lonely out here by herself, and she'd already admitted there had once been someone in her life... Blaine, was it? Blair? It didn't matter. What mattered was that she once had a taste of love in her life and had lost it. Perhaps she was hungry for it again.

If he could make her fall in love with him, perhaps he could prize out of her where she'd hid his sealskin. It would take some convincing on his part, but given the attraction that was already there... perhaps it wouldn't be as hard as he thought.

He admired the graceful way she stooped to put the book back, the way the dress clung to the slight curves of her body as she moved. The single lock of hair that fell down her back. He felt the lust curling in his stomach as he watched her.

No, it wouldn't be hard at all.

CHAPTER 6

RONAN STOOD, TAKING IN the careful way she brushed the metal implement on the top of the mantle with her fingertips, an almost unconscious gesture. He noted it for later, then cleared his throat. "I need to leave a note for my second-in-command. My clan has to know where I've disappeared to."

Una frowned. "If you leave, how do I know you'll come back?" Ronan stared at her, letting the weight of his displeasure settle on her. She pursed her lips, a nervous habit, and then looked away. "Fine. But you should be back before nightfall. The water's not safe at night."

"I know how safe the ocean can be," Ronan said in a tight voice, his anger simmering under the surface. She flinched, and he felt a rush of unease. So she was a little scared of him? That wouldn't do, not if his goal was seduction. He pitched his voice to a neutral tone to put her more at ease. "I'll be careful," he promised.

"Take my boat. You know how to get back?"

He nodded.

She tore a sheet of paper from one of her father's journals and passed him a writing implement. He frowned down at the paper. What to say? He would have to get a lot of information across in a short space. If he wrote that a human had captured him, Ceannas was sure to rush to his aid, armed and ready to kill. That wouldn't do either. He needed her safe.

"Something came up—a side mission. Let's meet, this cave, two nights at dusk." There, that should keep him at bay long enough for Ronan to get this curse business sorted out. He didn't plan on being here longer than a fortnight, anyway. Surely he could exert his considerable skills in seduction for this lonely woman to fall for him in that time. He would have to ensure that he utilized the time they had together to do it. If he was lucky, he would meet Ceannas in his seal form in two days and they could shepherd the clan to safety.

But what if it took longer than that? He paused. Should he tell Ceannas about Una? Though he trusted his second Anchor with his life, something told him Ceannas would take her as a very definite threat and would act upon it, with or without his consent. Best to keep that part of his situation secret from his friend and only reveal that he would be gone for a time. He could get information from Ceannas and advise him as needed to keep the clan safe in his absence. He'd have to trust Ceannas was up to the job.

Una was watching him closely, and he forced a smile. "I leave you now. I will be back as soon as I can."

"If not, I will come for you," she warned. "I need you too much."

He checked the surge of irritation that flared at her words. He needed her too much, as well. She had no idea how much. His skin was life to him—there was no way of knowing how much she understood about the ties between him and the sealskin, and he had no intention of telling her.

HE MANEUVERED THE BOAT awkwardly, not used to how human arms worked the oars. But he remembered the path as if he'd traveled it hundreds of times, and soon made his way up the inlet to the cave mouth, though it took longer than he liked. He docked the boat in the same place she had, hidden by clumps of sea grass, and entered the cave.

He scanned it with sharp eyes but saw nothing out of place. Nowhere she could have hidden it, even if she was stupid enough to keep it in that very cave. No, she was too clever for that. She would have hidden it somewhere else, somewhere safe from his prying eyes and intuitive gaze.

He dropped to his knees on the sand of the beach, looking for any sign that Ceannas had already been there. There was no sign.

With a sigh, he stood and pinned the note in place on top of a boulder by a rock the size of his fist. He hoped Ceannas would see it, though he knew his second Anchor's sharp eyes missed little. But there wasn't much else he could do, aside from waiting in person for him to come. He would come for Ronan soon, Ronan knew, would trace his path back to this cave, where he knew Ronan had gone to change. He would see the note and understand that something had waylaid Ronan beyond what he could control. Though Ceannas could be hotheaded and rash, being as young as he was, he was sensible and would follow Ronan's lead. If Ronan wasn't concerned, Ceannas wouldn't be.

He sighed. He just had to make sure he came across as confident and in control of the situation, however untrue that was. He could fake it long enough to get his skin back and return to his clan.

Returning to the boat, he pushed it with more force than was necessary to unbeach it from the sand. He hopped inside, hating the feel of his wet trousers clinging to his skin. Every time he had to wear clothes was awful, for that matter, and clothes that felt like binders were even worse. But he couldn't avoid it. He had to pass as human for now, and that meant clothes.

He thought of how Una had looked in her clothes, wearing them as easily as he wore his sealskin. He needed to get under her skin, needed to put her off her game, as haughty as she seemed to act. "You're not getting your skin back until I lift that curse," she'd told him, as if she knew she held his life in her hands. He would have to offset that.

Maybe the secret to putting her in a vulnerable position was to strip her of her version of the sealskin. To get her as naked as possible around him so that she would learn to cling to him, to love him to the point of trust.

The thought of her naked underneath him, her pale flesh pressed against his, brought a certain amount of heat to his body. He would enjoy that part of things, that was for sure. It had been a long time since he'd mated. Though he never bonded with his partners past the physical joining, it would be interesting to see what happened when he did it with her, given the level of attraction that was there, the insatiable pull that she had over him. It was a unique position for him, and he intended to make it a unique position for her, too.

Already he could feel the bond tightening around him, an awareness of her presence that felt very similar to the pull of his sealskin when he was separated from it. He felt drawn to her, slightly anxious for being away from her, and in such a short time. Despite his anger at her actions, he couldn't deny that he wanted her, and badly. He had the bond to thank for that.

His mouth tightened to one side. That was a complication he could have done without. He would do well to avoid encouraging the bond, if possible. He didn't need an actual mated bond—it would derail everything he'd set in order in his life.

No, he would have to remain above it, to keep the bond from strengthening as he seduced her. Must exert all his considerable willpower against it.

He was certain he could do it. There were few things in life he had found himself unable to do once he became determined to do them. And he was determined with her. Determined to force her to submit to him, to his will, to force her to give him back his sealskin.

The thought of her bending to him filled him with a great deal of satisfaction. He could bend her, given time. And now time was all he had. He rowed with a renewed sense of purpose. He would return to her as quickly as possible and begin her seduction immediately. Would play the part of the caring suitor, the intent lover. And then he would get what he wanted.

He always did.

CHAPTER 7

WHEN HE ENTERED UNA'S home, the look of relief she turned on him made something flip inside his stomach. She hadn't believed he would return so fast, if at all. That he followed through on his promise was good—it would train her to take him at his word later.

"So, where do we start?" Ronan asked Una, feigning casualty, as if he was unaware of her distress while he was gone. He dropped himself into an armchair, wincing at the lack of stuffing as his buttocks sank through to the wooden frame beneath. He hoped he appeared as comfortable as she did upset—it would put her off just a little, just enough for him to assert himself as the dominant one in the relationship.

She frowned, thinking. "It's late. Why don't we start first thing in the morning?"

Ronan bit back a surge of frustration. "Why wait? Let's get started now."

Una shook her head. "I'm exhausted. And you said you'd had a rough day," she shot him a rueful, apologetic glance, "so we start tomorrow at first light."

Ronan growled and rose in a fluid movement. He strode over to her, appreciating the way she recoiled from his closeness as his chest bumped hers. "We start now," he said in a seductively soft tone. Her lips were inches from his. He could kiss her right now if he chose to. The thought was tantalizing. He found himself staring at her lips as she licked them nervously.

She put her hands on his chest and pushed. It wasn't enough to unbalance him, but he did rock back a step. She glared up at him. "Stop trying to intimidate me. It won't work. I get that you're powerful and used to being in charge. But around here, I call the shots, not you. And right now I'm too tired to think, so *we. Start. Tomorrow.*" She poked his chest with each word. She put her hands on her hips and glared up at him, daring him to contradict her.

He stared down at her, eyes blazing. How long had it been since a female fired back at him? One who didn't obey without question? He felt a surge of appreciation that dampened his irritation at the defiance. He knew he could intimidate—it was a tool he employed often when needed—so for her to stand up to him spoke of courage. Or extreme desperation.

He forced himself to back up and put up his hands. "Fine." He spat the word. "Tomorrow then." He glanced around the house until his eyes settled on the bed. He strode over to it and tossed himself down on it. It was surprisingly soft, and the way the cushion underneath sank under his weight was like a full-body hug. It was a pleasant sensation that reminded him of the way strong currents felt against his fur when he was swimming.

"Oh no," Una said, moving over to tug on the hem of his pants leg. "You're not sleeping in my bed. You're on the couch."

"That lumpy thing?" Ronan complained, not moving. "I won't sleep a bit. I'm not staying on that." He turned a glare on her. "You wanted me, you got me. And this is where I'm sleeping." He bounced his head on her pillow for emphasis.

With a growl, she leaned over and tugged the pillow out from under his head, then hit him over the face with it. "There's no way you're kicking me out of my own bed! Now get up!"

He swung his legs over the side so that his knees brushed against her dress. He grinned up at her. "There's no need for you to be kicked out. It's a big bed. We can share."

She stared at him in shock. He saw the flush creep up her neck, blazing into her cheeks like beacons in the dim light. "There is no way in hell you are sharing my bed this night or any. You are no selkie husband. Now *get. Up.*"

He liked the way she growled the words at him. He stood, once again uncomfortably close to her, but liking the way she had to crane her neck up to meet his gaze with her own fiery one. Letting all his pent-up desire leek into his eyes, he felt the burn all the way down into his stomach, curling around his skin like fire, until he felt she would all but combust from the heat of it.

"Fine." He let the word slide out of his mouth, savoring the feel. He noticed the way her eyes flicked to his lips. He smirked. "But I'm not sleeping on that sad excuse of a couch. I'd rather sleep on the floor."

Una cocked her head, then smiled in a way he didn't quite care for. "Fine," she said, drawling the word out the salacious way he had.

Ten minutes later, she lay on the bed, still in her dress but without her boots, which she'd placed by the front door. She stared at the ceiling, wide awake. At the foot of her bed, Ronan lay on a pile of blankets she'd layered on top of each other to form a pallet, with one rolled up underneath his head as a pillow.

Ronan watched her feet twitch as they hung over the edge of the bed. She had rather small, dainty feet, he thought as he admired them. He wondered what she'd do if he reached up and massaged them. *Probably slap me*, he thought. The idea made him smile in the dark. He liked how feisty she was, how quick to anger. Yet she'd been thoughtful when he spoke about the curse and how to lift it. She had a knowledgeable streak in her, too, apparently. He liked that. And he knew Ceannas would appreciate that, as well.

If I ever get to see him again, he thought. No, that was the wrong way to look at it. *When* he saw him again. It was just a matter of time. He would seduce the lady, get his sealskin back, and be gone before she could say his name. It was just a matter of time.

UNA LAY AWAKE ON the bed, discomforted by the raw presence of the selkie on the floor at her feet. She figured it was better to think of him as a selkie instead of a man. Her attraction to him was too strong to ignore, but there were more important things than lust, as she'd well learned.

Yet, she couldn't fight the realization that this felt like more than just a simple attraction. She'd never felt this was with Blair, never had a desire to touch just to see what would happen, to find out if his skin felt different when warmed from her own pressed against it. She'd never thought about him constantly when he was away—and Blair had been away plenty—had never been consumed with thoughts of how he looked, never pored over moments frozen in time: the first time she saw him, the way his eyes looked with pinpricks of sunlight dancing in them, the way his hair tangled in the wind.

She wanted to run her hands through Ronan's mass of hair. Was it soft like her own? Or coarse, like Blair's, from the sea air and salty waves? Even now, her fingers itched to find out, to just lean over the edge of the bed and trail a fingertip through the long hair resting on his shoulders. She bet it was soft, like his sealskin's. Maybe permanently damp from being soaked in the water all day long.

A rustling noise came from the foot of the bed, as if he had rolled over. She wondered what he was thinking. Probably scheming about how to get his sealskin back, she figured. It's what she'd be doing in his situation. *Good luck with that*, she thought. There was no way in hell he'd be getting that back until after they'd lifted the curse. If that's indeed what they were dealing with. *Don't think like that*, she told herself. She had to give him a certain amount of trust for this to work—he obviously wanted to be rid of her just as fast as she wanted to be rid of him. So it was in his best interest to help her.

So a curse. How to lift a curse? *Let's look at what we know*, she thought. It began twenty-four years ago, when she was small. What happened then? No biological events, according to the selkie. *Ronan*, her mind whispered. It was dangerous to think of that creature by name, but she couldn't very well go calling him "selkie" everywhere, especially when they were around the townsfolk. That would call all the wrong kind of attention. No, this feral man would be Ronan to her. And what to the town?

She frowned up at the ceiling. She hadn't considered that. For a strange man to show in a place where outsiders rarely came... What story could she concoct that would be believable? She sighed. A single woman, suddenly living with a handsome man? What else would the town think but that they were lovers.

On second thought, she might pass him off as a long-distance relative. A third-cousin, perhaps. Twice removed. That was it, she thought. Forget what the town figured. He'd be out of their lives soon, if they were lucky. And all that would be left would be the rumors. She snorted a laugh to herself. She'd weathered worse.

Now, back to the curse. What had happened twenty-four years ago? She remembered little of town events. Maybe someone else in town would have a better idea.

The Mayor, Adair Barron! Of course! Who else would remember the town history better? She smiled. He would be the first person she visited tomorrow morning. She would ask him what events had happened about two decades ago and go from there. Hopefully, he'd be able to shed some light on the situation.

She frowned. And what to make of her own situation? Stuck with an aggressive selkie who would just as easily bite her hand as help her. He'd certainly shown his teeth, jumping on her bed like he owned the place. She remembered the way he'd looked at her when she told him to get off. Like she was a choice piece of meat he'd happily devour. She shivered. Those eyes, with their dark, liquid promises. And those lips, the full redness of them, like ripe strawberries. What kind of man had lips like that?

A *selkie* man, her brain supplied. And weren't the selkie women considered the most beautiful and fertile? Why would she think a selkie man would be any different? Preternaturally handsome, his face seemed cut from stone, with his strong jaw that clenched and unclenched so frequently and that long, straight nose. She wondered how his beard stayed cropped so close to his face—she couldn't imagine that he'd shave in his human form. Maybe it always stayed that way as part of the magic?

She realized she was fixating on how attractive he was and shook herself. "Stop it," she whispered.

"Did you say something?" Ronan's voice floated up from the floor, and she blushed, caught.

"Not to you." Then she realized how curt she sounded and amended, "Just go to sleep. I'll be quiet."

"I know what you're thinking."

Una cocked her head and put her hands behind her head, feeling shame rush through her. Surely he couldn't read minds, too? "How so?"

"You don't have to do this alone, you know. We'll get this figured out." He sounded determined. She wondered if he'd at last realized he had no choice and had resigned himself to helping her. "The curse, I mean."

Una smiled. "Of course. The curse. I was thinking," she said, testing the words as she said them. "I will need to introduce you as something to the people in the town. You can be my third-cousin, visiting for the season. To help with my fish shop."

There was a moment of silence. Una waited.

Finally Ronan said, "Why not just introduce me as your husband?"

Una sat up in the bed. "What?"

Ronan's head appeared at the foot of the bed, and he rested his chin on his forearms. "Hear me out: a strange man appears in your house. You've lived here, what, all your life? Wouldn't they think it strange that a long-lost relative suddenly appears on your doorstep? It makes much more sense to say you met me inland and fell in love." He grinned wickedly. "We could put on quite a show for them."

Una shook her head. "Absolutely not. When would I have met you for this sordid love affair to have occurred?"

Ronan cocked his head, thinking. "Have you been off the island recently?"

She nodded. "About a month ago. To send a letter."

"To whom?"

"None of your business."

"That's what you'll say then. You met me inland, fell instantly in love, and we married quickly. They'll have to accept it, seeing as how I'm here. And nobody will know where I really came from."

"What if they ask questions?"

He smirked. "If your clan is as close-knit as I suspect, they won't. They'll probably talk behind your back plenty, but they won't dare say anything to your face."

She cocked her head. "How do you know so much about humans?"

He looked at her, deadpan. "I was talking about selkies."

Una snorted and covered it with her hand. "That might work. Just be aware that you're going to get a lot of attention. Especially from the women in the town."

"Because I'm a stranger?"

"Because you're attractive," she blurted, then blushed. She was glad it was so dark he couldn't see.

But he chuckled. "I'm glad you think that."

"Why?" Una asked, her cheeks hot.

"Because it will make it easier to believe that I swept you off your feet. Just pretend to be madly in love with me and it will all work out."

Una smiled weakly and lay back down on the bed. This conversation seemed to raise more problems than solve them. Pretend to be madly in love? How was she supposed to pretend to feel something she never had before? She'd seen women swoon over men they thought were attractive, but she'd never felt that same pull towards Blair. Had never shared those secret glances she'd seen Bridget Christie share with her husband when they thought nobody was looking. Or the small caresses Elspeth Leishman gave to her fiance's shoulders when they were looking at fish at the market. Those small moments were foreign to her, and now she had to perform them as if they were natural?

At least he's comely, her mind supplied. And there was no denying an attraction was there. He made her stomach clench—with anger, admittedly—when he looked at her with those smoldering eyes, but perhaps she could turn those feelings into something convincing to the others. *Just look at him like he looks at you.* Now, there was an option. She frowned, thinking. He looked at her like he wanted to devour her. If she could pretend the same, there would be no question as to her devotion. Newly weds always looked hungry for each other.

She would do it, she decided. Just mimic whatever expression he gave to her. She could fake her way through this.

How hard could it be?

CHAPTER 8

THE NEXT MORNING, THEY rose with the dawn. She commanded him to turn around as she changed into new clothes, and he'd done so with a smirk. But when she'd glanced over her shoulder as she pulled her dress over her head, she'd noticed him staring at her naked back. She hastily pulled the dress down, telling herself that human nakedness probably meant nothing to selkies, and fastened the closures at her breast with flaming hot cheeks. But when she turned to confront him, he was staring at the ceiling.

"Have those cracks always been there?" he asked, pointing. She looked up at the spiderweb of cracks in her ceiling, noting for the first time how many there were. They'd always been there, at least a few of them had, and the roof leaked a little when it rained, but she'd never taken the time to repair it.

"For a while, yes." She felt a little embarrassed after seeing them through his eyes. He must think her either poor or inept. But without Blair to do the handiwork around the house, it had fallen into disrepair.

Ronan nodded thoughtfully, then turned to her. He held out a hand. "Ready, wife?" He grinned at her answering scowl. She strode past him, ignoring his offered hand, and collected her boots from by the front door. As she sat on the couch to put them on, she noticed his bare feet.

"We're going to have to get you some new clothes. And some shoes." She thought for a moment, then hurried to the trunk at the foot of her bed. She withdrew a pair of leather work boots and a pair of woolen stockings. "These were... they belonged to someone. But I think they might fit you." She pulled out a cotton shirt and a pair of corded pants. She turned and held them up in the air, measuring him with a critical glance. "These might work..."

Ronan scowled. "I hate shoes."

"Yes," Una said, "but you'll look strange without them. And strange is the last impression we need right now. Our situation will look shady enough as it is. I don't want people thinking anything odd is going on other than how fast we moved." She scowled again. "They'll assume I'm pregnant, given how quickly we were 'married.'" She rolled her eyes. "Oh well. I've been called worse by better." She tossed the clothes to him, smiling a little as he fumbled to catch it all, and turned her back to him.

"What are you doing?" he asked in a cross voice.

"Giving you privacy."

He snorted. There was the noise of rustling cloth, then a swoosh that she imagined was his old clothes hitting the ground. She smirked. It was easy to picture him standing naked in her living room after seeing him shift into his naked form in the cave. The thought made things low in her stomach tighten. The memory of him shrugging into his clothing easily translated into a mental image of seeing his muscled stomach flex as he stepped into Blair's old pants. She pictured the rest of him, his long, muscled legs, the hair on his chest that went in a line down his stomach and tapered at the V-shape above his... She took a steadying breath.

"How are you coming?" she called over her shoulder, face heating. She hoped her voice sounded steadier than she felt.

"All done."

She turned and drank in the sight of him. His long copper hair trailed down either side of his shoulders, making stark contrast with the white fabric of his shirt. His broad shoulders were bigger than Blair's had been, and the fabric stretched tight across his bulging pectorals. Even his thighs, so strongly muscled, stretched the fabric of his pants in a way that was hard to ignore. He looked every inch the Scottish warrior, from the build of his body to the careful way he held himself, as if holding an immense amount of power in check.

He stared at her in baleful resignation. "Is this good enough?"

Una straightened her shoulders and nodded. "Let's go." She paused. "Ronan." It would take some getting used to.

He smiled as she said his name, and she smiled back at him.

"Of course." He paused with a mischievous glint in his eyes. "Una."

THEY MADE THEIR WAY down the path that led to the docks. As they walked, Una pointed to different sections of buildings, some houses set back away from the sea, like hers, and others the storefronts of the local shops and businesses.

"The town of Selbane is an inlet set on Loch Cree," Una explained. "It faces east, away from the prevailing winds, so we don't all get blown away when we walk out our doors." She laughed, and he found himself smiling at the musical sound of it. "Selbane was a planned fishing village on the northern edge of the loch built when introducing sheep farming about a hundred years ago. Most of the people here came from Glen Carron, further inland, and found the fishing to be so prosperous, they never went back."

"So the town grew around the docks or the other way around?" Ronan asked.

"Definitely around the docks. We're set very close to the ocean here, so we can do deep sea fishing other towns can't. They have to travel further and it's more expensive to do so. So we capitalize on that."

"And what do you do?" Ronan's tone was intimate. He leaned towards her as they walked, and Una pretended not to notice.

"I sell fish off the docks. The boats bring in their loads every day, and I buy their shipments at cost. Then I sell for profit at my shop."

"Will I get to see your shop?"

"Of course! After we visit Adair Barron, the Mayor."

"What's a Mayor?" Ronan asked in a suspicious tone.

"He runs the town. Sort of like our leader. He helps keep the town running and tells the fishermen how to run their businesses according to the town rules."

"So he bosses everyone around." The statement wasn't a question.

"Not necessarily," Una said. "He's more like a manager. The businesses are free to run their stores however they like, so long as they abide by town rules. If you don't follow the rules, you don't get to have a business."

"And what goes into starting a business here?"

Una laughed. "Thinking of going into business yourself, are you?"

Ronan gave her an affronted look. "If I'm going to be staying with you for any length of time, do you make enough to support both of us? My assumption is that I will need to work to help out."

"I don't anticipate this taking very long," Una said.

Ronan stopped in his tracks. "You think we're just going to waltz into town, solve a curse that's been plaguing the town for nearly two decades, and then make it home for dinner?"

Una frowned. "Not that easy, no. But how long do you think it'll take?"

Longer than it should, he thought. But to her he said, "Long enough." Then he smiled at her, a slow, languid movement of his lips. "Long enough to make things interesting."

Una flushed and turned to keep walking. "You could just get on one of the ships as a deckhand," she continued in a conversational tone. "They're always looking for strong men who aren't afraid of an honest day's work."

Ronan noticed the glance she gave his strong arms and flexed them slightly under her gaze. It was good if she appreciated his body—it would make her seduction all the easier. He smiled smugly to himself.

"I don't take orders from people." he said.

"Ah," Una said, in a knowing tone. "You like to *give* the orders instead, don't you?"

Ronan gave her a frowning glance. "Is that so bad?"

Una sighed and gave a rueful smile. "I don't think so. I don't take orders from others very well either. Never have."

"I noticed," Ronan said dryly. Una gave him a sideways glare.

"*So*," Una continued, "that's why I have my shop. I set my own hours, nobody tells me what to buy or when, or how much to sell for... I love it."

"You're used to being on your own, aren't you?" Ronan observed.

Una nodded, tucking a flyaway hair behind her ear. She smoothed her apron down in the breeze. "Ever since Blair died."

"He was someone special to you?"

"My husband."

Ronan felt something twist in his stomach. He found the idea of her having another man in her life distasteful. He pressed his lips into a thin line. "How did he die?"

"The ocean took him. Went out on a run one day and never came back."

"Did you love him?" The question fell out of his mouth before he could call it back.

Una gave him a strange look. "He was my husband."

"That means nothing. He wasn't your True Mate."

"Is that a selkie thing?"

Ronan nodded. "Something like that. But my question still stands." He found he very much wanted to hear her answer.

Una looked ahead, squinting against the sun, and they walked in silence for a bit. The dirt path and sea grasses gave way to small trees and a larger main road. Wooden docks appeared along the waterline, with brightly painted large and small wooden ships tied to them. Ronan saw small fishing boats moored next to larger fishing vessels made for the open water. On some docks, lobster traps sat in neat pyramids. The building fronts came into view as they made their way into the heart of the town.

"I cared for him. But I didn't love him, no. It wasn't like that between us."

Ronan felt a swell of excitement in him that had nothing to do with his strategic seduction and everything to do with the True Mate bond between them. If only she could feel it, too. "What *was* it like between you?"

Instead of answering, Una stopped in front of a large circular fountain with painted blue tiles lining the bottom to make it look like the ocean floor. She gestured behind it to a large stone statue he hadn't even noticed as they'd approached. It was of a woman standing on one foot, her body stretching high towards the sun as it she were preparing to dive into the fountain. Around her neck was a thick fur cape that flew behind her, as if lifted by an invisible breeze. Her dress was a simple tunic whose hem flared behind as she moved.

"What's this?" he asked, disgusted. The face seemed wrong somehow, the patina on the metal warping her face from what was supposed to be a picture of ecstasy into a grimace of pain. Her hair tumbled behind her, looking ragged and disheveled, and the mossy rust growing in patches on her dress made her appear unkempt. The whole scene made him uneasy, though he couldn't place his finger on why.

"The selkie who saved the town," Una explained with a fond smile as she looked up at it.

"The one who gave up the... what did you call them... honey holes? And then never got away?"

Una grinned at him. "It's an old myth, but one of our favorites." She sighed with deep satisfaction. "I love coming here and seeing her. The joy on her face as she prepares to transform, her eagerness to return to the ocean. It fills me with hope when I see her. Hope that things will get better."

Ronan gave her a careful sideways glance. Hope? He would have thought a desperate woman like her would have no room for hope. He noted the exchange, then cleared his throat. "And the rest of the town? Do they have hope, as well?"

Una's smile slid away from her face, and he regretted his words, though he felt a surge of irritation at himself for the feeling. He didn't owe her anything. She deserved to feel sad after what she had done to him.

Still, for a moment her face had appeared lighter, almost girlish, though she still appeared to be a young woman. He rather appreciated her youthful expression a bit more than the hardness as the lines settled back in her face as she frowned.

"I certainly hope so," she said and set off without looking back at him to see if he'd follow. The action galled him, that it made him trot after this human like a puppy on a leash, and he stalked after her.

A few minutes later she stopped in front of a standalone building set apart from the others. Above the door read a sign that said, "Town Hall." The building was rough-hewn gray stone and had a red painted door and red windows.

"We're here."

Inside was a sparsely decorated great room with a single desk in the middle. Behind it sat the Mayor.

Adair Barron was a swarthy man, dark-headed, with a shock of gray hair at each of his temples. It was cropped short to his neck, with a styled swoop of hair that fell down over one eye. It seemed to Ronan to be a calculated style, given the man's habit of brushing it back with a small flick of his head. He had the look of a muscular man who had since gone to seed, with a bulbous pot belly that pressed against the buttons of his shirt. He'd neatly pressed his pants, with a sharp crease running down each shin. His leather boots were as dark as his hair and so shiny Ronan imagined he could see his face in them.

Ronan noticed there were few items on the walls for decoration, aside from a framed compass rose made of wood and an impressive painting of Adair himself, standing with one food propped on a rock. The picture showed a more muscular, younger version of the man in front of him, and he wondered how long ago the picture had been painted.

"My dear, Una!" Adair boomed. His voice was over-large in the small area and hurt Ronan's ears.

"Adair, good to see you," Una said in a quiet voice.

Adair waved her away with a smile. "And you, of course. What brings you to my office today? What can I help you with, dear woman?"

Una turned a knowing smile on Ronan. "My... husband... and I had a brief question for you, sir. Was there any particular event that happened about twenty-four years ago? Something significant to the town?"

Adair frowned and looked back and forth between them. His shrewd eyes passed over Ronan with a squinted, calculating look. He stood, straightening his shoulders and pushing his stomach out in front of him, then moved around his desk to approach Ronan.

"I don't believe I've met you, young man." Adair held out a hand to Ronan, who glanced questioningly at Una. Una surreptitiously held out her hand and raised it up and down next to her side.

Ronan reached out to grasp the Mayor's hand. Adair clasped his hand and squeezed, grinning at Ronan with narrowed eyes. Ronan responded by squeezing back just as hard, and for a moment, the two men stood together with shaking hands, each daring the other with his eyes to let go first.

Finally Adair let go, massaging his hand with his other hand. He gave a rueful laugh. "Strong young man you have here, Una. Very strong. He'd be a handy man to have down on the docks, don't you think? I'm sure Donnan Morgan could use him on the *Boy Liam*—he's been shorthanded since young Dougal got injured."

Una nodded her head, as if considering his words. "He might consider that, sure." She shot Ronan a quick glance. "But I'm hoping to use him in my—"

"Where did you say you hail from, boy?" Adair interrupted, with an inquiring look at Ronan. He didn't notice the angry flush that worked its way up Una's cheeks, but Ronan did.

"It's Ronan, sir. Ronan... Tod."

"Of the Leister Tods?" Adair inquired. "Oldest family on the mainland, they are. Glad to say they've had me over for dinner several times now." He winked at Una. "Old money," he whispered loudly.

Ronan forced a smile. He found this old man's blustering to be wearying. "No, sir. From further inland. Small town, you probably wouldn't have heard of."

"Try me," Adair challenged with a smile.

But Ronan just smiled his tight smile even wider. "I'd heard tell that the town's fallen on hard times of late," he said in a conversational tone. "I'm sorry to hear that."

Adair's smile wilted, and he cleared his throat. "Ah, yes. Well. We're working on that." He straightened his shoulders and pushed out his stomach, bumping Ronan with it. He took a deep breath, obviously getting prepared to launch into some prepared speech.

But Una stepped forward. "About that thing, sir? Twenty-four years ago? What happened? Was there anything strange?"

"Strange?" Adair asked. He seemed thrown off by her interruption. "Strange how?"

"Was there anyone new to town?" Ronan offered. "Anyone not from here?"

Adair thought for a moment. "Can't say that I know of anything around that time. I had just gotten married that summer, you see. Mainland girl, my Harper." He smiled at them in a conspiratorial manner. "Bit of a whirlwind experience, if you catch my meaning. But I seem to recall a few newcomers to the town, now that you mention it."

Ronan and Una exchanged urgent looks.

"The butcher got a new apprentice that year, I remember. Thin young thing. Ethan, I think his name was."

"Ethan Wallace?" Una asked in surprise. "He came around then?"

"Yes," Adair nodded. "Came over from Castle Kerrick, from the South. And the doctor, Old Man Scott." He gave another booming laugh that made Ronan and Una flinch. "He was older than time, even then. Can't imagine how he's lasted all these years." He peered at them for the first time since they'd entered. "Now, why is this a concern of yours?"

"No reason," Una said with a wide, toothy smile. "Just curious. I was trying to catch my man up on some town history."

Ronan nodded. "Town history, yes. Fascinating town, Selbane."

"Now, if you want history—" Adair began, puffing up, but Una cut him off.

"Thank you for your time, Mayor. I've got to see to my shop now." She tugged at Ronan's sleeve to pull him toward the door. The Mayor waved and smiled at them as they left.

Once outside, Una hissed at Ronan, "What was that back there? Haven't you ever shaken hands before?"

"Why would I have?" Ronan asked.

Una made a frustrated sound. "Whatever. Fine. Let's just go." She gathered her skirts and stalked off down the road. Ronan followed a few steps behind her.

"I noticed one thing in there, though. That picture on his wall."

"What about it?" Una grouched.

"The compass rose?" Ronan grabbed her hand to stop her. She whirled on him, then stopped as she noticed his urgent expression. "It had seals along the border."

"So what?" Una said. "Seals are good luck charms. You'll see them all over here."

"Really?" Ronan said, oddly pleased. Una nodded.

They looked at each other for a long moment, then he realized he was still holding her hand. *And she hadn't pulled away.* He smiled at her, then glanced back over his shoulder.

"Kiss me," he said in a low voice.

Una snatched her hand back and clasped it to her chest. "Of course I won't," she hissed.

"He's watching," Ronan said, with a small motion of his head back towards the Town Hall, not knowing if Adair was watching or not. "We need to be convincing, remember?"

Una scowled at him, but stood still as he reached down for her hand again. He pulled, drawing her closer to him, until their chests touched. Her breasts pressed firmly against him, and he felt that low pull in his stomach again.

Reaching up to cup her jaw possessively, he bent and pressed his lips to hers. At first, her lips were firm and unyielding against his. But as he worked his mouth, bending her head back until she had to give way or crick her neck, she softened. Her hand slid up to caress the back of his neck, and she kissed him back, her tongue flicking over his lower lip in a way that brought a gasp to his lips at the electricity that shot through him. He pulled her head closer, increasing the pressure of his lips against hers, letting his tongue slide over hers as they kissed. His other hand crept up to her waist and pulled her closer, so that her body lay flush against his. He could feel her hips pressing against his sudden erection. The feeling was unbearably pleasurable.

He pulled back, noting the high flush in her face and the tendrils of hair that had escaped her tight bun on one side of her face, where his hand still cupped her cheek. She looked dazed, her lips pink and swollen from his kiss. He looked down at her triumphantly, his eyes blazing with emotion. That had been the most satisfying kiss he'd ever experienced. And from the look on her face, he imagined she felt the same.

He watched as she took a step back, composing herself, and tucked the stray hair behind her ear. She licked her lips, and the movement made his erection throb. But the look she gave him was steely as she smiled at him through gritted teeth. "Do that again, and I'll break your hand."

He grinned at her. "If I get to do that again, it'll be worth it."

She gaped at him, then turned and strode away down the street. He watched her backside move against the material of her dress as she moved, then followed behind.

Yes, it would be worth it. Every single bit.

CHAPTER 9

UNA WALKED RONAN THROUGH the rest of the town, down the main street, hollering the occasional greeting at shipmen coming in from the docks. Ronan marveled at the way she seemed to know everyone and how everyone seemed to know her—there wasn't a single person they passed Una didn't greet by name.

He got more than a few curious glances, but he was prepared for that. He smiled and waved as best as he could manage, trying not to feel too uncomfortable about being surrounded by so many humans. The feeling of their eyes on him made his skin crawl. *So close*, his inner seal worried. *So close.*

He followed Una down a few close streets, then into a small blue doorway just off the docks. Inside reeked of fish, and he quickly saw why: there were barrels of them everywhere, making a small trail he had to weave to get to the counter Una disappeared behind. He saw pike in one barrel, perch in another. Above his head, rows of salted greylings hung by hooks through their eyes, tails dangling dangerously close to his head.

He grimaced. To see such waste in one place...

"Surely you don't sell all of this?" he called.

Una reappeared from a back room, now clad in an apron that he could tell had once been white cotton. Dark brown stains ran the length of it across her thighs and chest. He noted how the drawstring at her waist accentuated her slight curves.

"Not even on a good day, no," she said in a melancholy tone. Then she gave him an inquiring look. "Why?"

"It's just..." He gazed around, trying to convey what he was feeling. "We have starving pups in the lean months and barely find enough food for all of us to eat as seals, and here you are with such a vast wealth of food at your disposal." He gave her a derisive glance. "Not all of us know what it's like to not have to eek out a living."

Her eyebrows arced on her forehead as she gazed at him in disbelief. "Vast wealth of food?" She indicated the small shop. "This is a vast wealth to you? This represents over a month's wages that may or may not get earned. The lean months you speak of? Those have been the last twenty-four years for this town. And every day is a day of not knowing if you'll make enough to eat that night." She cast a scathing glare in his direction. "You at least have other avenues of getting food. If you seals don't get food, then you humans can. But we don't have other opportunities. It's just us and what we can glean from the sea. If she doesn't produce, then neither do we."

She smoothed a hand angrily down the front of her apron and turned away to glare at the wall.

This wasn't going how he needed it to go. He sighed and raked a hand through his hair. This was going to be difficult if they were going to butt heads at every turn. He took a deep breath to calm himself and straightened his shoulders. *Don't forget your mission!* he told himself.

"We're more alike, I think, than I realized before," he forced himself to admit in a rueful tone. It wasn't entirely untrue, but he wasn't willing yet to concede that they shared the same hardships.

To his surprise, the look she gave him was wary, but not angry. "We are?"

"Both of us know what it's like to go hungry," he offered with a small smile. "And it seems your town is as close-knit as my clan. It's hard to see your clan members hurting. I see how it hurts you."

She gave him a surprised look. "I suppose you're right," she admitted. "It's not easy."

Now to turn the moment, he thought to himself. His smile widening, he stepped forward and leaned over the counter railing. "So now what?" he asked in a low, seductive voice. He leered at her. "Care to show me your back rooms?"

Una rolled her eyes. "Now we wait for the captains to unload their stock and bring them in. They know where to find me."

Ronan nodded, glancing again around the store. "And what do I need to do?"

"Go make yourself useful. Know how to clean a fish?"

"I handle fish all the time," he scoffed.

Una smiled at him and flipped a knife into her hand. "Good. Get to work in the back then."

TWO HOURS LATER, RONAN was covered in sweat and fish bits and had shredded not one but five fish carcasses into uselessness.

"What the hell are you doing?" Una cried from behind him. "I told you to clean the fish, not hack it to pieces!"

Ronan glared at her. "I'm trying," he growled. He scowled down at the fish in his hands. "But it's not cooperating."

"Here," Una said. She stepped up behind him, pressing her chest to his back, and wrapped her arms around his middle. She could feel the strong muscles of his back tense under her chest, but she ignored it and leaned around one side of him. "Like this." She placed her hands over his gore-covered ones and showed him how to use the knife to cut along the gill line and then down the belly. Then she flipped the knife, expertly spinning the handle around in her palm, and pressed it back into his hand. She cut along the backbone toward the tail, then lifted the fileted piece and placed it in his bloody palm.

"Now just take the skin off and put the meat over on the ice." She pointed to the trough she'd just filled.

He pivoted so that he was facing her with her arms still around his ribs. "You'll have to show me that again," he said in a low voice. He stared down at her hungrily, letting the heat from her nearness creep into his gaze. He could feel his erection bump against her hip as she leaned into him.

She watched his mouth as he spoke, then licked her lips. "I can show you everything," she murmured. Her eyes widened, and she took a step back. "About fish! I can show you everything I know about—"

His lips fell on hers as his hands reached around her to crush her to his chest. He kissed her, not caring that he'd heard someone's footsteps enter the front of the store. She responded immediately, her forearms pressing into his ribs as she held her fish-grimed hands behind his back. Her lips slid over his as she ate at his mouth, hungry for his kiss. He pressed his erection against her hips and she moaned into his mouth with need. He felt her breasts crushing against his chest and wondered what they would look like when free of that apron and dress. The thought of her nipples pressing against him undid him and he moaned her name into her mouth.

"Ronan," she gasped, pulling back. Her face was flushed, and she was breathing heavily. "I need to tend to the front. I need you..." She trailed away, gazing at his lips again. "I need you—"

"To slice the fish," he finished with a smile. "Got it." He leaned down and slid his tongue across her lower lip teasingly. She closed her eyes, regaining her composure. "Your wish is mine."

She stepped back and smoothed her hands down her apron, leaving a bloody streak behind. Then she took a deep breath, straightened her shoulders, and gazed at him with naked lust in her eyes. "How do I look?"

"Delicious," he told her, and she smirked.

"Get back to work," she said as she turned and headed through the door.

He wasn't much better at slicing the rest of the fish the way she'd showed him, but he tried not to butcher them more than he could help—he couldn't shake their earlier conversation and was acutely aware that every fish he mangled was another coin she couldn't make. If their roles had been reversed, he wasn't sure he would have been as patient a teacher as she had been. And the memory of her body against his, the feel of her mouth as she moaned into him... it all sparked something deeper inside him he didn't know himself capable of feeling.

It's all an act, he reminded himself as his knife tore through the flesh instead of cutting it. *Just seduce her and you'll be back home soon.* But the thought of her body underneath his on her uncomfortable bed at home was too tantalizing. *Soon,* he promised himself. *Very soon.* If she responded so eagerly to his kiss now, after threatening to break his hand earlier, there was promise in getting her to fall for him. It was just a matter of time.

HOURS LATER, AS SHE was entering numbers into her work ledger, Una heard the door open.

"Una!"

Una looked up from her ledger to see her childhood friend, Lyall, sweep through the door. "You'll never guess who just commissioned a handfasting dressing from the Grey Lady." Lyall's round face flushed with excitement. She approached the counter and leaned over it to put her face close to Una's. Her eyes were very wide with the secret she was holding back. "Donalda Roid! That young fisherman she's been dating—"

"Tamhas?" Una supplied, smiling down at her friend as she closed the cover of the ledger.

"He finally asked for her hand! Of course, it's a scandal, with her father being out at sea for a fortnight still, but she said—"

"Of course she said yes," Una said scornfully. "She's besotted. They've been dating since they were five, it seems. I'm sure her father won't be too unhappy to have him as a son-in-law, given how long he's been around. Practically part of the family now, anyway."

Lyall grinned. "Isn't it beautiful? I hope I have that kind of love someday. The kind that seems like it's been around all your life."

Una's smile froze on her face. She'd known Blair all her life, and that hadn't mattered when it came to love. But Lyall continued, sweeping a hand over the backs of a pile of fish in a nearby barrel, too absorbed in her news to notice Una's reaction.

"I'm sure he treats her well. Someday I'll have that, too."

"You haven't even been kissed yet. What makes you think love is on the horizon now?"

Lyall paused and threw her a haughty look. "I'm almost twenty-two. In a few weeks, I'll be a woman, and that's always a desirable thing for a man to have."

"Mm-hmm," Una mused, with a smile teasing her face. "Still have your eye on Rory?"

Lyall pursed her lips together and flashed Una a coy smile. "He smiled at me the other day, you know. Came by the Grey Lady to pick up the dress I hemmed for his mother. And he not only smiled at me, he called me by name!" She squealed and did a small dance. "He looked me dead in the eyes and said," she dropped her voice to a low baritone, "'Good day, Lyall. You look well.' And I gave

him my best smile and said, 'Thank you, Rory. As do you.'"
She grinned at Una.

"So you think marriage is just around the corner now."
Una smiled at her friend.

"*Obviously.*" Lyall drawled the word.

They laughed in unison. "Well, I wish you the best with him," Una said. "He's too hairy for my taste."

"I like them looking like some hairy bear," Lyall said. "Anything to help keep me warm at night."

Una gave her a mock-scandalized look. "For shame, Lyall! What would your father say if he heard such talk?"

Lyall rolled eyes. "He would wave his cane at me and threaten to skin me with it." She pointed an accusing finger at Una. "Or send me to you and have you do it!"

Una laughed. "I'd never skin you at his request." She gave Lyall a sideways glance. "I'd charge double for it."

Lyall groaned and put her hands on her hips. "Besides, that would require him to pay attention to something I said, which we both know will never happen." She gave Una a deadpan look.

"I don't know," Una admonished. "Uncle Hugh listens to you." She paused. "Sometimes..."

"He never does. He listens to you more than me."

"He was my father's oldest friend, and I'm like a daughter to him. Besides, I'm older than you—he probably sees me as the responsible one."

Lyall rocked her head back and forth. "He probably sees me as the responsible one," she mocked in a sneering voice. Then she scowled. "That's not wrong." She sighed deeply. "I just wish he would see me as my own person instead of some extension of my mother."

Una stepped around the counter to clasp her friend's hands. She looked earnestly into Lyall's eyes. "You are your own person. You are not just a smaller version of your mother. And someday he will see that."

"I just wish he saw that now," Lyall said, looking down at their clasped hands. Then she brightened. "At least once I'm twenty-two, he'll have to see me as an adult. I'll be my own woman. He won't be able to ignore that, will he?" Her voice held such naked optimism, Una couldn't bear to burst her bubble.

"Of course he will," she agreed, feeling slightly ashamed of the lie. After her father had died and with no mother since she was an infant, she had grown up with Lyall, who was only a few years younger. Her Uncle Hugh had always seemed to treat them as sisters, with deference being given to her as the older of the two. She'd had to earn her independence by marrying Blair, and only then did Uncle Hugh treat her as an adult. She knew he wouldn't treat Lyall the same until she, too, was married off to an honorable man. But she couldn't bring herself to say such things. It was easier for Lyall to believe that turning twenty-two in a few weeks would bring about a magical transformation. She was not ready to hear the voice of reason.

"I've got to get back," Lyall said. "Madam Ruadh will want me back for those trousers of Mr. Sgot's." She hefted a deep sigh and flashed a forced smile at Una.

"Shall I come by tonight to bring out your father's fish supply? I'm sure he'll be wanting pike again."

Lyall blew air from between her lips noisily. "He does love pike, doesn't he?"

"I think he is half-pike. Or at least half-seal, given all the fish he eats."

Lyall grimaced. "Ick. Give me a nice roast lamb or some beef."

Una thought about the visits she would have to make to the butcher and the doctor and hustled back to the door that led behind the counter.

"Actually don't worry about the fish," Lyall said, stopping Una in her tracks. "They're gone."

Una turned with a frown. "Gone where?"

"To the mainland to sell a shipment of black pearls and abalone. There's a jeweler there that will pay twice the going rate for them." Lyall gave a smug smile.

"But why would they pay twice as much?" Una asked.

"Because they don't know any better." Lyall grinned wickedly, then plucked an imaginary speck off her shoulder. "Both mother and father went. They won't be back for several days."

"Why didn't they take you with them?"

Lyall gave her a haughty look. "Somebody had to keep up with the house while they were gone, earn a respectable keep. We can't all go gallivanting off to the mainland whenever we please." She gave a disdainful sniff and Una had to hide a smile. It was all an act—Lyall would have jumped at the chance to visit the mainland if offered the opportunity. She figured Aunt Leannán and Uncle Hugh were grateful for the getaway. They never seemed to leave the island.

Of course, neither, did she. But that was fine by her. She was born and bred here. It was in her blood in a way she knew wasn't in her uncle's and aunt's.

"Well, I will be by soon to visit you, I promise. In the meantime, let me know how Donalda's dress turns out."

"I'm sure it will be perfect," Lyall preened. She fished out a few copper coins and set them on the counter in front of Una. "After all, Selbane's best seamstress is on duty!" She pretended to examine her nails and grinned.

Una laughed and leaned forward to kiss Lyall's cheek. "Good day, Lyall. I will see you later." Lyall smiled, her eyes crinkling at the corners, and swept out of the shop.

Only as the door swung shut did Una realize she hadn't mentioned Ronan at all. She knew how islanders talked—it would be horrible if Lyall learned about him through the town's gossip channels instead of from her best friend. She would have to rectify that soon, before everyone began talking about her "new man." The thought made her roll her eyes. She didn't even know what to think about him herself, let alone how she would break the news to Lyall. And later, to Uncle Hugh and Aunt Leannán.

But that was a problem for another time. She opened her ledger again and began tallying prices for her newest shipment. She had enough issues on her plate as it was right now. And one large one was in the back room as she wrote.

CHAPTER 10

By the end of the day, Ronan had no idea how long he'd been working, but he felt as if he'd tried swimming a few hundred leagues in one day. His back hurt from stooping over the cutting table and his hands were cramping from misuse. They hurt so bad, he had to pry his fingers away from the knife handle so he could put it down. The smell of fish guts was all over him, and grimy, scaley fish bits caked his hands. He felt disgusting, nastier than he'd ever felt as a human before, and wanted nothing more than to slip on his skin and slide into the salty, cold water of the ocean.

Then Una came through the door looking radiant and he forgot all about it.

"I got something," she said. "A lead."

"How's that?" Ronan asked, leaning back until his spine gave a loud series of cracks.

"Something Adair said, about the doctor, Iain Scott. Adair said he was 'older than time' even when he came. How long do your kind live?"

Ronan frowned, thinking. "I don't know. A few hundred decades, I suppose. We don't really keep track."

Una paused in surprise. "And how many decades old are you?"

Ronan thought for a moment. "I guess I'd be around sixty, maybe seventy turnings old?"

"But you don't look older than twenty!" she exclaimed.

He shrugged, a motion seeming to indicate *I don't know what to tell you.*

Una shook her hands. "Nevermind that. If he is an older man, that could mean he is the one who put the curse on the town."

"And what indicator does age have for a curse?"

"He may be an old enough creature to know how to put one on. I wouldn't expect anyone young to know how to cast a curse. So we talk to the doctor first, then the butcher's apprentice, Ethan."

Ronan frowned, his eyebrows furrowing. "Does it matter?"

She shrugged. "I suppose not. I have some business with the butcher. We might as well approach Ethan then."

"Can we close up shop now?" Ronan asked plaintively.

Una took in his fish-grimed hands and laughed. "Yes, I think so. Wash up over there"—she pointed to a washbasin filled with water—"and we can go see the butcher afterward."

She watched as Ronan went to the washbasin and began cleaning his hands and arms. The muscles of his shoulders bunched beneath his shirt as he bent over the basin, reminding her of the way his back had tensed against her chest when she pressed against him. That had been exciting, if unwise.

Don't get too close to this one, she reminded herself. *He's just out to save his skin.*

But it was too easy to remember the feel of his mouth on hers, the salty aftertaste his kiss left on her lips, as if he was made of the sea himself. It was a heady feeling that made her body tighten in anticipation and warmth rise between her legs. He was a fascinating man, for sure. But she would have to keep her distance.

Ronan turned, surprising her with a smile. "Ready?"

"Very," she murmured, and answered his questioning expression with her own smile. "Let's go."

The butcher's shop was only a few stores down from hers, so they didn't have to walk far. She opened the door and a small bell sounded. Ronan looked up at it in surprise.

"That's neat!" He turned to her. "Why don't you have a nifty bell for your door, too?"

Una rolled her eyes at him. To have some cat's bell ringing every time someone walked through the door? *Not in this life or the next*, she thought.

"What can I do for ya'?" a man called from somewhere in the shop.

Una craned her neck, trying to see where it had come from. After a moment's searching, a man's head popped into view from behind a shelf. The man was bald, with bushy sideburns the color of flames running down each cheek and culminating into a long, scraggly beard that covered his beefy neck. The man waddled around the edge of the shelf and put his hands on his hips. A bloody, white smock hid his clothes. "Una MacCallan? What brings you in today?" He nodded affably to Ronan, who nodded back.

"I'm here to speak with Ethan, actually, James. Is he available?"

The man scowled. "What's the lad done now? He doesn't owe you money, does he, Una? Ethan!" he hollered over his shoulder. "Get out here and pay the woman! You know better than to leave behind a debt we can pay!"

A few moments later, a young man came around the doorway from somewhere in the back. He skirted the counter, wiping his hands on his apron and leaving a bloody streak on his thighs. "Sir?"

He was Una's age, tall and broad-shouldered, with black hair that stood out in curls around his head. When he caught sight of Una, he flashed her a winning smile that made Ronan's neck stiffen with dislike.

"I told ya' to always pay yer debts! How many times have I told ye?" James slapped one hand in his other palm for emphasis. As Ethan walked past him, he delivered a slap to the back of Ethan's head, though he had to reach up to do it.

"He doesn't owe me anything, James!" Una said quickly, as Ethan deftly ducked another slap headed his way. "I just needed to ask him about a few things. And get my beef ration for the night. I'm afraid I'll need an extra tenderloin for my... my man here." She gestured at Ronan.

James eyed him with open interest, but had too many manners to ask questions. "Oh, right then." He glared at Ethan. "Get to it, then! What are you waiting on, an invitation to the ball?"

Ethan shot him an irritated look, but then smiled at Una. "Ms. MacCallan, follow me to the back. I'll get that chopped right up for you."

They followed Ethan back behind the counter and into the back room, where they butchered the meat. Una passed a skinned hog hanging upside down by its legs, held to the ceiling by a thick chain around its fetlock. On one table, a slab of bloody ribs lay with a butcher knife sticking out of it like a pincushion.

"Over here," Ethan directed. He walked to a bin and pulled out a hunk of red meat. Then, from a holster hidden beneath his apron, he pulled out a small knife.

"Ethan," Una began. "I wanted to ask you something."

The man grunted in acknowledgment.

"How old were you when you became James's apprentice?"

Ethan paused in his cutting. "Oh, I was a wee lad. Maybe eight or so? My parents couldn't afford to keep me and my brothers, so they sold us out as apprentices around town. My older brother, Dougal, went on as midshipmen on Donnan Morgan's ship, *The Boy Liam*, and my younger brother, Gregor, went to work Fergus MacRob's sheep farm."

"Yes, I heard Dougal got injured recently..." Una said with false concern in her voice. She didn't have time for chit-chat.

But Ethan grinned at her and shrugged. "He was likely being an idiot, as usual. Probably deserved it."

Una gave Ronan a surprised look.

"So you grew up on the island?" Ronan asked.

Ethan shot him a grin over his shoulder. "Born and raised."

"Do you get to see your parents often?" Una asked.

Ethan shook his head. "My Da died a few years back. Had an attack of the heart. It's just me Ma now and her two farmhands. I help there, on the weekends, when I can. It's hard work, but I appreciate it." He grinned. "Nothing like the cushy job I have here."

He hacked at a tenacious strip of flesh holding a small cutlet to the hunk of meat and set it aside. "There you go. I'll get that wrapped up and you can be off."

"Before you go," Ronan asked. "Did you ever see anything strange around the island, maybe twenty years ago? Something not quite right?"

Ethan paused and frowned at him. "Like what? Like somebody doing something they weren't supposed to be?"

"Or any strange event, really," Una supplied. She knew how weird they must sound based off the odd look Ethan was giving them. "You would have been just a boy, I know."

He shrugged. "I see plenty of people doing what they shouldn't. But nothing overly strange or out of the ordinary. It's just a regular town here."

Ronan opened his mouth, seeming about to launch into more questions, but Una gave him a warning glance and put a hand on his arm to stall him. "Thanks, Ethan. We were just curious."

Ethan gave them another strange look, then took the small cutlet over to another table and wrapped it in waxed paper. He tied the bundle with twine and handed it over. "Here you go! One cutlet, fresh off the block." He smiled at them.

Una fished a copper coin from her purse and handed it over. "Thanks for the help, Ethan."

He pocketed the money in a smooth motion and led them back to the front of the shop.

As they opened the door, with the bell tinkling loudly, James called, "Don't be a stranger now, Una! Come back any time!"

She turned and waved, then closed the door behind her.

On the street, she tossed the wrapped package back and forth in her hands. Her mouth skewed to one side as she thought. "That seemed rather..."

"Uneventful?" Ronan supplied. She nodded.

"Did you get any otherworldly sense off him?"

"Like what?"

"Any selkie senses that he wasn't what he seemed?"

Ronan shrugged. "It doesn't work like that. We can't tell non-humans from humans that easily, especially if they look human. But nothing about that kid screamed anything other than human to me."

Una scowled. "I thought so." She sighed. "Well, I suppose that just leaves the doctor."

"And if it isn't him, either?"

She gave Ronan a grim look. "Then we're back where we started. And in trouble for having wasted the time."

CHAPTER II

A FEW BLOCKS OVER, Una led them to a stop in front of a door labeled "DOCTOR." She stopped outside and looked him over with a fretful look on her face.

"What's the matter?" Ronan asked, frowning. To his mind, all they needed to do was go in and ask a few questions. He didn't understand her worry.

"We need a reason to come in here." She looked him in the eyes, pinched his cheeks, and said, "I think you aren't feeling well."

"What?" he exclaimed. "I feel—"

"No, you definitely don't look right. I think you need to see a doctor."

Ronan scowled at her. "I will not be poked and prodded just so that we—"

"Can lift the curse and get your skin back?" she asked pointedly.

He closed his eyes and gave a deep sigh. "Just know, I am not okay with this."

Una smiled at him. "That's okay, you don't have to be. Just go with it." She straightened his shirt by plucking at the shoulders, then turned and opened the door. Ronan sighed again and followed.

Inside was a small reception area, where a long-faced woman listened to Una explain why they needed to see Dr. Scott. The woman's eyebrows seemed to be permanently raised, so that she had a perpetual look of surprise. She pointed to a set of empty chairs on one side.

"Wait there and the doctor will see you soon." Message delivered, she turned back to the papers in front of her, obviously dismissing them.

Una gave Ronan a quick frown, then motioned for them to sit.

Moments later, the door behind the reception area opened and a stoop-backed old man in a white coat stepped through. "Ronan Tod?" He wore a pair of small round spectacles perched on the end of his nose and they made his eyes appear very round, like an owl's.

Ronan stood and Una jabbed him in the ribs.

"Wha-?" He turned to her, and she gave a wiggle of her eyebrows that he took to mean *look sick*. He coughed into his hand and saw her lips turn up in a slight, satisfied smile.

They followed the doctor down a short hallway and into a small room with a single table padded with cotton cloth. The doctor closed the door, then turned to Ronan. "What seems to be the problem, young man?" His voice had a warble to it that sounded as if he were singing.

Ronan gave the doctor a wide-eyed look, then turned to Una. Both men looked at her expectantly. She sighed in exasperation, then put a hand on Ronan's arm. "My, er, husband here... well, he... fell... off a ladder." She cleared her throat, then hurried on, warming to the story. "Yes, he fell off a ladder and bumped his head. Hasn't felt well since then, so we thought we'd see you."

Dr. Scott nodded and moved closer to Ronan, indicating for him to sit on the padded table. He put his hand over Ronan's heart and cocked his head, as if listening to something. Ronan gave Una a sideways look, but she was frowning in thought.

After a moment, the doctor straightened and said, "Your heart beats a bit fast, young man. Is that normal for you?"

Ronan raised his eyebrows and nodded, hoping he looked like he was confident in his answer. He had never thought about his heart versus a human's, though differences were likely.

He froze as the doctor turned to pull a device out of a drawer.

Of course he would seem different from a human! Why hadn't he thought of that before? He tried to give Una an urgent look, something to indicate to her that they needed to leave, but she was cupping her chin in her hands, lost in thought.

"Doctor," he began, "I'm actually feeling better now. I don't think you need to—"

"Hold still, young man," the doctor commanded, and raised a small triangular stone with a handle on one end to tap it against Ronan's knee.

Nothing happened.

The doctor frowned, making several deep creases appear in his forehead, and tapped again.

Again nothing.

"Doctor Scott," Una began, oblivious to Ronan's rising anxiety or the doctor's increasingly firm taps on Ronan's knee, "where did you practice before you came to Selbane?"

"Oh?" Doctor Scott asked, setting the triangular device on the table next to Ronan. Ronan eyed it, wondering how he was supposed to have responded if he'd been human. "What's that, my dear?"

"Where did you practice?" Una said in a louder voice. "Before Selbane!"

The doctor nodded in understanding and turned back to the table. He put his hand down to pick up the triangular device, but it was gone. He patted his hand a few inches around where it had been, then peered down in surprise. When he looked at Ronan, the younger man shrugged.

"I..." Using his hand to balance on the table, the doctor leaned over to peer at the floor. "I used to be at... oh blast, where did it go?"

Ronan leaned towards Una. "We need to go now!" he hissed in a whisper.

She gave him a quizzical look and leaned forward to hear better.

"We. Need. To. Go!" he hissed again. He glanced at the doctor, who had turned his back to look through the top drawer of his cabinet. "*Not human!*"

"What?" Una whispered back, but the doctor turned around and peered at Ronan through his round spectacles.

"Young man, have you seen my—"

"I think I'm doing much better now!" Ronan said loudly, sliding off the table. "Thank you for your time, Doctor

Scott!" His chest bumped the doctor, who stumbled backwards a step.

Doctor Scott scowled. "Now look here, young man. Let me just check your eyes in case of a—"

"That won't be necessary!" Ronan gripped Una's hand and pulled her towards the door. "Thank you again for your expertise, doctor!" He thrust her out the door and down the hall, smiling back at the confused doctor over his shoulder. They burst through the door to the reception area, and smiled crazily at the receptionist, who jumped and put a hand to her chest, as Ronan propelled Una out the front door and out on to the street.

Once outside, Una rounded on him. "What the hell was that about? I didn't even get to ask him any questions!"

"He was going to find out that I'm not human," Ronan said, mindful to pitch his voice low so it didn't carry to the people passing them on the street. "He was already suspicious."

"Because you were acting like a lunatic!" Una hissed furiously. She scowled and strode down the street. "And now we'll have to come up with some other way of asking him about where he came from." She flung an arm backwards towards the office. "He could have set the curse! And now we've lost our chance to find out."

Ronan jogged to catch up with her, aware that others were staring at Una as she stalked on. Her body language radiated anger, from her crossed arms to the forward pitch of her upper body. "He was going to find out I wasn't quite normal," he said, trying to reach her ear. "You were the one who said we didn't need that kind of attention. There will be other times to talk to him." He stepped in front of her, stopping her forward progress. She scowled up at him. "We'll figure this out," he said, gripping her arms.

From his peripheral vision, he saw a few people stopping to stare at them standing in the middle of the street. He changed his grip so that he was rubbing his hands up and down her arms instead, and her scowl deepened.

"Careful," he said softly. "We're on display."

She glanced to the side, noting the spectators, and ducked her head as she schooled her expression into one of loving kindness. She smiled up at him and he noticed it didn't quite meet her eyes. "My love," she growled through gritted teeth. "You're right." He realized that though her tone was rough, it was also sincere. "We will find another way to talk to him," she said ruefully.

He turned so that he was beside her instead of in front of her and slid one arm over her shoulders. Together, they started walking up the street.

Ahead, Ronan saw they were approaching the statue, and he shuddered at the thought of having to pass it once more. If he never saw that thing again, he'd live a long and happy life. He noticed someone standing near it, not moving but staring up at the statue while everyone passed by. There was a smile on his face, a wistful fondness much like the one Una had when she'd looked up at it. It seemed others weren't immune to the statue's effect, either.

"Isn't that your Mayor?" he asked, pointing.

Una looked ahead and nodded. "He often visits that statue. I see him sometimes when I make night deliveries. Usually just standing there, staring at it. I think it reminds him of better times."

"Maybe it gives him hope too," Ronan mused. He still didn't see what was so inspiring about the statue, but perhaps he would have had to been born here to get it. "So now what?" he asked, changing the subject as he steered her away from the statue and back to the path they'd used to enter town.

She cocked her head, thinking. "I suppose now we look elsewhere until we can circle back around to the good doctor. Maybe my father's old journals can give us a clue...?" At his inquiring expression, she shrugged. "It's as good an idea as any, I suppose."

He nodded thoughtfully, noting the unconscious way Una had begun to lean into his side as they walked. When he tightened his arm around her shoulders, she leaned into him a little more, without seeming to realize it. He grinned to himself.

Today. He would try today, when they returned. He savored the feel of her lean body against his as they walked. He tried to imagine how she would feel pinned beneath him on that uncomfortable bed of hers and grinned wider. This was going to be the best part of his imprisonment, if he could get her to go along with it.

He looked down at her shining dark hair as the sun cast copper and tan highlights through it. Yes, he was going to enjoy this very much.

CHAPTER 12

AT HER HOUSE, RONAN gripped Una's arm as she made to open the door.

"Wait," he said. He walked close to her so that she backed up against the door. The whole walk home, as they discussed the mystery of the curse, he felt that he needed to act on her. She couldn't just view him as a partner in this curse-breaking business—he needed her to see him as a lover.

He thought of the image he'd had of her earlier, with her hair spread out on the pillow. He leaned forward and held eye contact with her. "Una, I want you. And I know you want me, too."

Indignation flashed in her eyes. "You have no idea how I feel about you!"

He leaned forward and saw her tilt her head ever so slightly upward, lips parting expectantly. He paused. "I have an idea," he said with a smile.

She flushed and looked down at her hands, but gave a rueful grin. "I suppose I have an idea of how you feel about me, too," she said, peeking at him from beneath her lashes. She glanced pointedly down at his erection straining against his pants. "I have a *little* idea."

He lifted an eyebrow at her. "Little?"

She spread her fingers a few inches apart. "A small one." He grinned back at her.

He leaned forward again, loving the way she parted her lips and closed her eyes in anticipation of his kiss. Then he reached around her and opened the door.

She fell backwards, only to be caught around the waist by his strong hands. "You did that on purpose!" she accused.

He grinned at her. "Any reason to touch you is on purpose."

She stood, shooting him a baleful glare, and smoothed her skirt down her stomach in a nervous gesture. When she turned to walk away, he stepped close behind her. She froze at his nearness and watched as he reached up and pulled on the tie at her chest. The front of the dress fell open, revealing the swell of her breasts. The sight galvanized him.

He paused, hands hovering in the air in front of her. He frowned, scanning her dress. She smiled at his obvious uncertainty.

"I don't have a lot of experience with clothes," he admitted.

She gave him a patient smile and gathered the hem of her skirt in her hands. With a smooth movement, she pulled the material up over her head and dropped the dress onto the floor next to her. She stood in her chest wrap and underwear. She reached behind her and undid the tie on her wrap. Then, keeping eye contact with him, she unwrapped the binding and let it slide down her body.

Her breasts were perfect, creamy white with dull pink areolas and nipples. The sight of them made his erection throb against his pants, and he hurriedly shucked out of them, never taking his eyes off her body.

"Take that off," he said in a low voice, indicating her underwear. She pulled them slowly down her legs, giving him a long look at her smooth stomach and lean thighs.

He pulled his shirt over his head and stood there, naked and erect. His nudity didn't cause fear or shame, as it seemed to for her, for she flushed again, even as she watched him with hungry eyes.

"I don't have a lot of experience with men," she admitted. She looked like she wanted to move, but wasn't sure what to do.

"Touch me," he whispered. She stepped forward hesitantly and let her hands smooth over the thick pelt across his chest. The hair was soft and slightly oiled.

"Oh," she said and drew back. "That's... unexpected."

He grabbed her hand and placed it back on his chest, holding it over his heart. "Don't worry. I don't bite." He cocked his head and grinned at her. "Actually... that's a lie."

She smiled back at him and pulled her hand away. "How much of the seal are you?"

"Enough."

He ran both hands up the side of her head, burying his fingers in her hair as he kissed her. He leaned her backwards, just enough to control the kiss. The motion pressed her breasts against his chest, just as he'd imagined in her fish shop. The thought made him throb with need. He pulled back, and her eyes remained closed with a small smile on her face.

Good, he thought. *This would be easy, after all.*

He picked her up, causing her to squeal with shock, and carried her over to her uncomfortable bed. He set her down gently and eased himself next to her on his knees. Matching him, she sat up and knelt, too, so that they were both facing each other.

He grabbed both of her hands and ran them through the hair on his head. "See? Oiled against the water."

"You're waterproof!" She grinned and leaned forward to kiss him.

As their lips met, he slid one hand down her sternum, between her breasts, and down her taut stomach. Reaching lower, he slid a finger inside her. "And you're all wet."

She tried to kiss him again, and this time he let her. He crushed his lips against hers, his tongue plunging inside her mouth to glide across her tongue and slide ever so wetly against the roof of her mouth. She sucked on his tongue as if it were candy and he moaned into her mouth.

Her other hand reached down, grabbed the base of his manhood, and gripped it firmly. She began to slide her hand up and down his shaft.

"Gods, you are so beautiful," he ground out. He pulled back, his hand still clenched in her hair, and gazed down at her. He looked at her as if she were a meal and he was a starving man.

"I love this," she whispered. She felt him tense beneath her hand.

The desire drained from her body as she stared at him in shock. How could she have been so stupid? How could she say that to him when she'd only just met him?

She looked down at her knees on the bed, licking her lips. "I didn't... I mean..."

"What did you mean?" he asked. His voice was low and husky. He was still on his knees in front of her, and, she saw with surprise, still hard and erect. He took a kneeling step toward her so that the hair on his chest brushed against her nipples, sending a shock of desire through her.

"I just..." she stammered. "Don't read too much into it. It's been a long time since... and I—"

His hand snaked through her hair again and pulled her face close to his. "I love this, too," he breathed as he stared into her eyes. She saw that his were three shades of gold: a dark brown center, ringed by a bronze circle, then flecked with bits of amber throughout. But his pupil was oblong, not round like a human's.

She stared at him in surprise. "You do?"

"Of course I do. You are incredible—so strong, so beautiful. And," —he reached up to cup her breast and slid his thumb over her nipple, sending a wave of pleasure through her— "I want to do more," —he leaned over and pulled her nipple into his mouth and sucked— "of this." She gasped and leaned into his touch.

He shifted to the other breast, sucking and nibbling at her nipple while pinching her other nipple between his thumb and forefinger and rolling it gently back and forth.

"Oh gods," she moaned and arced backwards, her hands on his chest for balance. He reached behind her and gripped her buttocks with both hands, squeezing and pulling her hips close to his as he sucked and nibbled along the length of her neck.

He pulled back and kissed her again, slowly this time, as if he were savoring the taste of her. Then he let go of her buttocks and pushed her shoulders so that she fell backwards on the bed.

"What are you—?" she started, but stopped as he stretched out between her legs and grinned up at her from the shelter of her thighs. He bent his head and nuzzled her soft folds, using his nose to brush against her clitoris. Then he used his tongue and lapped long, wet strokes through her.

She writhed on the sheets, gripping a fistful of the bedspread in each hand. "Yes," she breathed. She moaned as one hand slipped inside her and the other reached up to flick and roll her nipple between his fingers.

The hand inside her spread her wide with the first two fingers, and his tongue delved deep into her wetness. "Oh god!" she shrieked and arced upwards into his pressure. His tongue circled her clitoris as his fingers slid in and out of her, pushing her folds wide to receive him.

She closed her eyes against the feel of him inside her. "Ronan, yes!"

"Say my name again."

"Ronan," she moaned.

"Say you're mine."

"I'm yours." Her voice was breathless with need.

He raised his head and paused the motion of his fingers inside her. "Always for me," he growled against her lips and nibbled her folds lightly between his teeth.

She shivered with delighted anticipation.

He released her. "I want to hear you say it," he said, as he began flicking back and forth across her clitoris and gliding in and out of her again with his fingers.

"Mmmm," she moaned, as the tide rose inside her.

He slid faster in and out. "I want to hear you say it." She could hear the smile in his voice, and she groaned.

"Oh gods, always for you!"

"Just me," he murmured. His breath was warm against her skin and she shivered again. She could feel the desire rising in her stomach, burning like an ember.

"Only you. Nobody else!" She quivered under his touch.

Screaming, she rode the crest of her climax as it came, drowning her in wave after wave of delightful sensation. For a moment, she thought she felt two heartbeats galloping together out of sync, but when she tried to focus on it, the feeling was gone and it was just her own body's frantic beating and ragged breaths. Her fists relaxed their grip on the bedspread as her body quieted, and when she brought her legs together, her delicate area felt deliciously swollen and slick.

"That was amazing," she murmured as sleepiness stole over her. "That was—"

"A small trick," he said smugly. When she looked at him, he held up two fingers a few inches apart. "A little one."

She grinned at him. "I love this," she said again.

"As do I," he responded, rising to move between her legs. His hard length slid against her slick folds as he shifted his weight so that his upper body lay across hers. He kissed her and she could taste her own muskiness on his lips.

For a moment, he had the dizzying feeling of an echo of a heartbeat, an instance where he was back at the cave by the sea feeling a ghost of a heartbeat after his, the doubled feeling of multiple sets of lungs expanding and contracting in unison. Then the moment broke and he was back in himself again with his own single heartbeat pounding in his chest.

He looked down at her in surprise. "Did you feel that?"

"Feel what?" she said, smiling up at him. "All I feel is you. And me. And this. And I want to do that again," she said as she wriggled her hips against his. "And again." She leaned up to kiss his neck. "And again." She sucked on his earlobe.

Ronan shook himself and smiled down at her. "Can you go again and again and again?" he teased. He flexed and pushed himself deep inside her, so deep she cried out from the pressure and pleasure of it.

"We'll see."

And they certainly did.

CHAPTER 13

AFTERWARD, HE WAITED UNTIL she was drowsing, mostly asleep, before leaning over and speaking in her ear.

"Una?"

She made a noise of irritation and he smiled.

"I need to visit my second-in-command at the cave. I need to let him know not to look for me while I'm with you. Okay?"

She rolled over, blinking at him with bleary eyes. "Sure, but you must be back before nightfall."

"Why is that?"

"We have dinner plans tonight," Una told him with a playful grin.

He couldn't help but grin back. "We do? Who with?"

"The Mayor and his wife."

The smile slipped from his face as he frowned. "Shouldn't we be focusing on this? We don't have time to waste."

Una sighed. "I know what I said earlier, and you were right. We need to work the problem, not focus on what we don't know. Adair stopped by the shop earlier today and invited us over. I think he wants to get to know you better."

"And why would he care?"

"He was an old friend of my father's. He's always kept a friendly eye on me after my father passed, always been nice to me. I think he sees me as the daughter he never had, since he and his wife never had children." She lowered her voice to a whisper. "He let slip once that she was barren, despite their hopes." She gave him a significant look. "But I didn't just tell you that, okay?"

Ronan nodded reluctantly. If she wanted to waste time with this Mayor, who was he to argue. They had been operating on her deadline the entire time.

He rose, got dressed, and crept out to her boat. As he pushed it off the shore and into the ocean, leaping in at the last second with practiced grace, he wondered at what he'd experienced with their lovemaking. That moment of remembered heartbeats, of shared lung space. It was just like what he'd experienced back at the cave the day he met Una, and, he was now sure of it, because of Una. Somehow he'd sensed her at the cave, just like he'd been aware of her body in such a heightened way when they were joined.

He stopped rowing for a moment, struck by a sudden, horrifying thought. Was that a True Mate bond trying to form? He'd often heard of them growing up, knew the stories of selkies who had found the other half of their souls in someone else. They were the only ones for whom fate paused. And that gave him pause.

True Mate bonds were strong, stronger than typical loving affection or lust. They surpassed mating ties even, for those unlucky individuals who made up one half of a mated pair only to find their True Mate later. Even then, the True Mate bond was the penultimate goal, as those bonds metaphysically linked one selkie to another. He didn't understand it fully, but like Una knew her town's stories of selkie lore, he knew the lore of the True Mate bonds.

It was a sobering thought. He had never heard of it to happen outside of selkies, and certainly not with a human, of all creatures!

That can't be it, his mind rebelled. There had to be another explanation. It made more sense that he was tied to her somehow by his sealskin, that her having ownership gave him a heightened sense of her. Or something like that. Anything other than a True Mate bond.

For an Anchor sworn to his clan, that was a fate worse than death because it meant being torn between two masters: your heart or your duty. It went against everything he'd dedicated his life towards, to have a mate suddenly thrown into the mix. And that wasn't something he could afford to be distracted by.

"It can't be a True Mate bond," he said to the empty sea air. It made him feel better to say it aloud, as if by speaking the words they became solid, tangible truth. He would see if the feelings persisted, but this in no way deviated him from his plan to seduce Una and get his sealskin back.

It was a minor inconvenience, but nothing he couldn't handle.

After several more minutes, he made it to the inlet he was looking for. He rowed around to the cave and docked the boat against the shore. Striding around to the mouth of the cave, he saw Ceannas waiting on the pebbled shore for him when he entered.

"I was worried," the second Anchor said. His flaxen hair stood in wild tangles on his bare shoulders. He was naked, his strong body lean and well-muscled. He was heavier than Ronan, with more bulky muscle than Ronan's lean body naturally held, but Ronan often outmatched him when they sparred together. Ceannas may be heavier, but he didn't know how to wield it against a slighter opponent, something Ronan frequently tried to get through his head.

Ronan sighed as they clasped hands and bared their teeth at each other. It was a similar greeting to how they met as seals, where they slapped their flippers against each other and showed their pointed front teeth to display dominance. For these two, however, it was an empty display and not a true show of aggression.

"Well met," Ronan said.

"Well met to you, too," Ceannas responded. "Now what is this side mission that is so important? The clan grows restless with the siren threat."

"Which is a threat no more," Ronan said, ignoring the first question. He didn't want to jump into that can of sea snakes just yet.

Ronan took a deep breath. This was important, but it wasn't what he was focused on. He forced himself to settle. "Yes, they offered this." He pulled the necklace from his pocket and handed it over.

Ceannas squinted at it as he held it a few inches away from his face. He examined it as one might a small, very interesting bug. "They think to buy our peace with a bauble?" His voice was scornful.

"No, it is more than that. The white bones on the sides are said to be from the siren princeling's own fin tips, his metacarpals. The civil war was more than an uprising, it was a declaration. There were some in Clann Dorcha that wished to turn him over to us and who quietly disagreed with the royal's handling of the matter and their refusal to admit guilt. Once the war between us began, they became more vocal—they didn't see why they should die for his sins. They weren't willing to fight on behalf of the royal army, so they banded together and assassinated the royal family a week ago. News only just reached us when they sent an emissary with this."

Now Ceannas examined the necklace with more interest. "And this was made from his bones?"

Ronan nodded. "The flyspeck cerith on the end is supposed to be very rare. Something of a sacred find in their culture. It's meant as a valuable peace offering to show they wish no more war between siren and selkie."

"We had no issue with sirens, in general," Ceannas groused. "Only Clann Dorcha. But there is no need to remind them of that." He handed the necklace back to Ronan. "For a decade, they refused to give us the information we wanted and continued to convey their princeling had nothing to do with the attack. And now they want peace? I don't buy it."

Ronan's mouth twisted into a grimace. "What always got me was that I even caught him in the act!" Those damnable sirens never allowed their pride to get put aside for anything reasonable. All they had had to do was admit their prince's part in the attack that had occurred—the destruction of Lord Prion's sealskin—and they could work out retribution. But instead they played dumb for twenty-four years, as Ronan had suspected they would. Sirens were nothing if not full of guile.

"If only he hadn't escaped..." Ceannas mused with a sideways glance at Ronan.

Ronan flashed him a warning glare. "I did my best to capture him. He was too fast."

"If you weren't so weighed down by all that blubber," Ceannas offered with a sly smile, "you might have been able to keep up. And then our war would never have happened."

Ronan looked affronted. "How dare you." But the comment held no heat. There was nothing but amicability between the two and they knew it.

Ceannas grinned at him. "Did you know, the sirens, in addition to their little *peace offering*—" Ceannas sneered the words "—they have demanded an apology."

Ronan's eyebrows raised in surprise. "Have they? That's news to me. And what slight do they figure we gave?"

"For us to initiate war against them. For us slaying so many of their kind in a senseless war."

Ronan snorted. "Of course, for so many of *their* kind. Their clan is responsible for more selkie lives lost than ever before." He rolled his eyes. "It figures."

He turned serious eyes to Ceannas, who was looking around the cave with interest. Ronan glanced around, too, noting the sparkling set of water on the stone near the ground from the last high tide. Glittery things always caught Ceannas's eye. He snapped his fingers under Ceannas's nose, and the other man turned startled eyes back to him.

"Focus! What does your reconnaissance tell you about the fighting size of their clan now?"

Ceannas's expression was grave. "Too large. They outnumber us five-to-one, despite their losses."

"How did that happen?"

"They took on a new clan into their group, so their size nearly doubled. In a real battle, we would have half a contingent of Anchors available, while the rest shepherded the rest of the clan to safety. We do not have a favorable outcome should that happen."

Ronan ground his teeth together. He'd feared the same. If the peace offering was a ruse and the sirens attacked, his clan would have difficulty defending themselves. Though Prion had agreed to accept the peace offering, it could be a ruse to make the selkies let down their guard. They would have to be extra-vigilant until the royals signed the peace treaties.

"We need to figure out how to bolster our defenses. Take a third of the Anchors and let the sirens know we accept their peace offering and wish to schedule the signing of a peace treaty. Make a show of force against the territory edge of their clan. Show them we aren't afraid of them."

"Won't that have the opposite effect of what we want? If we incite them to attack, we're—"

"Still in control," Ronan supplied. "They respect boldness. Their culture favors the bold and the impetuous.

It will show us to be a formidable fighting force, even if numbers aren't on our side."

Ceannas nodded in understanding. "It will play to their culture as a show of boldness. Where we see arrogance, they see power. "

Ronan nodded his head in agreement. Ceannas was not slow, he'd give him that. "And that will buy us time to figure out how the King and Queen want to play the peace treaty signing."

"Do you think they'll be willing to ignore the damage done?"

"King Righ may go along with it, as he's the more rational of the two. But Mairi lives up to her name. She may want something more than a peace offering, some show of subservience to make up for the injury they caused their son."

Ceannas grimaced. "That won't go over well. Their clan is proud."

"As are we." Ronan bared his teeth in a fearsome smile.

Ceannas grinned back, baring his own teeth. "If they want a fight, we will bring one." Then his expression sobered. "But I hope, for both our sakes, that the offer of peace was genuine. I weary of all the fighting."

This surprised Ronan. Ceannas loved a good fight as much as any of them. Perhaps too much, but that was a lesson for another time. Right now, Ronan was glad of his youthful exuberance and impressed at his temperance. The young Anchor would be a good leader someday.

"Lord Prion will want to make sure his pearl shipment arrives on schedule. It is imperative the humans believe he is another of their kind, making a living from the sea, like they do. We must jeopardize his stability at our peril."

Ceannas rolled his eyes. "For a banished Prince, he sure gives a lot of orders."

"Banished though he may be, he is still Queen Mairi's son. He may command the battle forces but his parents have the ultimate say when forging alliances and peace treaties. If he wants a cushy life as a human, since he cannot have one as a selkie, who are we to begrudge that?"

"When it takes up my valuable time hunting baubles and trinkets for humans, it begrudges me!" Ceannas exclaimed.

Ronan grinned. "I'll let Lord Prion know of your feelings next time we meet."

Ceannas blanched. "Don't you dare. I don't wish to lose my head as well as my skin. Besides, I heard he won't be available for another week, anyway." At Ronan's inquisitive look, he added, "I was told he is off selling his last shipment."

Ronan's stomach sank. He had been counting on getting his Prince's advice on how to deal with the Una situation. And he still had to deliver the news of the siren peace offering.

But Ceannas saw the doubt on his face and gave Ronan a skeptical look. "Are you all right? You look as if this news had more impact on you than I expected. Does it have to do with this side mission you've been avoiding talking about?"

Ronan sighed. He knew it would come up, eventually. "There's been a new development." He cleared his throat. "I seem to have found myself in a predicament with a human woman."

Ceannas's eyes narrowed, and he smiled knowingly. "Ah, like that, is it? Well, give the babe your protection and be gone. You won't know if it's selkie or human until it turns twenty-two anyway, so—"

"There's no child, fool! A woman stole my sealskin. Says unless I help her with a personal problem, she won't give it back."

Ceannas shrugged. "Then kill her." Ronan blanched, and Ceannas grinned wickedly. "Now, Ronan, you were never one to shy from what needs doing. Why the weak stomach now?"

"She hides it from me. If I kill her, I won't get the location from her."

"Then torture her for the information."

Ronan's mind raced. "How do I know she will tell the truth? That she won't give me the wrong information just to spare her life? I have no guarantee she will tell me."

Ceannas looked at him in disbelief. "This is not a hard thing to figure out, Ronan. Convince her to give you back the skin. Do whatever is necessary. End of story." He raised his eyebrows in sudden inspiration. "Can I help?"

Ronan shook his head quickly. "No!" Then, at Ceannas's confused expression, he softened with what he hoped was a reassuring smile. "No, my friend, not this time. This is a small matter, something that will—" he ground his teeth together as he smiled "*hopefully* not take longer than a few weeks. I may be out of reach for a while. In the meantime, you must take over my duties as Anchor."

Ceannas's eyes widened. "That's... that's an honor." He clasped his fist to his heart. "I will not let you down!" His eyes shone with eagerness, such that Ronan smiled gently.

"I know you'll do a fine job. Just don't let your lust for battle overrule your common sense when handling the sirens."

Now Ceannas looked affronted. "Please! Have more faith in me than that."

Ronan laughed and clapped Ceannas on the shoulder. "Well met, my friend. And safe swimming."

"Well met to you, too." Ceannas said and clasped Ronan's hand again. Then he turned, pulled his sealskin over his shoulders and collapsed in a crouch onto the sand.

The human shape curled inward, becoming larger and more bulky as the sealskin flopped over his head, covering it like a cape. The seal's head dipped, nudging about at its stomach. Then it raised its head, as much a seal in appearance, with no trace of his human form visible. It gave a loud bark in parting, then slid into the sea.

Ronan watched with a pang of jealousy. He'd never given any thought before to donning his sealskin, securing it, then disappearing into the water as a seal. It was as natural an action as breathing to him. But to see someone else do it when he couldn't tore at him.

Soon, he told himself. He already had a good bond with Una, one that was growing stronger every day. It wouldn't be long until she trusted him enough to reveal where his skin was, he was sure of it, especially if it was a True Mate bond growing between them.

He just had to be patient.

CHAPTER 14

UNA REREAD THE PASSAGE her eyes had just traveled moments ago, then sat back from the journal and rubbed her eyes. She had been trying to read the same journal entry for the last hour of afternoon light and had nothing to show for it. None of the words made sense, jumbling over one another as she tried and failed to think about what Ronan was doing while he was gone. He had said he had to meet his second-in-command to let him know why he would be gone for a while. At least, she thought that was what she remembered him saying.

But what if they were plotting about how to get his skin back? What if they came for her, tried to hurt her? She knew Ronan was a warrior of some kind, what he called an Anchor. It sounded too much like a soldier for her liking. And soldiers knew how to hurt people.

Then she shook her head. Ronan wouldn't hurt her. If he was going to, he would have already. The gods knew he'd never been angrier than when he first discovered she'd hidden his sealskin. If there would have been danger for her, it would have been then.

She thought of how tender he had been when they made love. The memories made her body heat with desire. How loving he had been! How attentive. It had been better than anything she'd ever experienced before, especially with Blair. They had attempted lovemaking a few times. But it had been nothing but a chore for her, and a painful one at that. He had been willing, but lackluster in performance, finishing quickly and just as quickly redressing, as if ashamed that she had seen him so unmanned.

Ronan was nothing like that. He languished in his nakedness, letting her luxuriate in the sight of him. And he seemed to enjoy cuddling afterward, which she also liked. It was nice to feel safe in someone's arms, especially someone as strong and capable as he was.

Yes, he had certainly surprised her. Though nothing had surprised her more than her own feelings. She yearned for his touch again, craving it like a child after long-denied candy. She wanted to touch him, feel his long hair running through her fingers as she clenched her fist in it. Wanted to feel his tongue on her bare skin again.

Without realizing it, her hand had crept to between her legs, pressing to hold back the sensations the memories invoked. Yes, he had been especially attentive there—

A knock at the door interrupted her thoughts. She pulled her hand away from her legs in a startled jerk, flushing as if caught out.

"Una! Open up! I know you're in there!" Lyall's voice called through the thick door, and Una grimaced. Of course, she would pay a visit now. Una was just glad she hadn't shown up earlier when she'd been otherwise engaged.

Una looked down at her father's journal and closed the cover with reluctance. His secrets would have to wait a little longer.

She opened the door and jerked back as Lyall rushed into the room, heedless of an invitation.

"Donalda's dress is going to be the talk of the town for *years!*" she gushed. She stopped, hands on her hips, and turned a circle. When she faced Una, her expression was shrewd. "Okay, where is he?"

Una flushed. "Um... who?"

"This new man everyone's talking about. The one with the eyes like fire."

"Oh." Una pursed her lips, trying to think of how to explain him. "He's... well, see, I met him on the mainland—"

Lyall's eyes widened. "Ooh, a *mainlander!* That's positively scandalous! Why would anyone want to come out to Selbane when they could live on the mainland? It's so...*fishy* out here and all-the-time damp." Her nose wrinkled in disgust.

Una scowled. Though Ronan was not a real husband, she felt piqued at the thought that she was not enough for someone to come over from the mainland for. "We're in love," she growled.

Lyall paused, her mouth frozen in a small O. "In love?" she queried in a small voice.

"Yes," Una ground out, mindful of the fact that she must choose her words carefully. "He's my... my..."

"Your what?" Lyall clasped her hands in front of her as if to protect herself from the news she feared was coming. "Your beloved?"

"My husband." Una sighed the word. She braced herself for a scream, for a cry of indignation. This would not go over well.

But, to her horror, she saw tears fill Lyall's eyes and her lip began a tiny tremble. "And you didn't tell me? How could you not tell me?" Her voice was full of betrayal.

Una closed her eyes. This was worse than she had hoped. She rushed to hold Lyall's hands, but the other girl jerked them away. Her face contorted as tears began falling. "You... you... we... I thought we were best friends!" Now she began to show some kind of anger. "How could you get married without telling me? No, worse: how could you *fall in love* and I not know about it?"

She tossed her hands down as if throwing something to the floor. She paced in front of the couch, along the well-worn carpet. Una feared her stomping feet would tear it further, but there was no way she was going to say anything. Best just to mend the holes later.

"How could you fall in love without me? I thought we told each other everything. Everything! And here I find out you've gone and married some... some... *mainlander.*" She spat the word as if it were an insult. "And brought him here to this horrid little fishing town because you're in love and you..." She whirled and pointed an angry finger at Una. "When were you going to tell me about all this?" she demanded.

Una flinched and offered a small smile. "Today?"

A shadow fell over Lyall's face. She scowled. "When today? It's almost dinnertime."

"Um... now?" Una put her hands out in a placating gesture. "Lyall, it's not... it wasn't like that. It was a... a.. whirlwind sort of romance. The kind that sweeps you off your feet the moment you meet. I met him when I went to send a letter and he was so..." She cast about, waving her hands in small circles as she thought about how to describe the fictitious love affair. "He was so confident and caring." She thought of the way he held her after they made love. "And so strong. He touched me in ways I never felt before."

"But you had Blair," Lyall grumbled.

"That was different." The vast differences between Blair and Ronan almost made her laugh aloud, but she knew that would be disastrous. "Blair never made me feel like I was the only person in the room when he was around. As if I was something to be treasured, prized, sought after. Not like Ro—"

"So he's a big man, then?" Lyall asked in a softer tone. Una knew how much she longed for the love Una had just described.

"Not so much. Bigger than me, obviously, but not huge. Muscled. Lean." She thought of his hands caressing her body. "Big hands." She blushed, and Lyall smiled a little.

"And he treats you right, this husband of yours?" Lyall's voice still held a twinge of jealousy, but Una sensed she was coming down off her cloud of anger and hurt.

Una's memory was filled with the way Ronan looked at her, as if she was something he hungered for, the desire he let fill his eyes when he gazed into hers, and she shivered. "Very much so, yes."

"Well, where is he?" Lyall demanded again. "I want to meet him."

"He's... out."

Lyall scowled. "Out where? When will he be back?"

Una sighed. "I'm not exactly sure, to be honest. He had to go meet... a friend. He should be back soon, though." *I hope*, she thought fervently.

Lyall looked at her through narrowed eyes, as if suspecting Una was lying to her. "How soon? Should I wait for him? Or should I come back another time?"

Una thought. She needed to prepare Ronan before meeting Lyall. He might not appreciate coming home to the inquisition she knew Lyall had planned. Her friend was loyal, and she wouldn't be satisfied until he had answered all of her questions about his intentions with Una.

"You know my father is going to be furious at not having met him. I assume he doesn't even know yet?"

Una pursed her lips. She'd forgotten all about Uncle Hugh and Aunt Leannán! Yes, he would be upset. He had been like a father to her since her own had died, and he would wonder about the rushed nature of her marriage. "I will visit him when they return and let him know."

Lyall pursed her lips and glared. "They're back already."

"Since when?"

"Last night. And they'll be expecting to see you. Especially after my father hears the gossip the way I had." Lyall's mouth puckered as if she tasted something sour.

Una ignored that last jibe. "He doesn't visit town that much, so I doubt he will hear about it before I get to tell him. Lyall, promise me you won't say anything."

Lyall gazed at her mutinously.

"Lyall," Una said in a warning tone. "Promise me."

Lyall rolled her eyes. "If he finds out I knew and said nothing—"

"Promise!

"Ugh!" Lyall groaned. But she nodded. "I promise." She pointed a finger at Una. "But you'd better tell him before he or my mother finds out. It'll be worse if they find out from someone in town. *Like I did.*"

Una stepped forward and hugged her friend. "Thank you, Lyall, and I'm sorry. I should have told you earlier in the shop. I just had other things on my mind." Lyall's tense shoulders softened as she hugged Una back.

"But you owe me the full story later. I want to know *all* about it. How you met, what he does for a living, how he likes his tea. *Everything.*" She pulled back and shot Una a warning glare. "I mean it."

Una smiled and kissed her cheek. "I promise. I will tell you about all of it."

Lyall gathered her skirts in her hand and, with one final glance around the house, as if to make sure he wasn't hiding somewhere nearby, she left.

As Una closed the door, she let out a sigh. This was going to be harder than she'd thought. She had just told the mother of all lies to her best friend. And later she'd do the same to her surrogate father and mother. She would craft a convincing love story to prove how they met and how in love she was. This would require some collaborating with Ronan. He was good at these kinds of cover stories, apparently.

When would he return? She glanced out the window, hoping to see his lean figure striding towards the house.

But it was just the same familiar view she'd seen every day for twenty-four years. It mocked her with its sameness, which used to give her a sense of ease and peace. But now she longed for it to look different with his silhouette against the horizon.

CHAPTER 15

WHEN RONAN RETURNED THAT evening, Una had already fallen asleep on the bed. She woke to his lips pressing against hers.

"Wha—" she began, but he pressed his body close against her and she realized he was naked. She ran her hands down his arms, feeling the muscles clenching like wooden beams under her palms.

He kissed her insistently, as if he hungered for her like no other and couldn't get enough of her. She responded to his ardor, letting him pull back enough to slide her nightshirt over her head and bare her body to him.

He ran his hands down her stomach, caressing between her legs for a moment before thrusting a finger inside her.

"You're ready," he growled in surprise.

He lowered his body over hers and slid between her legs, thrusting into her with his hard length. She cried out at the pressure, still warming to the sensations coursing through her, and held him as he thrust in and out.

In moments, he stiffened and pulled his upper body back. She made a sound of disappointment, but he said, "I want you to come, too."

She nodded, and pulled him back down, opening her legs wider to receive him as he thrust harder and faster inside her. She felt the wave of emotion rise in her, then it crested. Crying out with her climax, she took his length until the sensation was too much. When he felt her relax, he stiffened over her as he climaxed, too, his back hard underneath her fingers until he relaxed with a sigh of pleasure.

Something surged between them, like a cord so close to tightening it was almost painful. He could feel the sensations rolling through his body, echoed by a ghost of similar, yet separate feelings of satisfaction and desire. Then, as he tensed under the realization, the feeling faded, leaving him feeling strangely alone inside his own body. It was like before, yet different. This time, he experienced a pleasurable, languid satisfaction that felt apart from him and separate from his own feelings. It was almost as if he was feeling what Una had to be feeling, too.

The True Mate bond, his mind supplied, and he let the thought roll through his brain instead of pushing it aside.

Was it so bad if she's your True Mate? a voice that sounded suspiciously like Ceannas whispered. She was beautiful and smart and strong-willed. Exactly the kind of woman he'd want as a mate if he ever took one.

He rolled her over so that she lay on top of him and watched her as she drowsed in his arms, her head on his chest. He knew the emotional bond between them was stronger with their lovemaking, but he'd always heard that the True Mate bond wouldn't begin to strengthen until two climaxed together. The metaphysical joining of minds that occurred then would be unavoidable and that obviously hadn't happened yet. But he could tell from the pliant way her body conformed to his that she was closer to falling under his spell than before. Never would she have let him own her so completely if she hadn't felt that attraction already.

He gazed down at her, taking in the beautiful lines of her face, the weather-roughened tan of her skin, the sun-bleached highlights of her copper hair. This had become more than just seduction, he realized. Much more. He could feel himself falling in love with her, which hadn't been in the plan, but which he now couldn't imagine as anything but unavoidable after getting to know her.

"I want you to have this," he murmured in her ear. After getting up from the bed, he walked over to his pile of clothes. He picked up the pants, fished something from the pocket, and returned to her.

He held up his hand. In his fist was a small necklace of white bones with a curled shell on the end that looked like a unicorn's horn.

"It's lovely," she breathed, then looked at him in surprise. "Who was this intended for?"

Ronan scowled. "What do you mean? How do you know I didn't make this especially for you?" When she merely looked at him, he relented with a small smile. "It was originally intended as a peace offering from the sirens. I was entrusted to keep it safe." He looked at her gravely. "I want you to have this. As a symbol of my commitment, my heart." He moved the hair off her shoulder and leaned forward to tie it around her neck.

She looked down at where it lay between her breasts and fingered the end of the shell carefully. "It's beautiful."

"Not as beautiful as you." She looked up with a smile, but he was watching her with a serious expression on his face. He reached up to cup her cheek. "Nothing can match you." He kissed her, and she met his kiss eagerly.

But as she reached for him, he pulled away with a laugh. "Not again. Not now. Much as I would adore it. We have to get to town." At her inquiring look, he raised his eyebrows. "Remember? We need to meet the doctor again. Dr. Scott was it?"

Una laughed. "We don't have to meet him right this second." She patted the bed next to her and raised her eyebrows in invitation. "We have plenty of time..."

Ronan groaned and gathered up his clothes. He began to dress as Una flipped to her stomach on the bed. He glanced at her and drank in the sight of her pale buttocks and smooth back. She propped her head on her hands and frowned at him.

"I don't like this side of you," she grumbled.

"The proactive side?"

"The dressed side." Then, with a groan of effort, she rolled off the bed and began to dress herself.

"I'm not too fond of it either," Ronan groused as he tied the drawstring at his waist. Then he bent to put on the stockings and his shoes. "Just like this retched couch!" He made a noise of disgust and glared at her. "Can't you afford some furniture that was made this century?"

She glared at him as she tied the sash of her dress around her waist. "That couch was my father's. And his father's before him. It is a cherished family heirloom."

"It's only fit for kindling." Ronan glared back at her, then softened. "I could make one for you, you know."

Una paused with a surprised look. "You know how to make furniture?"

Ronan grinned at her. "How hard could it be?"

Una grinned back at him. "You might be surprised. Let's just focus on the curse for now. You can play house with me later."

Ronan's smile slipped from his face as she turned and moved to fetch her shoes. Play house? Is that what she saw this as? If she merely thought of him using her for sex, he would have to double his efforts. He had been serious in expressing his feelings for her. He would have to be more intentional with his affections to let her know how serious. "Playing house?" he asked, feigning misunderstanding. "What does that mean?"

She turned to him with a frown. "You know, we pretend to be together for a while. It's a mutually beneficial system."

"Aren't you worried about how that might make you seem?"

"I am lonely. And I suspect you are, too." The admission made him flinch in surprise. She was far more perceptive than he gave her credit for. "So we make each other happy while we hunt for this curse solution," she continued, unaware of his reaction. "And when it's over, it's over."

He narrowed his eyes at her. "So this is some fun diversion for you while we complete this task, is all?"

She narrowed her eyes back at him in mock mimicry. "And what is it for you?"

He pursed his lips. How much to tell her? He decided she needed to know it all if she was to understand his true feelings for her. "I know we are bound by something more than just physical attraction." He stalked towards her. "There is something between us, even a human like yourself must feel it." She cocked her head at him, considering his words. He approached her and stood very close to her, letting his nearness invade her space. He leaned towards her so their lips were inches away. "Do you feel it?"

"Yes," she breathed, her eyes on his lips.

"You, my lovely, fierce woman, are my True Mate." He paused, holding his breath as she frowned. He let her take in his words and puzzle over them for a moment.

She pulled back. "What does that mean?"

"It means you are my mate, the only one for me, the one I never knew I was looking for. And now you're here." He moved closer to her, pressing his body to hers. "And I'm here."

"But what does that mean for us?"

He decided it was good that she hadn't pulled away from him. The True Mate concept hadn't scared her off. "It means we are fated to be together. That you are the other half of my soul. We were made for each other, Una, on a physical and emotional level. This is more than just love. It's a lifetime of being together in the most intimate of ways."

"A lifetime?" She frowned up at him. "But I'm human. My lifetime is shorter than yours."

"Not once you accept the True Mate bond. Your life is extended to that of mine."

"But what if you die? What happens to me then?"

Ronan cocked his head thoughtfully. "I don't know," he admitted with a slow smile. "I've only ever known one person who was True Mated before and we're not exactly on intimate speaking terms."

"Then how do you know this is what's between us?"

He pulled her closer and was emboldened when she let him. "Because I feel it every time we make love together. It's like a second heartbeat or a flash of pleasure that I'm not feeling myself."

"You can feel my emotions?" Una squeaked in surprise, her eyebrows raising high.

Ronan laughed. "Only a glimpse. Nothing like when the True Mate bond is fully realized and in place. Or so I understand it."

Una's face shifted to a doubtful frown. "I'm not sure I'm ready for that kind of... intensity. That's a lot to take in."

Ronan leaned down to press his forehead against hers. "I understand. But you know what? We'll navigate this together."

She pulled back far enough to give him a skeptical, calculating look. "And what if I'm never ready for it?" she asked softly.

He sighed. "Then we navigate that together, too." He squeezed her upper arms. "But we make that choice together. I can't do it by myself." *And I can't force you to give me back my sealskin,* he thought. He understood that the original mission had changed—it was no longer solely about seduction for seduction's sake. But he had complicated feelings about the True Mate bond; was he truly ready to alter his future forever just for the chance to be a seal again? And if he didn't, what did that mean for both of them?

"How do we, you know, make the bond take hold? If we decide to do that?"

He pushed his doubts away and pursed his lips. "I'm pretty sure we have to climax together during our lovemaking. I think when two True Mates come together, their climax seals the bond."

"Then we'll have to be very, very careful until then," Una cautioned sternly.

Ronan grinned at her. "I have been this whole time. No reason to stop now."

"Good. Now we've got to head to dinner at Adair's. We can see the doctor tomorrow."

He straightened and moved away, letting the air swirl behind him, marking his absence. It was good that she felt some of the True Mate bond and even better that she now realized what was truly between them. She had no doubt assumed it was sheer lust, and that was fine. For now. But he would need more from her than just physical attraction if he was to convince her to give up his sealskin.

He pulled her into a hug, but his expression was sober as he gazed over her shoulders. The True Mate bond was not something to be ignored, and it ruined both of their chances at finding happiness with someone else. To be bound together but not actually together would be a horrible way to live his very long life.

But he knew he couldn't pressure her before she was ready. And, in time, she would give up his sealskin on her own once the True Mate bond was in place. It was just a matter of time.

He hoped it wouldn't be very long.

CHAPTER 16

DUSK WAS JUST FALLING as they made their way up the bluff towards the Mayor's manor house.

"Wow," Ronan murmured.

Una looked at it with new eyes. She had been to the Mayor's house many times, as her father and Adair had been friends, but now she looked at it from Ronan's perspective.

The home was large, much larger than Una's cottage. It was a two-story manor with gray stone laid on the outside. The windows shone with candles on each sill, even the ones upstairs. A large red door with a window panel at the top half stood in the middle of the house front, bracketed on either side by small green shrubs carved into little balls the size of cartwheels.

"I suppose it's impressive," she grumbled, irritated at his adoration when he'd compared her own house to a hovel when they'd first met.

The door swung open, and Adair Barron boomed a greeting at them.

"Welcome, my honored guests!" He stood to one side to allow them entry.

His wife, Harper, met them just inside the door. "It's so good to see you, Una," she said warmly, embracing her in a gentle hug. She was a lovely woman, several years younger than Adair, but with a single gray streak that ran from her forehead down the long, dark hair that hung down her back. The hair at her temples had been gathered back with a shell barrette decorated with small gold stones. Her dress was long and grey, with a simple brown belt that showed off her curvy figure.

She cast an appraising look at Ronan, who offered his hand. She put her hand in his.

"My lady, well met," he said in a smooth voice, and bowed over their clasped hands. Harper gave him a bemused look, then arced an eyebrow at Una as if to ask *is he always like this?* Una just smiled and followed Harper into the dining room, where a lavish table was set with plates full of food at their chairs.

"Please, sit," Adair said, with a grand wave of his arm. "I hope you don't mind that we served you before you arrived. We figured you would be hungry when you got here."

"Not at all," Una said in a bright voice. The tablecloth was a simple homespun but had been pressed to have crisp creases at the corners.

Ronan sat and picked up his fork and speared a small potato slathered in gravy.

It was halfway to his mouth when Adair said, "Perhaps we should say grace first..?"

Ronan glanced at Una, then put down his fork. They clasped hands at Adair's motion, and all bowed their heads, except for Ronan, who watched them all with a confused expression. As Adair began the prayer, he took the hint and bowed his head, too.

"Great Lord, we thank you for the generous and bountiful feast we have in front of us. Bless the hands that provided for us and continue to bless us into prosperity for the future year."

Una noticed he didn't finish in the customary way, where one offered blessings on the guests at the table, too. But perhaps he'd been raised differently than she had been. Though she followed the older ways of her father, she respected the churchgoers in town that stuck to their beliefs. Belief was an important thing to have. For her and her father, they'd always stuck to something her father had once heard and oft repeated, "don't let your religion get in the way of your faith." And she certainly had lots of that.

Adair finished the prayer with a giant smile that made the wrinkles at the corner of his eyes multiply and spread down his cheeks.

"Let's begin, shall we?" Harper said with a gentle wave of her hand to indicate their plates. Una thought her voice sounded musical, and suspected the older woman had a delightful singing voice. Maybe she would sing for them after dinner—it was more common at large gatherings, but maybe she'd make an exception for them tonight.

There was a knock at the door, and everyone paused, looking around the table at each other. A servant in a grey uniform appeared at Adair's shoulder and leaned forward to whisper in his ear.

"Excuse me," Adar said, standing in a smooth motion and setting his cloth napkin on the table beside his plate.

Una and Ronan looked at Harper, who gazed serenely back at them. She didn't seem inclined to continue the conversation, merely looked at them with a gentle smile on her face. She seemed pleased to have their company, though the silence felt a little awkward to Una.

Just as Una was about to comment on the tasty meal, Adair reappeared. He thumped down in his chair, slumping slightly. He ran a hand through his hair, and it stuck up in disheveled waves. "I just got word from Finlay," he said to his wife, ignoring Una and Ronan. "Dr. Scott is dead. And, to make matters even worse, the docks are drying up."

Una gasped and leaned forward over her plate. "Wait, what?"

Adair turned tired eyes to hers. He looked as if he had aged years in a few short minutes. He looked every bit of his sixty years of age. "Dr. Scott was found in his office by his intern. That young man..." he snapped his fingers to job his memory, "What was his name again, dear?"

"Lucas," Harper offered in a subdued tone. She had her eyes tuned demurely down at her plate.

"But what about the docks?" Ronan asked urgently. Una felt as if someone had punched her in the stomach.

"The water line is about a foot lower than it was before. Which is about two feet lower than it was a few years ago." Adair ran a hand through his hair again and leaned his elbows on the table. "Something's changing," he murmured, almost to himself. Una and Ronan shared a look. "The water is going down. Soon the larger ships will be dry-docked in the harbor because they can't make it through the shallower waters of the inlet."

Una glanced at Harper. A small smile played about her lips as she watched her husband with greedy eyes. *Surely this was some nervous reaction?* Una guessed. It was strange, for sure.

"But this has happened over time, right?" Ronan asked. "It's taken years to—"

"This happened overnight." Adair's voice was low and quiet. Una looked back at him, aghast.

Ronan looked around the table. "How could the water go down a foot overnight?"

Adair lifted his hands and shook them. "I don't know! The sea captains were clamoring about something when I went into town today, but I had other things on my mind. I didn't know..." He sighed and passed a hand over his face. "Nobody will have any catches to sell you tomorrow, Una. They're all too worried about the conditions of their boats—nobody went out for fear of not being able to get back in."

"Without that, the town will die." Ronan's voice matched the fear Una felt. The entire situation was unraveling too fast for them to process.

Adair gave him a look of dislike. "It won't die. I won't let it!" He slammed a fist on the table. "This town will be fine. I just have to think of a way to fix it, is all."

"But, Mayor, you're not a fisherman anymore. You can't control the tides."

"Perhaps we should move," Harper said in a silky voice. "Get away from this tiny town. Go somewhere else more profitable."

Adair shot her a dangerous look full of malevolence. Una got the sense that this was a conversation they had already had before. "We are not leaving," he hissed at her. "What would everyone think if I just up and—" He caught himself with a quick glance at Ronan and Una, as if he'd forgotten they were there for a moment. He sat straighter in his seat and smoothed his hair back using both hands.

When it was in place again, he looked more composed. He even managed a smile at Harper. "We will figure this out. The town will prosper. It's just a matter of hard work!" He nodded his head, as if proud of the idea now that he'd said it. "That's it! The fishermen will have to work harder, using smaller boats. We'll trawl the inlet until our numbers go up, and then we'll bring in some others from the mainland, perhaps. They can help increase our loads when the captains go out."

But that won't change the water level, Una thought grimly.

"Well," Harper purred, gathering her plate and standing. She leaned forward to pluck her husband's plate, as well. "This is certainly troubling news. But not the best topic for our guests to endure." She smiled warmly at them. Una rose, too, following Harper's lead, and gathered her and Ronan's plates. "Dessert?" Harper asked in a bright voice.

Ronan demurred, but Una forced a smile. "That would be lovely."

"We have Clootie Dumpling, if that's to your taste."

Una raised her brows in surprise. She only had that around Christmas time, and even then, had only had it once. It was a decadent dessert that her father hadn't often had the money to spare for the baking supplies.

"We would *love* some," she gushed. It paid to be in the Mayor's house, she thought. Despite the state of the rest of the town, they obviously were doing quite fine.

She followed Harper into the kitchen, which was twice the size of her own. There were bowls of fruit set out along the counters and plates set to one corner. In the middle was a long stone island with a large brown pillow of Clootie Dumpling loaf under a glass dome.

Una's eyes widened. Such decadence. It made her mouth water, just seeing it. She had such fond memories of sharing a slice slathered with butter with her father on Christmas morning.

"Would you care to take a whiff?" Harper asked, eyeing Una's reaction with interest.

Una nodded and set the plates down, hurrying to the island. Harper raised the glass dome and Una inhaled deeply, taking in the spiced, yeasty aroma. She closed her eyes and hummed in pleasure.

Harper looked pleased, and flashed her a quick, close-lipped smile before replacing the glass dome. "Good. Would you please get the custard bowl from the counter over there?" She motioned with her chin to an area to the left of the wash basin as she wrapped both hands under the Clootie Dumpling plate and hefted it into the air.

Una scurried around the island and grabbed the dish. It was still cool to the touch, which told her it had just been made. Which was odd, given how long they'd been sitting with Harper and Adair in the dining room.

"Did you make this?" she asked in a casual voice, as she followed Harper out of the kitchen.

"Oh no, dear," Harper said with a musical, tinkling laugh. "We had one of the servants make it fresh for you. Only the best for our guests." She smiled over her shoulder.

Una noted she seemed in a wonderful mood compared to her husband's earlier outburst. When they returned to the dining table, she noticed the lines in Adair's face standing out in stark contrast to his pale skin. He looked weathered, older, while Harper looked radiant as she set the Clootie Dumpling on the table with a flourish and motioned to where Una should set the custard bowl.

"Now, Ronan," she said with relish, as she sat down. Adair had been deep in conversation with Ronan as they entered and looked at her in irritated surprise at her interruption.

Ronan slid his hand over Una's thigh as she sat down and gave it a squeeze. She pressed her legs together at the rush of pleasure it brought and hoped Adair or Harper hadn't noticed. Ronan schooled his face into an expression of polite interest.

"I understand you aren't from around here," Harper said. She shot a sideways glance at Adair. "I, too, am from the mainland. Maybe I've been where you are from?"

Ronan opened his mouth, then closed it, then opened it again. "The mainland, yes. I'm from there." His hand tightened on Una's thigh. "I'm from all around, really. Here and there. We moved a lot when I was a child."

"What did your parents do?" she asked with raised eyebrows.

Ronan smiled at Una and she saw it was tense around the corners. She leaned forward. "His parents were woodworkers," she lied in a smooth voice. "But sadly, they died in a fire when he was young. He went to live with his aunt in Castle Kerrick. It was there that I met him." She gazed into Ronan's eyes like a woman deep in love when he looked at her uncertainly.

"Y-yes, that's all true," he stammered with a smile. His lips widened as he rallied himself. "It was a beautiful day, made more beautiful by her presence. I will never forget it." He gazed back at her, letting his desire for her edge into his expression.

Adair cleared his throat and gave Harper a pained look. "Yes, well. That's... lovely." He smiled at Harper. "I felt much the same way when I met my angel here."

Harper smiled at Adair, gazing at him from beneath hooded lids. "Yes. It forever changed our lives when we met, didn't it, dear?" Her voice was low and intimate. She turned her smile to Una and Ronan. "And now we have these two lovers here with us, in Selbane. We are so pleased, Ronan, that you came here and didn't take our Una away. It would have broken our hearts to lose her. She's been a staple of this town for as long as I have been here."

Una smiled. "That's very kind of you to say."

"I couldn't stand to take her away from her home," Ronan said. "I wouldn't dream of asking it. It would be like taking part of her heart from her body."

Harper's smile faded slightly. She glanced down as she re-situated herself in her chair, then turned a full smile on them again. "How beautiful. Such is the power of love."

Adair looked back and forth between Harper and Ronan. He looked confused—a line had appeared between his bushy brows. "Yes," he said drawled. "So it is." He opened his mouth to address Una, but Harper jumped in before he could get a word out.

"Ronan," she asked. "Being from the mainland, did you ever see the plankton shine in the ocean? It looks like a sheet of glowing lights under the water."

"I've only ever seen it once," he said. "When I was younger. The plankton moved out of season back then, didn't they?"

"That year they did, yes," she murmured, still smiling at him. Una thought her smile had turned predatory in its stillness. Then she shook herself. Predatory? Sweet Harper, who had been nothing but kind and generous since they had arrived? *It must be from the news of the tides,* she thought. It had her upset, so she was making more of things than was warranted.

Adair stared at his wife as if she'd said something he couldn't understand.

Ronan smiled, though his eyes were calculating. "Adair, have you ever seen it? Una?"

Una shook her head as Adair jerked his head to regard Ronan. This time, the line between his brows was deeper, almost frowning. "Never even heard of it. Plankton shining like lights? Preposterous. Plankton don't shine."

"That year they did," Harper assured him. Then she favored him with a sweet smile. "But that was ages ago. If Ronan was any kind of seaman, he would have seen it."

Then how did you *see it,* Una wondered. But she kept silent. She got the feeling the conversation between Ronan and Harper meant something more to them than she and Adair could grasp.

"They said it was a portent," Ronan said. "But I didn't know of what."

"Have you ever heard the story of Kore and Aides?" Harper asked him suddenly. "Like yours, it's a beautiful love story." When Ronan shook his head, she continued, "Kore was a beautiful young woman, and her father wed her to Aides, the god of the Underworld. But he didn't tell her mother, who loved Kore dearly. So, one day, when Kore was alone, Aides swept up from the Underworld and claimed her and took her down below. When her mother found out that she was gone, she wept bitterly, and the crops withered as she searched for her daughter.

"Eventually she found out what had happened, and she demanded Aides return her daughter unharmed. Aides agreed, but on the way back to the world of the living, he offered Kore a rare fruit and tricked her into eating a few of the seeds. Not knowing any better, she ate them, and so when she returned to her mother, was told she had eaten of the Underworld and so should remain there forever as Aides's bride.

"Her mother was incensed but agreed to a compromise: Kore would remain with Aides for three months of the year and would live with her mother for the remainder of the time. And whenever it came time for Kore to go back down to the Underworld, her mother mourned, turning the world barren for the time in which her daughter was gone."

She finished and gazed at them with half-lidded eyes. She seemed like she was waiting for their responses.

Adair stared at her with an open frown. "How is that a beautiful love story, my dear? They took her against her will, all for an arranged—" He purpled suddenly, his face turning blotchy with red patches on his cheeks. "This is hardly good conversation for our guests, my dear. I think you should excuse yourself for a moment to compose yourself and apologize to our guests for your rudeness at thinking that was suitable dinner conversation."

Harper scowled at him mutinously. "I don't think it was that bad, *dear*. It—"

"It was not appropriate. Please excuse yourself."

Harper's face darkened, and she stood.

Ronan and Una stared at each other in confusion. The conversation had taken a drastic turn, and they barely could keep up with it.

"I think it was kind of beautiful, actually," Una said in a tentative voice. Both Adair and Harper turned startled eyes to her. Both faces still held traces of anger in their expressions.

"My friend, Lyall," Una explained, "would have thought the forbidden love was a lovely concept. She values true love above all things. For Aides to pine for Kore is kind of sweet, and then to act in such a bold manner to take her to be with him. I can see how some might find it to be a love story."

Harper looked smug as she glanced at her husband. He frowned, then nodded at her, and she sat back down.

Ronan and Una shared a sigh of relief. It hadn't been that hard to diffuse the situation, after all.

"Well, let's dig in, shall we?" Harper asked, slicing large wedges of the Clootie Dumpling and settling them onto small plates decorated with small blue fish around the edges. Una wondered where the plates had appeared from. Perhaps some servant had appeared with them while they were in the kitchen.

"Whiskey?" Adair boomed with a forced smile. He still looked disgruntled from the earlier conversation. "It goes down best with a glass of whiskey."

Una demurred, but Ronan perked up. "I would love to try some of your whiskey."

Una squeezed his thigh under the table in warning, but Ronan didn't look at her. He seemed fascinated by Adair's movements as he fetched a large bowl with a narrowed neck and flared rim. He produced a few small cups and set them in front of everyone.

"Oh, I don't want any," Una tried, but Adair waved her objections away.

"Nonsense! It's my special vintage. You'll love it." Una sagged in her seat as he began pouring a finger's length into each cup. As he poured, he glanced at Ronan, indicating the jug of whiskey. "See, the bowl captures the aroma of the liquid, and the narrow neck directs it to your nose. See?" He held the jug up to Ronan's nose.

Ronan inhaled deeply, then coughed, his eyes watering. "It's splendid!" he choked out.

Adair looked satisfied, then sat back and took a small sip from his own cup.

As Harper spooned dollops of yellow custard over the wedges of Clootie Dumpling, Una tried a small sip of her whiskey. It burned her throat and nose, making her cough. The drink tasted like leather and orange peels, and she quickly spat her small mouthful back into her cup, hoping nobody noticed. She set her cup down with a smile and an appreciative noise.

Adair raised his glass to her at the noise, obviously enjoying her enjoyment of the drink.

Ronan took a deep drink and downed the contents in one gulp. He coughed, banging a fist to his chest, and set the cup down with a firm thud. "That's amazing!" He turned a surprised look to Una. "Wasn't that wonderful?" He held his cup up towards Adair. "May I have another?"

Adair looked surprised but pleased and refilled his cup again. Ronan downed the contents and sat back with a satisfied expression.

Una saw Harper roll her eyes and give a distasteful glance at the cup in her hands. She rolled the bottom of it gently on the table, careful not to spill any.

Una picked up her fork and took a bite of the Clootie Dumpling. The flavor hit her, and she closed her eyes in delight. It was better than she remembered having with her father. Back then, there had been no custard, which had a creamy, rich texture. The fruit in the dumpling gave small bursts of flavor as she bit into them, and the spiced pudding of the cake made her senses explode with delight. It was heavenly. She tried to take small bites to make it last longer.

"Is it good?" Harper asked with a smile, enjoying her reaction. In response, Una groaned in delight. Harper's smile widened, and she dug into her own plate.

For several moments, the only sounds were the scraping of forks on the plates.

Adair refilled Ronan's cup every time he emptied it, and it wasn't long before Ronan had begun to sway in his chair.

His eyes had a glassy look that Una recognized, and she pushed her plate away. "I don't mean to be rude, but it is getting very late for us. We have a busy day tomorrow, given the news of tonight." Adair gave her a solemn nod. "We won't infringe on your hospitality any further."

Harper and Adair waved away her offer to help carry plates into the kitchen and instead watched bemused as Una place one of Ronan's arms over her shoulders and steadied him as they walked to the door.

"Let me carry you home," Adair offered. Una started to protest, but Adair had already snapped for a servant, who appeared seconds later, as if conjured by magic. "Please prepare a carriage and take my friends back to Lady Una's home." The servant nodded and disappeared into the kitchen.

"You don't have to do that," Una said, irritated that Adair wouldn't be accompanying them himself at this late hour but forced one of his servants to do so. But she was tired of his company, his blustering and noise, and wasn't fond of the idea of continuing a discussion on the ride home. At least with a servant, she didn't have to pretend to carry a conversation.

Harper excused herself and disappeared somewhere into the house. A short time later, the carriage pulled around to the front door: a simple blue supply cart drawn by a chestnut drought horse with a bobbed tail.

As Una moved the heavy weight of Ronan towards the carriage, Harper appeared and put a hand on her arm. She pressed a small sachet into Una's hand. "Give him this tomorrow morning in his tea," she said in a low voice, too low for Adair to hear from his position by the door. "It will help the headache."

Una nodded and helped Ronan hoist himself into the cart. He nearly pitched out of the other side of it, but the servant dropped the reins to help steady him and get him seated on the small wooden bench.

Una waved goodbye to Adair and Harper, then wrapped her arms around Ronan's ribs, holding him steady as the carriage lurched forward and into the night. Ronan's head drifted down to rest on her shoulder as they rode, despite the bouncing of the cart over the road.

CHAPTER 17

THE NEXT DAY, UNA dressed early to get to her shop, but Ronan begged off as he held his head in his hands and sipped carefully at Harper's special tea.

"I will stay here today."

Una frowned. "You don't want to help me?"

"I'm not up to butchering more fish for you, no," he said with a laugh. "I'd rather do some work around here. Some curse work on my own."

He's going to look for his skin, her mind provided in a spiteful undertone. But she sighed inwardly. If that was what he needed to do, it was reasonable. She would do the same in his position. But a part of her hurt to think that he would mistrust her.

"Some curse work on your own?" she said, in what she hoped wasn't a dejected voice.

Ronan nodded. "I'd like to pore through your father's journals to see what I can find. With the doctor dead, we need a new lead."

Una looked at him for a long moment, trying to discern whether she believed him. Then she nodded. "All right. If that's what you want." She tried to keep the hurt from her voice.

She finished dressing and gathered her bag. As she moved towards the door, he reached up and snagged her hand, stopping her. When she looked back questioningly, he just grinned up at her. She grinned back, and they stood for a long moment gazing foolishly at each other with their hands clasped.

Then, reluctantly, she pulled her hand away. "I've got to go," she mumbled. He pursed his lips and let his fingers slide slowly out of hers, as if just as unwilling to let go. The second their hands released, she fought the urge to throw herself on the ground and cuddle him close. *There's work to be done*, she told herself sternly. *He'll be here when you return.*

At the door, she stopped and looked at him over her shoulder. "You *will* be here when I get back, right?" she asked in a playful voice, only half-teasing.

He grinned at her and the look was without guile. "And miss your return? Never."

Her smile faltered slightly, and she turned to keep the expression hidden from him. Since when was he the devoted lover? And how could he speak so openly of missing her, as if he wasn't pining for her to be gone right now?

But she pushed her thoughts aside as she stepped out the door and closed it behind her. It wouldn't do to doubt him, not when she knew she had something as important as his sealskin. *There's no way he'll find it,* she told herself. *He can't.*

She set off for town, repeating that mantra in her head as she walked.

THE SECOND THE DOOR closed behind her, Ronan was off the bed as fast as he could move, and ran to place his ear against the door. Was she truly gone? Or was she waiting to burst back in to see what he was doing?

He counted in his head, imagining her just on the other side of the door, waiting for him like he was waiting for her. He thought he'd seen her smile slip as she left. Or was he imagining things? He needed her to trust him enough to give him alone time to hunt for his sealskin in a way he hadn't been able to with her around.

When he was certain she was gone, he risked opening the door to peer out.

There was nobody in sight.

He moved quickly, not bothering to put on clothes, as he began searching her house. Lifting the cushions on the couch and the chair, he flipped them over to search for anything strapped to the bottoms. He went through all the drawers in her house, both the storage for clothes and blankets, as well as everywhere in the kitchen he could think of. After opening all food containers that could be large enough, he searched the depths of them with his hands, sifting through flour and sugar with his fingers. He checked underneath her bed, in the chest at the foot of it, and throughout her closet. He even checked the fireplace, sifting through the ashes with his hands to be sure it wasn't hidden flat among the soot.

Nothing.

Balling his hands into fists, he let out a cry of frustration that rang out in the silence of the empty house. Without the magical pull of his sealskin in his ownership, he had no way of knowing where it was, whether it was in this house or somewhere else.

He sat down on the couch, naked, and rested his head in his hands. *Think*, he told himself. *Just take a moment to think.* He didn't figure she'd had long to find a hiding place for the skin before he'd felt the lack of it, felt the pull of it disappear. But he'd long since searched the cave and knew it wasn't there.

She could have stowed it away in her bucket, he thought. He hadn't thought to check it when he'd found her, assuming it had been full of mussels. If she'd hidden it there, she could have planted it anywhere by now. If he had told Ceannas, he could have his second Anchor look for it while he was engaged in this curse breaking.

He ran his hands through his hair in frustration. It could be anywhere. It could be in a hole in the ground, for all he knew.

He raised his head and gazed bleakly out the window, not looking at anything in particular. He was at her mercy and was unlikely to find his sealskin without her help. It was a hard fact to accept, but he was nothing if not pragmatic.

Help her lift the curse. Or seduce her fast enough to get her to reveal it herself. Those were his two options. A grim smile lifted the corners of his lips. He knew which one he'd prefer.

Leaning back on the couch, he let his eyes wander. They came to rest on the mantle place, where the wooden box lay open, revealing the metal contraption he'd never really looked at before. He stood and walked over to it.

It was a sundial, that much he could tell. But there was more to it. The burnished metal shone like brass, tarnished from many obvious years of use. It had a weathered look about it, as if it had spent a great deal of time outside, exposed to the elements. The wood around it looked polished and new, however, as if the metal sundial had been placed in the box for ornamental looks.

He fingered the tip of the sundial and noticed a small hinge on one side. With his thumb and forefinger, he lifted the sundial up, revealing a small glass face on top of a compass dial.

A sea captain's compass, he thought. He'd bet his skin on it. And probably her father's. *Or perhaps her husband's,* a sly voice murmured in his mind. He scowled at it. He didn't like that thought, since it was obviously put in a place of prominence on her mantle, as if it were important to her.

She had spoken little of her husband, but Ronan knew it couldn't be because she missed him. She was too inexperienced with lovemaking, too hesitant and uncertain to have been truly loved well by the man.

Perhaps it had been a marriage of convenience? She certainly seemed not to mind this one. Maybe it was because she'd already had experience with that kind of relationship before.

Ronan didn't like the thought of another man touching her, putting hands on his True Mate's skin that weren't his. He liked the feel of Una's body beneath him, savored the way she bent to his will in a way she didn't outside of the bedroom. She was feisty and independent most of the time, but under his hands she was an attentive, curious lover who seemed as innocent in love as any he'd met. He loved seeing that side of her, loved knowing he was touching her in a way she'd never felt before.

At least, he imagined now from the way she was drawn to him. She seemed just as surprised as he was about it. Of course, he knew it was the True Mate bond, but for her, it could only be love.

Or lust, his mind supplied in that sly voice. She had said she was comfortable playing house with him. Perhaps she was just using him for his attentions.

He scowled at the wall and pushed the thought away. She was his True Mate, whether she liked it or not. She would fall in love with him. He was positive of it. But he did admit that seducing her in the bedroom wasn't enough. He could own her body, she'd given that to him willingly, but her heart? That would take more effort.

He glanced up, noting the cracks in the ceiling, and frowned. Una would never take care of that, he was sure. She'd let it get too bad already.

Then he had an idea.

If she needed more than the physical attention, he would give it to her. He would seduce her mind, as well as her body. Before long, he would have her heart.

He dressed quickly and set to work.

CHAPTER 18

UNA RETURNED THAT AFTERNOON, half expecting to find the house empty, her selkie man gone with nothing but a pair of empty shoes in the doorway. Instead, she found him on top of the house, shirtless in the sun, long hair flying in the wind.

"What the hell are you doing up there?" she asked, shielding her eyes from the sun as she glared up at him. "Come down before you break your fool neck, and I have to solve this curse by myself."

Ronan grinned down at her, then bent back to his task.

After a few moments, she said, "No, really. What are you doing?"

He looked down at her with a small frown, irritated at the interruption. "I'm fixing your roof. Now leave me alone to do it."

Una's eyebrows shot upward. "But... why?"

"Because it's got a hole in it. A few of them. When was the last time someone tended to this?" He squinted down at her, and she thought for a moment. When was the last time Blair had repaired the roof? Had he ever? The cracks hadn't started until after he was gone, she thought, so there hadn't been a need for him to.

She shrugged instead, then watched him as he bent back to his task. She admired the muscles that stood out on his shoulders, his back flexing as he worked. When was the last time a man had helped her like this? And of his own volition?

She smiled to herself, walked around the corner to make sure his ladder was securely settled against the house, then went inside. She half-expected to find the house in disarray, cushions on the floor and her bedding tossed about—any evidence to show he'd searched the house for his sealskin. But there was nothing out of place. The house was in the same state she'd left it in.

She glanced up at the ceiling and saw the cracks were gone, replaced by a patch of white clay that was newer than the rest of the plaster.

Her heart felt strangely moved by this gesture. He'd known exactly how to win her over, she thought. To settle into her life and fix what mattered most to her, her home. She smiled again and had an idea.

She walked over to the bookshelf and removed three bound journals, then took them outside.

"Ronan," she called as she stepped foot on the grass. "I've got something that might help..."

She looked up, smiling, but Ronan wasn't there. Her smile slid off her face and she glanced around, frowning. Then she saw him, splashing in the sea several yards down the grass, swiping one hand down his chest, then rising to splash water on his face. She watched him for a long time, hugging the journals to her chest.

Guilt gripped her. How must that feel for him, to be in the water again, but as a man and not as a seal? What did it feel like to be missing half of himself? Did he resent her? He never seemed to show it if he did. But how could he not?

Perhaps I should give it to him, she thought, then rejected the idea. How could she even think that, when they were no closer to lifting the curse than when they'd started? He would leave, and the town would die, and it would be all her fault. She had everything they needed to solve the problem right in front of her. She watched him sink under the water as he dunked his head.

He could leave right now and never return, the voice in the back of her mind spoke up. *He doesn't need you. He could search for his skin on his own, without you.* The thought made her heart pang painfully in her chest. To lose him now... the thought was unbearable.

A tear trickled down her cheek, and she dashed it away with an angry swipe of her hand. She was stronger than this. She would find a way. With him. Somehow. She just had to figure out the curse. That was the solution—lifting the curse.

So she sat in the grass, thinking hard about their options, and watching him as he pulled himself from the sea and stalked towards her, naked.

He flopped down on the grass next to her, beads of water shining on his pale skin. "This manual labor stuff stinks," he grumbled as he put his hands behind his head and closed his eyes. "My body feels as if I've been beaten with reeds."

"I found these," she told him, ignoring his complaints. When he opened one eye at her, she held out the journals. "My father's records. It occurred to me he might have left some clues about what happened twenty-four years ago."

At that, Ronan sat up and took one journal from her. He flipped through it, scanning the pages. After several moments, he shook his head. "There are hundreds of pages here. How can we hope to find anything in this? It's like looking for fish bones in a whale."

Una put her hand over his on the journal. "It's not, though. We just have to go back a decade. We don't have to look through *all* the journals. Just the relevant ones. If anything significant happened, he would have marked it."

Ronan considered this with a thoughtful expression. "I suppose you're right..."

"Of course I am!" Una exclaimed. She slapped his stomach with the back of her hand. "Now get dry and get dressed before someone sees you and suspects you of being indecent."

Ronan held out a hand, indicating the open land around them. "Who would see me? All the friends that come to visit you? The women from the church you don't attend? The men from the docks?" Though he said it jokingly, the thought of other men visiting her made his stomach churn with jealousy. He pushed the feeling aside. She was his. End of story.

But Una just smiled at him. "Get your clothes on. You're too much of a temptation out here like this."

Ronan sat up, his stomach muscles flexing as he did so. His look was predatory. "So I *do* tempt you?" He trailed a finger down her upper arm, appreciating the smoothness of her skin. She shivered and re-situated herself a few more inches away from him.

"I will not have you on this grassy outcrop where any passing fisherman could see us. I have more respect in this town than that."

Ronan turned grave eyes on her, the predatory look turning serious. "Una, I'm worried about how my presence here complicates things for you. Already people are gossiping behind our backs about our fast marriage."

Una turned fierce eyes on him. "I don't care what they say! Let them talk."

"But would you have them close their business to you? Or shut you out of their protective circle?"

"That won't happen."

"How do you know?"

"Because I'm one of them, and they take care of their own. So I've taken a stranger to my bed. They've bought the whole 'husband' thing, however strange they may think it. They'll respect my choice. And in time, they'll come to accept you, too, for the good man you are."

"In time?" Ronan's voice was carefully neutral.

Una paused, deflating a little. "What?"

"You said 'in time.' How long are you thinking?"

She shook her head, pleading with her eyes for him to understand. "As long as it takes."

"And then I get my skin back. Right?"

Now she looked hurt. "Ronan, of course. I promised you. You are no selkie husband." He sat up and fiddled with a long blade of sea grass. She put a hand on his muscled arm. "Ronan. Please believe me. You have no reason to doubt me."

He stood up, his eyes dark as he looked out at the sea. "Let's get started then," he said in a flat voice. He gathered his clothes and walked back towards the house. She watched him go with a confused look on her face.

Had she done something wrong, something to make him doubt her? It was too easy to fall into a lull with him, to think it could always be like this. *He* made it too easy. But, she reminded herself, he *was* no selkie husband. She couldn't keep him, regardless of the temptation. For all their lovemaking, he was a wild thing, and she shouldn't hope to tame him.

But he did seem tamer with her, a voice at the back of her mind suggested. Softer. Less rigid than he'd been when she first captured his skin. He had grown on her and she on him, she was sure of it. Would he actually leave when given his chance? She didn't like to think about it. The thought made her stomach twist with anxiety. Be without him, after the whirlwind of intimacy they'd enjoyed recently? It hurt to imagine.

She took a deep breath. *I'll catch that fish later*, she thought. *It doesn't have to be decided now.* She tucked away her hurt feelings, pushing them down deep where she didn't have to think about them. They burned like an ember in her stomach, but she pushed them aside. For now. Focus on the now.

She stood, gathered her father's journals, and followed Ronan into the house.

Inside, he sat on the couch, leafing through the other journal. He didn't look up when she entered, but said, "This is a lot of information. Your father was meticulous! Look," he leaned forward pointing to a line in the first section of the journal, "'I worked the loch today, instead of heading along the strait. Good fishing there: pike, salmon, sea trout, greyling, and some rockcook wrasse. About 2,100 fish in the pound nets. Will document specific poundage once docked.'" Ronan flipped the page. "And here you have the exact numbers. This man knew how many fish he brought in, what the total pounds were for each species, and what each catch sold for."

Una smiled fondly and nodded. "He was like that in life, too. Everything in its place, everything documented. He kept personal journals, too, with daily writings in it every morning. I used to wake up and sit at his feet and play with my dolls while he wrote before breakfast. After he died, I pored through all his notes, seeking some part of him, something more than what I always knew of him."

"Where was your mother in all of this?" Ronan asked. "I've never heard you mention her."

Una pursed her lips and sighed. "Run off when I was two, Da said. She was from off the island and didn't appreciate the life of a fisherman's wife. He said she pined for the mainland. Couldn't bear the stink of fish coming off him every night, couldn't take the worry when he was on a long haul where he was gone for days. When she left, he stopped the long hauls—he had me to care for—and kept mostly to the inlet. Some ocean fishing when I was old enough to stay by myself."

"What did you do?"

She looked at him proudly. "I managed the fish shop when I was younger, back when it was owned by my Da's friend, Graham. I bought it off him when Blair died, with what meager savings we'd had, and I've been running it ever since."

Ronan looked at her with a mixture of admiration and pity. "So you've been on your own for a while, then. First with your father, then once Blair was gone?"

She looked at her hands, flicked an invisible speck off the back of one. "Even with Blair, I was on my own for most of the time. He did long hauls. Would be gone for weeks, sometimes." She gave a bitter laugh. "It was hard, being without him at first, but I figured things out. I'd long since learned how to keep up after my Da, so keeping up after Blair was no effort. Then when he was gone, I kept myself mostly to myself."

"Didn't that get lonely?"

She nodded solemnly. "It was." She lifted her gaze to his, and he felt like his heart stopped from the emotion blazing in them. "Then you came along, and I wasn't alone anymore."

The naked admission shocked him. To be that desperate for company, for love, to be denied it for so long. No wonder she'd fallen for him so quickly, he thought. How could she have not, when he was putting all his effort into her seduction?

The guilt ate at him. To start off with duplicity was one thing, but now that he'd grown to love her, it was different. *He* was different. He didn't feel like the same selkie who'd come to shore a week ago. He wanted to be around her. Craved her touch. Gods, had he ever slept so well, so deep and trusting as he now did with her head on his chest every night? The longer he stayed, the firmer the True Mate bond grew, he could feel it.

And yet, just as strong was the pull in the other direction. For the sea. For the impending war on the horizon with the sirens. He'd just left that life behind, thinking to make this mission as quick as possible and here he was sleeping with this human *and enjoying it*? Actually falling in love?

He looked down at his hands in case his eyes betrayed him. This wasn't the plan. And he wasn't the kind of person who deviated from the plan once he'd figured it out. He needed to speak with Ceannas and soon.

He stood. "I need to go for a while. I need to talk with another of my clan. To make sure they are well."

She regarded him with serious eyes. Hearing him say the words "I need to go" left her feeling gutted in a way she had no business feeling. *It's just a few hours*, she told herself. *He can't leave without his skin. Not really.* Then she nodded, forcing a smile she hoped looked genuine.

He set the journal down on the table, then stepped towards the door. But as he passed her, he stopped and trailed a hand down her hair, cupping her neck. "I'll be back before sundown," he promised, and bent to kiss her.

The kiss was sweet, almost chaste, and she leaned into it. Then, all too soon, he was pulling away and walking out the door. She didn't watch him go, choosing to ignore the vision of his back walking away from her, the feeling that this time he wouldn't return. Behind her, she heard the door close.

Stop it, she chastised herself. Out loud, she scolded, "You're a besotted fool, and he's better off without you." Her words rang out in the empty room. Then she took a deep breath and gathered herself. He promised he'd be back. She had to trust him, just as she asked him to trust her earlier.

We're two sides to the same coin, she thought in frustration. *Each pulled away by things larger than ourselves.* She thought of the tender way he'd passed a hand over her hair, like she was treasured, cherished. "I wish for once it was easy," she breathed. Then she set about putting things away, tidying up what didn't need tidying. Anything to ease that ache in her chest that the house was emptier now than it had ever been.

It wasn't until she spied her basket by the door that she remembered her promise to Lyall that she would bring her uncle and aunt some supplies once they were back. She'd brought home the package of fish but had set it aside in surprise at Ronan's work on the house.

Now is as good a time as any, she thought, as she scrawled a quick note to Ronan saying where she'd gone. Then she gathered her basket and left.

CHAPTER 19

LESS THAN AN HOUR later, Una knocked on the door and after a moment it opened. A woman stood there, her wide mouth stretched into a smile. She was small, smaller even than Una by a few inches, and she'd plaited her dark blonde hair into a long braid down her back. Gray wisps of hair trailed down the sides of her face at each temple, and crow's feet branched at the corners of each eye as she smiled.

"Una! So good of you to come by." She stepped aside and gestured for Una to enter.

"Una!" Lyall called from the kitchen. "Glad to see you! Finally, you come by!"

"Aunt Leannan, how was the mainland?"

"Busy!" her aunt said with a laugh. Behind her, Lyall scowled, and Una pursed her lips to keep from laughing at the expression. "We sold all of our valuable stock and even had time to tour the city a little." She preened, and Una thought again about how glad she must have been to get off the island. They rarely left, but Una always felt it was because of her uncle's feelings about travel rather than her aunt's.

Una held up her basket. "Your weekly catch, as promised to your daughter while you were gone," she said with a smile. She crossed the room and set the basket in its usual spot on the counter. "Three greyling and one pike, as usual." She shook her head. "I would think, after all this time, you three would change things up a bit. Try a bit of variety."

"Yes, *Mother*. We should add more variety," Lyall muttered as she unloaded the paper-wrapped parcels from the basket.

The front door opened again, and a tall man entered, leaning heavily on a cane. He wore a tweed suit and a white undershirt with simple wooden buttons down the front. His hair was dark and streaked with gray, and his knuckles were white around the head of the cane. He turned a piercing blue-eyed gaze on the pair of them as he entered, his eyes sweeping the room carefully, as if expecting something out of the ordinary.

Leannán crossed to link her arm through her husband's. "Hugh dear, Una says we should have more variety in our eating habits. Says the fish we get are too ordinary. Too boring."

"It's true," Lyall groused, setting the fish on the counter.

"I didn't say quite all that," Una admonished as she crossed the room to give the man a huge hug. "Uncle Hugh, where were you?"

"Out enjoying a walk," he said, as he made his way over to a small chair and settled himself in it. "I love the beach at high tide. It smells so... fresh. So enticing."

"It reeks of fish," Una complained, wrinkling her nose. "I love to look at it, but at high tide I don't have the same the appreciation for the smell." Leannán and Hugh laughed.

"We come from a different place," Hugh said, with a gentle look at Leannán, as if they shared a secret nobody else knew. Then he frowned and peered at her. "Now, my dear, tell me: why has it been so long since you came to see us? We went into town yesterday to visit you, but you had already left for the afternoon. Most unusual."

Una blushed and studied her hands. "Well, you see. I've taken a... there's this man I met. We've been spending a lot of... time... together. I've just been so busy that I haven't—"

"I heard rumor of a new young man in town," Leannán said thoughtfully. A small smile played around her lips and her eyes twinkled at Una. "A strapping young man, from the sound of it. Very handy around the docks, they say. And very pleasing to the eye."

Una smiled. "Yes, he is very handy." *And handsome,* she thought. The thought of his dark eyes looking at her with dark promises popped into her head, and she struggled not to blush again.

"I've heard he's more than just some man you met, my dear." Leannán's voice was gentle, but there was a slight admonishing tone. Una's blush deepened. She glanced at Lyall to see her friend busy straightening the items in the pantry, her back to them. As Una watched, Lyall moved a loaf of bread from one side of the pantry to the other, then moved it back again.

"Now, my love, there's no need to needle the girl!" Hugh complained. He gestured to Una. "If she doesn't want to tell us about her new—"

"Husband," Una blurted out. "He's my new husband." She winced, steadying herself for the aftermath.

Hugh turned a startled look to her. "What? What kind of marriage was this that we have never met this boy! What fey creature would he have to be to sneak into our town and sweep our girl off her feet without us even knowing his name?" He stood, using his cane to help him up, and pointed a finger at Una. He raised his eyebrows threateningly. "What kind of man is this you've taken up with? Does he have no honor? What would your father have thought?"

Una gave him a rueful smile and gestured for him to sit down. "Uncle Hugh, really, it's not like that. It was a bit of a—" the Mayor's phrase passed through her mind and she grasped it eagerly "—a bit of a whirlwind romance, you might say."

Hugh pointed his finger at Lyall. "Lyall, you don't seem surprised in the slightest. Did you know about this?"

Lyall flushed and turned a panicked look to Una. "I... well, I... kind of," she finished lamely. "But I wanted to meet him first so I could—"

"Are you pregnant?" Leannán asked Una in a sharp tone. "Because if so, we will help. We can—"

"No, it's not like that," Una reassured her. "He is a good man. We just fell in love very quickly." It was close enough to the truth that it didn't feel like a lie when she said it. But the thought of it twisted her stomach into a knot just the same.

"I must meet this *whirlwind* young man," Hugh grumbled, his eyes intense on hers. He looked as if he was thinking angry thoughts. "I've known your father since before you were born, and when he died, I promised to look out for you." He pointed an accusing finger at Una. "And I can't do that if I don't even get to meet the man before you marry him!"

Una laughed nervously. The sound came out higher than she intended. "Don't worry, Uncle. You will find him more than worthy." But a trickle of doubt spread through her. Sure, he would be worthy, but for how long? What disparaging things would she have to hear when he was gone? He was a good man, she knew. And she didn't relish the vitriol that would come once he left her to return to his people.

"But that's something for another time," Leannán said, with her hand on Hugh's shoulder. She gave Una a quick smile, and Una wondered, as she so often did, at the way Leannán always seemed to read minds. Her timing, as usual, was impeccable.

Hugh nodded absently, then took a shuffling step forward. Una noticed him rubbing his thigh as he did so.

"It's bothering you again today, isn't it?" she asked in a grim tone. She knew the injury had come from an old fishing accident, but she had never heard the full story. It was always a story Hugh said was "for another day."

But he waved her worries away. "Just a twinge. The cold sea air brings it out." He waved the tip of his cane in her general direction. "You must bring this young man of yours around soon." His voice took on a steely note and his blue eyes glinted menacingly. "I want to meet the man who would swoop in and steal the heart of our practical girl so quickly." It was too close to home.

Una stood, smoothing her dress front. "I have to go, Uncle. I'm sorry it took so long for me to come by. I will be back soon with Ro—"

"Tomorrow." Hugh said in a flat voice.

Una cocked her head and frowned. "What?"

"You will be here with him for dinner tomorrow. And bring some pike with you, will you, dear? I do love pike for dinner."

Una's jaw sagged as she looked at Leannán for support, but the older woman just shrugged as if to say, *what can you do?*

"Two days."

Her uncle raised his eyebrows in affronted surprise. "Excuse me?"

"He's very nervous about meeting you," she lied. "It will take me a few days to prepare him."

Uncle Hugh scowled. Then he nodded his head. "Fine. Two days from now." He pointed an accusing finger at her. "But he'd better not back out. I will look very unfavorably on it if he does."

Una nodded. She knew it was not worth the argument. Her uncle could be quite intractable when he set his mind to something. "In two nights then."

Hugh nodded, mollified. "Make sure you don't forget the pike."

Una nodded again and picked up her basket. She hugged both of them, waved at Lyall—who gave her a reassuring smile—then left.

CHAPTER 20

THE NEXT MORNING, RONAN had to admit they were no closer to lifting the curse than they had been a week ago. It was beyond frustrating. And worse, that he didn't know how his clan was doing in the meantime. Things moved so quickly in the water, shifting like the currents themselves. How was he to keep track of all the changes that could happen in so short a time? He had to either work this curse out or complete his seduction of Una into accepting the True Mate bond and giving his skin back.

But he was increasingly perplexed by his attraction to her. The True Mate bond was stronger than ever from their intimacy, both in the bed and out of it. And he could no more imagine leaving her now than giving his skin away. And he was starting to suspect she felt the same level of attachment.

Maybe I should just ask for my skin, he thought. *What would she do if I just asked?* Maybe the seduction wasn't a necessary act anymore, however much of an act it had ceased to become. Could he draw on her love for him and ask for it back? But what if she said no? How could he bear the bond between them if she really only wanted him for his help with the curse now?

It was all too much to consider. He loved her, he was sure of it, and he thought she loved him back. He couldn't bear the thought of leaving her at the mercy of the curse, which would ultimately cripple the town to death. *Maybe we actually can break this curse,* he wondered. How quickly might they solve it if he gave his full attention to it? It was worth a shot.

"Why haven't you had any new ideas?" Una groused, bringing his thoughts back to the present. "We aren't any closer to figuring this out." It was enough of an echo of his earlier thoughts that Ronan was surprised.

"I've been a bit busy," he growled. Figuring out how to take care of his clan was just as important to him. How could she not see that?

"I just feel like you've been distracted lately," Una said, looking at her hands, which were twisted in her lap. "You haven't been giving much thought to—"

"And who was I distracted by?" Ronan shot back. "We've spent more time in bed than in handling these journals, it would seem." It galled him that she didn't notice that she wasn't any more help than he was. Did she expect him to carry the entire mission? He was magical, but not a magician. "I'm a warrior, not a curse breaker."

Una scowled at him. "I'm not trying to pick a fight," she said. "We just need a new angle. Something we haven't thought of yet."

"I'm trying!" Ronan shouted, standing up and spreading his arms wide. "If you haven't noticed, I've had a lot to deal with. Trust me when I say that solving this curse is at the *top* of my priority list! While I'm here with you, my clan is in danger of going against one of the largest predatory groups in our seas. And I'm stuck here, on this fool's errand, while they suffer without me."

"Well if you feel that strongly, why not come up with something new! Anything to get us out of this rut!"

He refused to rise to her bait. He sat down on the uncomfortable couch, ignoring the way the wood frame creaked a warning under his weight. "Okay, what do we know?" he asked, moving into triage mode. "What information have we gathered so far?"

"We don't know anything more," Una groaned. When he looked at her, he saw the worry lining her face, making the grooves on either side of her mouth stand out. He moved to kneel in front of her and took her hands in his.

"Hey," he said in a soft voice. "Stay with me. Work the problem in front of us, not the questions we still have."

Una took a deep breath and nodded her head. "You're right. What do we know? We know it started twenty-four years ago. We know there were two new people in town, but that it's not either of them." She rolled her eyes in frustration. "We know something supernatural set the curse, so we're looking for something not human." She pulled her hands away to flop them in her lap. "So we're right back where we started."

Ronan shook his head, thinking. "Not necessarily. That last part is important. What do we know of that can cast magic like that?"

"Don't you mean what *you* know of?" Una said sarcastically.

"I know of several. Sirens have their own type of magic. The Blue Men of the Minch can cause shipwrecks, as can mermaids—"

"But there haven't been many of those," Una pointed out. She thought of Blair and her father, who had both been lost to the sea. What if it had been one of those creatures who caused either of them to die? She pushed back those thoughts. That wasn't important right now.

Ronan pursed his lips and cocked his head. "It could be one of the Sidhe, perhaps."

"Fairies?" Una squeaked. "Those are real?"

Ronan smiled. "Very. But those sorts of curses usually revolve around a single person, not a town of people. We'd see someone in particular with the bad luck."

"Could any of your people do it?"

Ronan looked surprised at the idea. "We have magic, too, but there are no shamans among our kind. There is a rumor of one, but they don't actually exist."

Una frowned. "Then what else could it be?"

Ronan cocked his head. "Maybe 'who' isn't the right question yet. Maybe 'when' is."

"I don't follow."

"Maybe we need to find out what else happened twenty-four years ago. Who would know that?"

Una thought for a moment, with her elbow on her knee, chin resting in her palm. "My father has his ledgers and journals that go back that far. Or we could ask Innis, the town historian. She might know something we don't."

"That's it!" Ronan turned triumphant eyes on her. "Let's start poking around about the town's history with the town historian. When can we see her?"

Una watched Ronan as he spoke. The passion in his voice, the urgency, made her sick with wanting him. He was glorious when he was riled up. A part of her wondered if he was actually invested in ridding the town of the curse or if he was just trying to get his skin back. *Does it matter?* a small voice at the back of her mind asked. She decided it didn't. He was helping her, that was all that mattered.

"Today, if you like. The town shuts down for the Sabbath so the Christians can go to church."

Ronan nodded, considering. "Won't she be in church?"

"She's pagan, like most around here. We can find her in the library."

"Let's do it. What do we have to lose?"

INNIS PADARSAN WAS A wisp of a woman, slight and stoop-backed with age. Her short white hair clung to her head like a cloud, so thin they could see her age-spotted scalp through it. But the look she turned on them when they entered the library the next morning told Ronan without a doubt that she still possessed her mental facilities.

"Ms. MacCallan, so good to see you. It's been a long while since you came around these parts."

Una flushed. "Ms. Padarsan—"

"Innis," the older woman insisted, eyeing Ronan with interest.

"Innis then," Una smiled. "We have a few questions for you, if you had the time to spare?"

Innis lifted a thick book from her desk and raised it to place on the stack of books next to her. But the heavy volume wavered in the air, and Ronan rushed forward to relieve her of the burden. He placed the book on the stack and smiled at her.

Innis stared at him with shrewd eyes as she thanked him. "Much appreciated, young man."

"Ronan," he supplied, and she nodded.

"Interesting name. Means 'little seal.' You must have been quite the swimmer when you were young."

Ronan looked at Una in surprise, then at Innis. "I still love the water. Ever since I was young."

Innis nodded, as if she suspected as much. "What questions do you have for me? My spare time is limited these days."

Una stepped forward with an anxious look at Ronan. "Well, m'am, we were wondering about some events that happened several years back. Anything of significance that happened around twenty-four years ago."

Innis's mouth worked back and forth, pursing and unpursing as she thought. "Twenty-four years, you say? Well, there are a great many things that happened back then."

"I understand if you don't remember," Ronan began, but Innis gave him such a sharp look of indignation, he shut his mouth with a snap.

"Don't insult my memory, young man! I can remember the names of every person on this island. I know who their parents were and where they came from. And I remember every significant event that happened since I've been on this island. So don't lecture me about memory." She glared at him.

"I meant no offense," Ronan said, putting his hand on his chest in apology. "I just thought there may be more events than you can remember in that time frame."

"I may remember every significant event," Innis said slowly, "but what you seek may not be one of them."

Una cocked her head. "What can you remember?"

"Births, deaths, most marriages. I lose it a bit with the divorces, mind, but I can still keep track of most of them." She pointed a finger at Una. "I remember, for example, when your man died in that shipwreck two years ago. It was a Wednesday."

Una looked at her, surprised, and nodded. She remembered that day well, too. It was the start of some of the toughest times of her life.

"Shame, that," Innis continued. "He was a kind young man. Good with a ship. Better than most."

Una nodded again, unable to think of what to say.

Ronan watched her closely and put a surreptitious hand on her lower back.

"I remember the week you got married, too, with your father looking proud as could be." Innis smiled, showing several missing teeth. "He was a good captain, too, your father. Had my eye on him myself, though he was several years my junior. But he married that offshore girl, your mother, and that was that." She gave a small sigh, as if to say, *oh well.*

"But was there anything of significance that happened about two decades ago?" Una pressed. She didn't want to discuss her mother.

Innis smiled. "For this small fishing town, yes. We had the biggest catch this town has ever seen."

Ronan sighed in frustration. This was going nowhere. "Yes, but, anything else? Anything of significan—"

"This was significant, boy!" Innis snapped. "You don't see the likes of this haul as anything other than magical, even for non-magical folks like yourself. This catch"—she pointed at Una—"brought in by your father, nonetheless, was of epic proportions. There were more fish in his boat than it could carry. It was spilling out of his catch tanks, overflowing his nets. His boat almost couldn't bear the burden." She chuckled. "That was the day two boats arrived with newcomers. The Mayor's beautiful wife-to-be, and those two that live out by themselves... the artifact dealer and his wife..." She snapped her fingers, trying to recall.

"Uncle Hugh and Aunt Leannán?" Una said in surprise. "That was when they came here?"

"They'd been here before," Innis said, "many times. But that was the year they settled down here for good. Your father had picked them up from somewhere and brought them and that amazing catch back. The town called it the Catch of the Century, and for good reason."

Ronan thought for a moment. For there to be such a good haul, followed by such lean times. Surely that wasn't a coincidence? He tapped Una on the arm. "We need to go back to your father's journals," he said in an urgent voice. "I think our answer is in there."

Una nodded, though he could tell from her expression that she wasn't sure of his line of thinking. "Thank you for your help, Innis," she said. "That was what we needed to know."

Innis nodded. "Can't say I gave you anything of value," she lamented, peering at them. "But you're quite welcome. Come back any time. I don't get many visitors." She smiled at them as they left.

"What was that about?" Una asked when they were outside again. Ronan explained. "So you think we missed something earlier?" He nodded, and she shrugged. "Then let's try again. Oh," she added as an afterthought, "we also have dinner plans tomorrow night."

Ronan gaped at her. "Again? I'll not go back to the Barrons. That whiskey hurt me."

Una laughed. "No, not with them. With my aunt and uncle. Lyall's parents. They're dying to meet you, and I couldn't put them off."

Ronan gave her a stern look. "And when will we work on the curse? Why isn't that a higher priority?"

Una's smile slipped. "Because these are my family. They are important to me. And I want them to meet you." She took his hand and squeezed it. "Please? For me?"

Ronan stared at her. Was this what playing house was like? Meeting the family? Going to dinners as a couple? Why couldn't they just stay at her house and make love and investigate there? Why all this show for her family?

Because she loves you, a voice murmured in his head. And the second he thought it, he felt lighter, because it had to be true. Why else would she go to the trouble of making sure he was well met by the people in her life? He swelled a little, puffing his chest out, and managed a gentle smile. "For you, anything."

As they started up the street, she took his hand as they walked and squeezed it. "I'm grateful for your help," she said in a low voice. She didn't look at him as she spoke.

He knew it was as much of an apology as he was going to get. He smiled and squeezed her hand back. Then his smile faded. Did he have a choice?

The thought made him think of his clan, and the fact that despite their progress with the curse breaking, he had no way of knowing how things were going with his people. Had Ceannas learned anything new? He had no way of contacting his second without revealing his clan's location, which he would never risk. He would just have to assume all was well, and trust that Ceannas would inform him if they needed him.

Not that it would do any good, his mind spoke up. What good was knowing of trouble when he had no skin to change into to go help them? It was a troubling thought. He knew Una was only acting out of concern for her town. But he had his own concerns to deal with, as well. He would have to come to terms with that.

But the sun shone warm on his face, and his hand was tucked securely into the hand of his True Mate. It was hard to focus on anything serious when he was near her. She turned her head and gave him a sweet smile, one filled with so much love and tenderness it made his heart hurt.

It wouldn't do to dwell on things he couldn't change right now, he thought. Better to focus on the problem in front of him. What had he told Una earlier? *Work the problem.* That was what he would do.

He squeezed her hand again and felt her grip tighten on his. That was exactly what he would do.

CHAPTER 21

FOR THE REST OF the day and into the next morning, they spent their hours poring through her father's journals looking for something, anything out of the ordinary that might indicate what Innis had mentioned. Though Una knew they'd already gone over most of them, she just knew the answer was there somewhere. They just had to find it.

They worked in silence, pulling each journal from one tall stack near the fireplace and placing them in smaller stacks next to them when they were through. Una worked on the kitchen table, while Ronan sat on the floor in front of the couch. Each time one would grab a new journal from the pile near the hearth, they would touch the other with their fingers as they passed: a caress over the hair, a lingering touch on the shoulder, a brief kiss to the palm. There were no words exchanged, but they had no need of them—the small contacts were enough.

They made a small, quiet breakfast, neither speaking to the other, each lost in their own thoughts.

Finally, as the morning waned, Una pushed her hair out of her eyes and rubbed them with the heels of her palms. "I'm beat. Any luck?"

Ronan shook his head and tossed a journal aside with a disgusted expression. "Nothing. Years and years of records about fish. If I see another tally mark, I think I'll rip my eyes out." He scrubbed his cheeks with his palms.

Una smiled tiredly. "We've been at this for hours. Let's take a break." She walked over to where he sat on the ground and gave him a coy smile. "I can think of several ways I'd like to spend my time."

But instead of smiling at her, Ronan stood, hands at his sides. "I need to meet with someone," he said. "My leader. He can tell me what I need to do here."

Una's smile fell away. "What do you mean? Now?" She gestured to the stacks of journals. "We've still got work to do."

"We just said we were done for the day. I need a break. I need to confer with my leader about the best path forward. We found nothing today. We need outside help, and he can give it to us."

Una scowled and crossed her arms under her breasts. "Why now? What makes this meeting more important than what we're doing?"

"My leader hasn't been available until now. This is the first I've been able to contact him. For something this important, I need—"

"I need more from you," she said.

Ronan froze, his expression guarded. "Like what?"

Una flapped her arms at her sides. "I don't know. More time, I guess?" She sidled close to him. "I just want you. All of you. And I feel like you're holding back." She knew he was, but she hadn't dared ask before. But now she felt bold, empowered by the strong feel of his body under her hands, the nearness of him. "What are you keeping from me?"

Ronan pulled away. "I'm not keeping anything from you!" he said. "I just... this thing you feel for me, this—"

"Love."

The admission shocked her. For her to say it aloud made every past doubt swirl in her head. Was she ready for this? She felt she was, but what if she didn't fully understand what she was committing to?

Ronan winced. "This feeling... it's the True Mate bond trying to establish itself. It's the magic talking, not you."

She wondered why he was pulling back. He appeared uncharacteristically uncertain, unwilling to meet her eyes. Was he scared too? Or worse, was he regretting his feelings for her?

Una frowned. "So you're saying that this is all a hoax? That you don't feel it, too?" She dropped her arms away from him, and it felt like a chill passed between them.

"That's not what I'm saying at all," Ronan said, running his hand through his hair in frustration. It's just... it's difficult to explain."

"Then try harder." Una frowned in consternation. Of all the times she needed him to reassure her that they were fine, he wasn't doing it. Why wasn't he doing it? She stepped towards him again, reaching for him, but he stepped back, widening the gap between them.

"Maybe I can't give you what you want," he said softly, his expression wretched. He turned his back to her and walked to the mantle place. He fingered the necklace, then asked, "Why did you take it off?"

"It made my skin itch," Una said. "So I put it there. It's where I keep my prized possessions, the things from the people I love."

And lost, her mind finished, but she banished the thought. Ronan wasn't leaving her. He would never do such a thing. Not if she really was his True Mate.

"Why are you feeling this way now?" she asked in a soft voice. "What brought this on?"

Ronan turned to face her but wouldn't meet her eyes. "It's just, when I first met you, I felt like... a captive. And I thought I'd do anything to get my skin back. But now, being with you has changed me. I feel... differently. I care for you too much." He spoke haltingly, seeming frustrated by his inability to express himself.

She stepped closer to him and clasped his hands. He squeezed hers back, and she felt a rush of compassion. He was having difficulty telling her how he felt, was all.

But is that all? her mind supplied. *What would he have done to get his skin back?* Not hurt her, not directly, because he didn't do that, she told herself. But what else was he willing to do? There were other ways to hurt someone.

"Your feelings for me," Ronan began again, in a stronger voice. "The True Mate bond is tightening between us. It's getting stronger every day."

"Which means what?"

But he turned away. "I need to go. Before it gets too late."

Una felt a flash of irritation sweep through her. He was running away. Backing down when he needed to talk to her. *Typical*, she thought, then immediately felt regret. That wasn't quite true. He had always been honest with her, never lied to her or manipulated her. It wasn't fair of her to expect him to be perfect, to be able to articulate his feelings when he hadn't had to before.

So she plastered a smile on her face. "Of course. We can continue this conversation another time."

Ronan's smile was bright, as if grateful she understood, and she felt another flash of regret. Lying to him wasn't right either. But if it mended this discomfort between them, perhaps it was forgivable. He kissed her, long and deep, and she let herself get lost in the feeling of his lips on hers. Then he backed away, sending a rush of cool air between them, and left.

In his absence, Una brooded. Then, realizing she was brooding, she broke out her father's journals again. Innis had said there was a great catch twenty-four years ago. The Catch of the Century, she'd called it. Perhaps there was something here that would shed some light on it.

Then, an hour later, she found it:

"My greatest hour is upon me. I've been waiting for this moment all my life, and finally it has come. I snagged a job today, honeymooners out to visit family—or so I was told. The adventure has brought my wildest fantasies into reality.

"But there is more, so much more, and I hesitate to put it into words. I've met more than just people today. A legend—a living legend, one which shouldn't exist but does! It's nowhere in the lore that I've heard of, but then, as a human, that's not surprising."

This caught her attention. "*As a human*"—what did he mean? Did he mean something other than human lore? Something supernatural, perhaps?

"This creature, this myth, is incredible. Power beyond compare. And angry. So angry at being caught. He has great plans for her, plans I can't yet articulate, and which frankly make me sick thinking about them. But I was unable to do more, and I will take that to my grave. Outside of this, I can say no more."

That was the end of the entry.

Una sagged in frustration. That wasn't as helpful as she'd hoped. Who was "he?" And what plans made him sick to think about? Obviously, this creature had something to do with the curse, that much seemed obvious.

Angry. So angry at being caught.

Yes, this creature had set something wicked down upon the town. Una just wished it was more apparent what this creature had been!

"Some description would have been nice, don't you think, Da?" she grumbled, flipping pages.

Then again, in an entry dated one week later, she found something that seemed unusual:

"He thinks to buy my acquiescence, but it won't work. Still the price gained will see me and Una well into our next few years. We will be provided for most fortuitously."

Una flipped through the next several entries, even skipping ahead several more, but there was no other mention of any windfall or money or anything out of the ordinary. She checked the date of the last entry, the one referencing the mysterious "he" again. That was the year they'd had the Clootie Dumpling, she remembered with a small smile. She had been young, but old enough to know those things weren't common for her or her father to come by.

The two entries were related, she was sure of it. But did he sell the creature? Was that how he got the money, however unwillingly? And what happened to it? The creature may be gone, the curse set to run in perpetuity. That was a sobering thought. What if there was no solution because the curse caster was dead?

She shook her head. No, that kind of thinking was futile. There had to be a way out of this, there just had to be.

She looked out the window at the darkness that covered the sky. She wished Ronan were here to bounce ideas off. She wished he were here to hold her and tell her their plan would succeed.

Mostly, she just wished he were here.

CHAPTER 22

RONAN MADE HIS WAY away from the house, feeling wretched yet determined. Leaving her had been hard, though he knew there was nothing else he could do. He couldn't get lost in his feelings for her, especially since he couldn't truly give her what she needed. His clan was the most important thing, and he needed to be sure things were still going well without him.

He didn't like the feeling that war was on the horizon, and he was trapped here with no way to protect them. He was an Anchor, duty-bound to protect his clan, and here he was playing house with a human. A human who held his skin hostage as a weapon to keep him compliant. It didn't matter that she'd never brought it up again, past that initial threat when they'd met. The threat was still there, inescapable. And he'd do well to remember that.

But every step away from her pulled at his heart. Every part of the bond called him back to her, called him to forget what he was doing and rush back to hold her. *Why is this so hard?* he worried. The True Mate bond was strong, he knew, but to make him want to forget all his duties and responsibilities? Surely it wasn't *that* strong.

He made his way down the bluff, waving to the few travelers he met along the way. They all greeted him happily, and he felt a twinge of guilt. He was posing to everyone. Posing as Una's husband, posing as a human, posing as her lover. It was hard to keep rationalizing these things when his heart was on the line.

The bluff gave way to barren land dotted with sea grass clusters, and he met fewer people the closer the got to Lord Prion's house. Having lost his own sealskin to a siren princeling nearly two decades earlier and being unable to shift into his seal form, Lord Prion lived his days passing as human with his lady and their daughter on the Isle of Selbane, where Una lived. However, despite the loss of his shifting ability, Lord Prion had not lost his identity and remained a strong leader of Liath Clann.

Ronan approached the small stone house, neatly set against a cliff facing the sea so that the stiff sea breeze buffeted the windowed wall of the home. He approached via a well-worn path that faced the door, where Lord Prion could easily see him coming through the windows that braced either side of the front door.

He knocked once, then three times, the pattern to announce himself as a friend, and waited.

The door swung open a moment later, as if Prion had been waiting for him to appear. Lord Prion stood to one side, allowing Ronan to enter, then closed and locked the door behind him. Prion was a tall man, about a half head taller than Ronan. His hair was dark and streaked with gray, and his knuckles were white around the head of the cane that he leaned on, favoring his left leg. He wore a simple white tunic shirt over a pair of faded blue pants. His stark blue eyes pierced Ronan as he examined him.

Ronan jerked his head at the locked door and raise his eyebrows in an unspoken question.

Prion smirked. "One can never be too careful in times of war." He had been playing a game with his daughter, who now gave him an uncertain glance. "Lyall," Lord Prion said, "can you please give us some privacy? We have some business matters to discuss. Why don't you help your mother hang the washing on the line?"

Lyall rose, gathering the playing board with a sour expression on her face and putting it away on a shelf. Ronan knew she didn't like him, though he had always been polite to her when they met at this house. He suspected she had an inkling that their "business dealings" weren't exactly what her father portrayed them to be, but he had heard nothing from either her or Lord Prion to confirm this.

Once Lyall left the room, Ronan cleared his throat. "Did you have a good trip, my Lord?"

Prion sniffed disdainfully and glanced at the door. "I got the necessary business done. My wife enjoyed the trip more than I did." Then he turned his piercing gaze to Ronan. "What brings you here?"

Ronan explained his situation.

Prion gave him a scathing glare. "You don't need to be involved in this town's mess. It's up to them to deal with. Your only priority is our clan."

Ronan growled. "I know! But I just can't..."

"You can and you will. Human problems are not our concern."

Ronan stilled, jaw clenching and unclenching in anger. "Yes, sir."

Prion nodded. "This human girl you're hung up on—"

"Don't talk about her like that." Ronan's voice was low and dangerous.

Prion paused and cocked his head, looking at Ronan full in the face for the first time. "Oh? And how should I talk about her?" His voice was full of curiosity, but it didn't deceive Ronan—Prion was a dangerous wielder of words and could lash out at a moment's notice, and he wasn't known for his temperance and grace.

"She's my..." Ronan took a steadying breath. "My True Mate."

Prion's eyes widened in surprise. "You, Ronan? The truest Anchor I've seen in half a century? Taken so easily."

Ronan let out an anguished cry. "I didn't plan on this! It just happened. It's not like we can control it."

"Of course we can't." Prion's voice was soft, surprisingly tender. Ronan shot him a wary look. "These things of the heart, they take us by surprise, don't they? These... *whirlwind romances...* that come upon us so suddenly? And they catch even the most unsuspecting humans in their net." He was looking out the window at a petite woman with long blonde hair hanging in a braid down her back. Ronan recognized her as Leannán. She was hanging sheets on a line to dry in the wind, and the breeze whipped her white dress against her legs like a banner. As they watched, Lyall joined her, and the two each took a corner of a sheet and hung it on the wash line to dry in the wind.

The look on Prion's face was gentle, with a small smile playing at the corners of his mouth. Ronan felt as if he was watching some intimate moment between the two of them and felt a flush creeping up his neck. To see his prince in such a vulnerable expression was disarming.

He cleared his throat. "Highness? What do you want me to do?"

"Do?" Prion sounded distracted as he gazed out the window. He turned and his expression was vague, as if he'd forgotten Ronan was even there. "What else can we do? Obviously, you must work this out."

Ronan cocked his head. "I don't take your meaning, sir. I'm asking for direction."

"I can't tell you what you're supposed to do, Ronan. True Mate bonds are not to be taken lightly and you cannot break them. To leave her to return to our clan will break a part of you into pieces you cannot put back together—you will forever be half: half a man, half a heart. But you cannot forsake your duties to your clan. They need you and will be in danger without you. The longer we wait to handle the sirens, the bolder they get. We cannot risk being away from them when peace is on the horizon."

Ronan passed a hand through his hair in frustration. Behind him, the door opened, and Leannán came in holding a wooden laundry basket. "Ronan! Good to see you again." She crossed to kiss his cheek, balancing the basket on one hip. "What brings you out our way?"

Ronan locked eyes with Prion, who wore a grim smile, as if he knew what Ronan was thinking. "Advice. I came seeking advice."

Leannán grinned at him, her eyes sparkling. "And did you get what you were looking for?"

Prion arced an eyebrow at him as if to ask, *yes, did you?*

Ronan forced himself to smile down at the small woman. She barely came up to his shoulder. "I have enough to work with, yes. I think I know what I need to do."

Leannán's smile widened, her wide mouth stretching into an easy grin. "Good! Then you will stay for lunch. We are having cullen skink." She winked at Prion. "It's a human specialty here." Once again, Ronan felt he was watching an insider's scene from the outside and felt strangely guilty for having seen it.

"I'm not sure what that is," he said, "but I'm afraid I can't stay to find out. I have to be getting back... back home." He had caught himself from saying "back to Una."

Prion's eyebrow arced again, as if he were enjoying Ronan's discomfort, but he gestured toward the kitchen table. "No, sit. We have much to discuss. You will stay for lunch."

Ronan heard the veiled command in his tone and sighed inwardly. He glanced out the window. Una would be worried when he wasn't home soon. But he couldn't refuse a command from his prince, so he smiled instead. "I would be honored to."

Una wiped down the counter of her kitchen table for the fifth time. It was lunchtime and Ronan still hadn't returned. Had he been so angry when he'd left? He'd said he would be back in a few hours, but obviously something had kept him. Maybe he was hurt? She dashed the thought from her mind. It wasn't likely. Her selkie man could take care of himself, she knew that.

But what then? In her secret heart, she feared he was looking for his sealskin, turning every rock in the inlet, trying to find it before she could return it to him. Again came the nagging sense that perhaps she should give it back and let him make his own decision. Would he stay with her once he had it back? She knew how she felt, could recognize the telltale signs: longing for him when he was gone, missing the sound of his voice and the touch of his hands on her body. She hungered for him when he was in the room, to the exclusion of all else. This was no puppy love, as she'd originally assumed. No mere lustful craving of the body for the fleshly pleasures he was so adept at giving.

This was love. Pure, unadulterated love. And she was head over heels in it for him. Perhaps it was the magic of the True Mate bond he spoke of, but she knew it was something strong and binding, whatever the cause.

She wondered what she would do if he came home and asked her for his skin in earnestness. Could she give him up if he asked it? Could she give him his freedom if he truly longed for it? That thought wasn't comforting in the slightest, so she pushed it away. She would handle that moment when and if it came.

Until then, she would wait for him, pray for his safe return, and hope to the gods that he would return to her.

CHAPTER 23

RONAN WASN'T PLEASED WHEN she told him about Uncle Hugh's desire to have dinner that night. He had returned from Lord Prion's home quiet and unwilling to speak. He was lost in his own thoughts, and when she'd told him what she'd found in the journals, about the strange creature and the mysterious "he" referenced within, he took in the information with a sober nod.

"Can I see it?" he asked. The emotions within him swirled like a whirlpool, and snippets of his conversation with Lord Prion kept pushing forth for prominence in his mind. A quick scan of the journal entry told him nothing new that Una hadn't already clued him in on, but he needed time to think, so he pretended to pore over the entry as Una straightened the house, casting him anxious, curious glances.

He wrestled with himself and his thoughts until it was time to leave. Then he put away the journal and held out his arm to Una. "Ready?"

She responded with a tight smile, still wanting to ask him questions but holding back.

They started walking, letting the cool night air whip at their clothes as they strode along the coastline.

After several minutes, Ronan couldn't stand the silence any longer. "We can't afford to waste time visiting family when the curse is ramping up. It's becoming dangerous now. We need to figure this out."

"You think I don't want that?" Una cried. She pressed her hands to her breast. "But this is important. This is my life." She scowled and flung a hand at him. "Besides, you didn't mind sneaking off to visit your second-in-command all those times. Why is it okay for you to do it but not me?"

Ronan scowled. "That's different."

"Is it? Because it seems like the same thing to me. Your family isn't more important than mine, Ronan."

"I didn't say they were. It's just—"

"It's just what?" Una's eyes blazed in her face as she put her hands on her hips. "Take your time. I'll wait," she snapped.

Ronan closed his eyes and took a deep breath, searching for calm. This was getting them nowhere.

"Fine. We'll meet him." He pointed a finger at Una. "But this is going to be an inquisition, not a dinner, and you know it. They want to know what kind of man would sweep you off your feet, and I'm tired of explaining myself to all these humans."

Una frowned, hurt. "'These humans' all matter to me. Why can't you see that?"

Ronan's heart twisted, but he held firm. This was the True Mate bond talking, he could sense it. This wasn't rationale, and therefore couldn't be reasoned with. He would play the part of dutiful husband once more. Then they would sort this out. The town had little time.

"We're here."

Ronan looked up, not having paid attention to where they were headed. Then, with a jolt, he realized he knew the house they were approaching.

He stepped in front of Una as they reached the door, pressing his hands into her shoulders. "Una," he said in an urgent voice, "you don't need to be here. It is very dangerous for you."

Una stared at him quizzically. "What do you mean? It's just—"

Behind him, the door opened. "Una?" a man's voice said. "Is that you?"

Ronan froze. Una gave him a curious look, then stepped around him. "Uncle Hugh!"

Ronan turned and saw Una's uncle give her a long hug. Over her shoulder, their eyes met, blue eyes blazing into brown. Ronan felt his face drain, and he felt weak. This was not what he expected.

"Come in, my dear," Una's uncle said, moving back toward the open door and waving them through.

Once inside, Ronan dropped to one knee and bowed his head. "My lord!"

Una looked on, shocked, then looked at Leannán and Hugh, who were sharing a grim look. "Uncle Hugh, what is this about?" Behind them, Lyall bounced into the room with a large smile that faded when she saw the tense looks being exchanged.

Ronan straightened in a fluid movement and clasped a hand over his heart. "My Lord Prion, what is this about?"

"Ronan, how do you know Uncle Hugh? And why are you calling him Lord Prion?" Una asked.

"Una—" Leannán attempted, but Prion interrupted.

"I had suspected she was the human you were talking about. Given the gossip of Una's new man scampering around town and your sudden True Mate dilemma, it made perfect sense."

"You *told* him about that?" Una said, turning on Ronan. "And now I'm just some human?"

Ronan looked at Una, then at Prion, in obvious bewilderment. He looked at Una and pointed at Prion. "How do you know him? This man is your Uncle Hugh?"

But Una stared at him in stoney silence and crossed her arms. Her mouth was a thin line in her face.

"Ronan," Leannán interjected, stepping between them all and putting her hands up as if afraid they would come to blows. "I think we all just need to sit down and figure some things out."

Ronan gave an angry glance at Una. "Yes, I suppose we do."

Lyall stepped up to meet them. "Una, what are you doing with my father's business partner?"

Una turned an incredulous gaze to Ronan, who took a deep breath, not meeting her eyes.

Prion's gaze was inscrutable as he watched Ronan. Ronan looked at Una, then at Lyall's confused face, then at Leannán's grim one. "Lord Prion, do you have any whiskey?"

"Okay, so let me get this straight." Una pinched the bridge of her nose with her fingers and squinched her eyes shut. "Ronan is a member of your clan, Uncle Hugh," she looked at her uncle. "Because you're a selkie. And you, Aunt Leannán, are one, too." She looked at her aunt, who nodded. They were all seated around the dining table, sharing a jug of whiskey.

"Which would make me... what?" Lyall asked in a breathy voice. She looked at her parents with a fearful expression. "I've never changed into a... never been... I'm just a human! Aren't I?"

Prion looked at her with a sad expression on his face. "We were waiting to see what would happen when you turned twenty-two. That's when you would shift for the first time." He jerked his chin towards his bedroom. "We have a sealskin waiting for you, in case you turned out to be a selkie after all."

"Why wouldn't I be?" she asked in a hurt tone. Una's heart broke for her—to suddenly find she was not the person she'd always thought herself to be, and now to face the possibility that her birthright might not reveal itself after all... it was a lot to take in.

"Sometimes the offspring of selkies who give birth while in human form never realize their selkie forms," Leannán said gently. She covered her daughter's hands with her own. "We won't know until you turn twenty-two if you will be able to shift."

"And you can't shift, Uncle Hugh," Una broke in, "because your skin got... damaged?"

"By a siren princeling," Prion growled. His eyes blazed with anger. "He wrecked my skin, and I couldn't repair it."

Una looked between her aunt and uncle. "So you two have been passing as human ever since? Aunt Leannán, how could you bear to never shift back?" Ronan's face echoed the same question.

Leannán smiled and it held a lifetime of heartbreak in it. "Because of my love for him." She turned glistening eyes to her husband, who smiled back at her. Ronan watched the love shine between them and felt a momentary longing for the same. To have someone who meant more than your skin. What kind of love must that be?

"And you're a prince?" Una squeaked the word. Her eyes were very wide.

Prion smiled at her, and it was the gentlest Ronan had ever seen him look. "Strategic Anchor Commander, nowadays. My mother and father still rule our clan, but I advise our fighting contingent, the Anchors. I am still responsible for protecting our clan. It is all I can do in my altered state."

"So you don't actually hunt for sea treasures?" Lyall asked in a skeptical voice. "And Ronan isn't your business partner?"

"Ronan is Anchor for his clan," Una explained. Leannán and Prion shared a quick, surprised glance.

"Not while he's human, he's not," Lyall snorted, then quieted as everyone turned on her with an angry glare.

"That *is* a source of contention," Ronan said dryly, with a sideways glance at Una. Una flushed with guilt.

"So you stole his skin to..." Prion asked Una. "Save the town? From what?"

"From the curse."

Prion's face darkened. "The curse."

"Ronan said the town was cursed. I enlisted Ronan's help to stop it." She sagged in her chair. "But so far, we have no idea who laid it down."

"I do," Prion said. "The wretched *buidseach* that refused to help repair my skin did it."

"The what?" Lyall asked. She narrowed her eyes at her father.

"A selkie witch," Ronan explained to her. "What we call *buidseach*. But those are just a myth." He looked at Prion. "They don't exist. Do they?"

"Oh, they do," Leannán said in a grim voice. She cast a dark look at her husband. "And we know who she is."

Una leaned forward with excitement. "Who?"

"The Mayor's wife."

"*Harper?*" Ronan and Una exclaimed together.

"That can't be right," Una said, frowning.

"It is," Prion said, leaning back and fidgeting with his cane. "But that wicked woman won't lift the curse. And I don't blame her."

"But why did she curse the town in the first place?" Una asked.

Prion's eyes blazed with triumph. "Because Adair, back when he was a simple fisherman, tricked your father and captured her. He stole her sealskin, the same way you did Ronan's. Then he took her as his wife."

"Like the folklore says," Una breathed, her eyes wide. "How awful." She shared a pained look with Ronan. "But why would my father allow such a thing?"

Ronan ignored that. That was a question for another time. He leaned forward and rested his elbows on the table. "So we get her skin back and she lifts the curse. Easy, right?"

"No," Prion said curtly. "That evil woman deserves her fate."

"Uncle Hugh!" Una said, shocked.

"No!" he said, slashing a hand through the air. His expression was fierce. "Where was she when I needed help? Why should I help her? She left me like this, with this half-life that no selkie should have to endure. And now she knows what it's like to lose her skin." He sat back with a smug, satisfied smile. "Got what she deserved."

"We can't leave the town like this," Una said, looking at all of them. "We just can't. We have to try to lift the curse." Prion folded his arms and pursed his lips. Una scowled at him. "Fine. You don't want to help? Don't help. But like it or not, this town is your home, too. And if it dies, so does your livelihood."

Prion's expression turned sulky, but he looked away from her, not meeting her gaze.

"And you," she said, turning fierce eyes on Ronan. "You need to help me find it. It's got to be somewhere in his house."

"She'd find it somewhere in the house," Leannán pointed out.

Una thought. What did they know about Adair? That he had been a fishing captain with her father. That he had kidnapped Harper and taken her sealskin to bind her to him. She closed her eyes and pictured Adair in her mind. She remembered the way he gripped Ronan's hand in competitive greeting when they first met. Then later how they'd seen him passing through the town square, pausing to smile fondly up at the statue of the selkie woman. He had looked at it the same way he looked at Harper: possessively, happily.

"Perhaps it's somewhere in plain sight," Una said, thinking her words through as she said them. "The statue in town square. Remember how he looked at it? Like he was looking at Harper herself."

Prion cocked his head thoughtfully. "He had the statue put in the day they elected him Mayor, shortly after Harper arrived. I remember it well. It was a celebration day for the entire town. And Adair presided over the event like it was his birthday."

Ronan shuddered. "It's a hideous thing," he said, surprising Una. She'd always admired the beauty of it, the way the woman's body arced like a seal curving through the water. "No selkie would appreciate that thing," Ronan continued. "It's too exposed. Too much metal. It would be like fairies being surrounded by iron."

"So there's a chance Harper wouldn't even know it's there?" Una said with rising excitement. "So she wouldn't be able to get it back because it's hidden from her somehow, maybe buried somewhere around the base of it? And in plain sight, too." She shuddered. What kind of man would do that to his own wife? Especially given how much he professed to love her?

Then guilt crashed over her. But wasn't that exactly what she'd done to Ronan, hiding his sealskin near the cave where she'd found it? And how deep was her love for him, if that was something she could live with? She pushed those thoughts away. That was a conversation to be had at another time. Right now, they needed to plan how to break the curse.

"Why don't you just go there and get the skin for her?" Lyall asked Una. She'd remained quiet throughout the conversation, and now she sat up straighter as she spoke. Her eyes shined with excitement. "Give it to her, make it right. She gets her skin back, lifts the curse, and we save the town."

"It won't be that easy," Prion spoke up. "Her husband is a jealous man, and a powerful one. He will not be so keen to lose his wife of nearly a decade. He's worked very hard to make a life with her. He won't give it up easily."

Ronan turned fierce eyes on him. "We'll make him. By force, if we have to."

Prion smiled. "Now you sound like Ceannas. So rash and ready to jump into the fray." He shook his head. "No. Trust me when I say the Mayor is a dangerous man." He looked at Una. "I don't want you to go anywhere near him."

"When I was small, I knew he was my Da's competitor. But since he died, Adair always spoke highly of him, as if they had been friends since before I was born," Una said. She pushed aside the sick feeling she got at the thought of why the Mayor would speak so. Could he have seen her father as an accomplice to it all? *He thinks to buy my acquiescence, but it won't work.* That's what her father had written in his journal. Did Adair somehow think her father had led Adair to Harper in the first place? It was more than she cared to think about. "He would never hurt me."

"Because you were never a threat to him before," Leannán broke in. "Now that has changed. You threaten everything he holds most dear with this knowledge." She gave Una a warning look. "You must be very careful, my dear."

"The Mayor's throwing a huge party at the Town Hall for his twenty-four-year wedding anniversary," Lyall explained. "We were invited, and I was going to go with Rory, but..." She paused and glanced at her father. "Then you said we shouldn't go. I never knew why until now."

"You shouldn't feel special," Una said dryly. "The whole town was invited."

Lyall scrunched up her face. "What I don't understand is why he would make a wedding anniversary a public spectacle..?"

Una shrugged. "Adair has a penchant for the dramatic."

"The Town Hall is just a few blocks away from the statue," Leannán suggested. "That would be the best time to do it, when everyone's distracted at the party."

Una bit her lip. "We must get that skin back. It's the only way to lift the curse." She looked at Ronan. "Do you have any ideas?"

He sat back, looking thoughtful. "A few. But more than half of them involve me doing this and not you." As Una began to protest, he held up a hand. "No, don't even start. I'm not putting you in harm's way."

"I can take care of myself," she shot back, eyes blazing.

"I can't risk you!" he shouted, ignoring the looks the rest of the table exchanged. "Do you know what it would do to me if I lost you, too?"

Una looked back at him with a shocked gaze. His skin was such a vital part of who he was, and now, whether or not he meant to, he just declared her on the same level.

She felt as if she might explode into tiny pieces from the force of the exhilaration his statement filled her with. She wrapped her arm across her chest to contain it and tried to focus on the conversation at hand.

"Uncle Hugh... Lord... Prion," she stumbled over the unfamiliar words, "what is the best way to resolve this? You must have some ideas."

He glared at her, but wiped a hand over his face in resignation. "The party is the best time to try for it. You will need the skin. Ronan is the best bet to get it. You don't need to be involved in the actual retrieval." At her protest, he spoke over her. "I know you are quite capable, my dear. But I can't have you hurt. And, besides, Ronan is trained for this. He is our best warrior. If anyone can take care of this quickly and cleanly, it's him."

Una looked mutinous but sat back in her chair. After several long moments, she nodded. "Fine," she said in a flat voice. "Ronan, can you handle digging around the statue to look for it? It's something you said no selkie would ever do." His admission that he loved her like his sealskin still rocked her, and she was bitterly aware of the fact that getting Harper's sealskin back to her would change things between them forever. There was something much bigger at stake here than just the town now, and she didn't know how she would withstand it.

He nodded, swallowing hard, and she wondered what he was thinking. She wished they were alone so she could hold him and talk to him about what she was feeling without other eyes on them. But she didn't trust herself to speak of it just yet. There would be time later.

"Then that settles it." She stood, her chair scraping back on the floor. "We must go."

Leannán stood. "Stay and have dinner, at least. There is much to plan. You can't do anything until tomorrow night, anyway."

Una gave her a wan smile. "That is kind of you to offer. But this needs to be resolved immediately. Ronan and I will return home and plan what we need to do. The trickiest part is figuring out how Ronan can dig up the sealskin in plain sight without getting caught."

"We can figure that out when we get there," Ronan said in a firm voice. "If the party is *the* big event of the year, as you say, perhaps it will be just enough of a distraction that nobody will be around."

For a moment, everyone was silent. Then, as one, they all looked to Prion.

Prion shook his head, his eyes on Una. "This seems like the most solid plan," he admitted. "It makes the most sense. But, if anything were to happen while the two of you are gone"—he turned fierce eyes on Ronan—"I would never forgive you." His voice was cold and low.

Una suppressed a shiver. This was no father-figure speaking. It was the commander of the Liath Clann's fighting force. And he would not be denied. She had no doubt if they failed tonight, Ronan's life would be forfeited.

Ronan nodded. "She will be safe, sir. She will be at the party while I go alone to get the skin." He clasped a hand over his heart in salute. "My lord." He nodded to Una. "Let's go." She gave him a small smile and stepped past him towards the door.

"Well met, Ronan," Leannán said to their backs as they opened the door.

He turned and smiled. "My lady."

Then they left.

CHAPTER 24

THE NIGHT WAS STARLESS above them as they trudged back to Una's house. Una felt as if there were a thousand things she wished to say to him, but none of them sounded right in her head. She ached to talk to him, but there was a distance between them, the mission ahead, that loomed in the way.

"I'm sorry my Uncle was so hard on you," Una offered with a rueful smile.

Ronan chuckled. "They just want to know you're in good hands."

His words made Una's stomach twist uneasily. Was she? Was Ronan so eager to help because of his altruistic nature, or because he still wanted his skin? She had to know. She gave Ronan a sideways look. "So am I, Ronan?" she asked softly. "Am I in good hands?"

His face smoothed as he looked at her, then a scowl formed. The sight turned Una's heart to ice. "What kind of question is that?" His voice was menacing soft.

"It's just..." she floundered, "I've been wondering about your loyalties lately..."

"My loyalties," he growled.

Una lifted her chin. She would not let his assertive nature push her around. Did he not like being questioned? Too bad! She had every right to know what he intended. Her heart whispered at her to stop before it went too far, whispered that she wasn't doing the right thing. But she pushed the feeling aside as she pushed her hair back from her face.

"Yes, your loyalties. What is the real reason you're trying to help me now? Is it to help me save the town? Because you care about me?"

"Do you doubt how much I care about you?" he countered. Even in the fading light, she could see a dark flush of anger in his cheeks. "What would it take to earn your trust, Una? What more can I do to show you how I feel about you?"

"You can tell me the truth when I ask for it." Una's voice rang clear in the dusky twilight air.

"And what truth do you demand now?" Ronan's voice was rising. "Another sacrifice on my part? Haven't you already taken enough from me?"

Una stopped, as if he'd struck her. "What did you say?"

Ronan stopped too and leaned over her. "You heard me! What more can you take from me that I have to continually prove myself to you? What more can you possibly ask from me that I have to give?" He balled his fists at his sides.

She matched his body language, leaning forward into his face. "Fine! You want your skin back? Is that what this has been all about?" She slung her bag from her shoulder and fished around in it with one hand.

She had grabbed it days before, having planned to give it to him as a surprise. It had felt like a hot coal in her bag the entire time, so much that she could swear that he'd sense it being so close to him, in the same house for the last few days. But, to her surprise, he hadn't sensed it, hadn't mentioned it even.

Now she grabbed the sleek pelt, feeling its heavy oiledness, the magic that tingled along her fingertips at its touch, and balled in her fist.

She pulled it out and threw it in his face. "Here! Take what you so dearly want! Take it and be gone from here! That's all you ever wanted anyway, wasn't it?"

She wanted to cry. Wanted to sob and rend her clothes and weep for what she knew she was throwing away. But she wouldn't give him the satisfaction. The hot coal of anger burned in her stomach and instead of pushing it down, she fanned it hotter, letting the rage build in her so that was all she had to think about.

Una watched as Ronan pulled the skin away and held it carefully in his hands. He looked at her with a dark emotion that she couldn't place. She'd once thought it was love. But how could that be? All he'd ever wanted was his sealskin, she knew that now. Seeing his face go so still as he looked at the skin in his hands, seeing the tense set to his shoulders that she imagined was a fight-or-flight response. Was he calculating how fast he could get away? Was he already planning his return to the sea even now?

"What are you waiting for?" she said in a grim voice. "This is what you wanted."

Ronan stared at her with incredulous intensity. His eyes blazed from his face.

"Where was it?" he asked in a deadly soft voice.

"Near the cave where I first saw you," she said, matching his tone. "There's a rocky outcropping nearby. I buried it underneath some stones."

"And you had it all night tonight? Without telling me?"

"I was going to tell you when the time was right," she ground out. She suddenly couldn't stand to be here, talking to him while her heart was breaking into tiny pieces before his eyes.

He was predator still, his body held in such check she wondered how he wasn't vibrating with the effort of holding back. He caressed one hand down the skin's length, as if trying to convince himself it was real.

"This changes everything," he said in a low voice, and she tore her eyes from him as the salty air stung her face, making her eyes water. She felt one traitorous tear break free and trickle down her cheek.

"No, it doesn't." She inhaled once, twice, letting the sharp night air pierce her lungs as his words had pierced her heart. This was no time to be weak, she told herself. She straightened and pulled her shoulders back. "Go."

"Una," Ronan began, but she couldn't bear it any longer.

"Go! I was wrong about you. About us."

There was a moment of stillness, where she had a moment's hope that he would touch her, tell her it wasn't about his skin after all, that he truly loved her. Then the moment passed, and he was gone, moving past her close enough that his clothes brushed her shoulder. His footsteps were lost in the sound of the waves.

She heard nothing as the night sounds of the tide washed over her. She didn't know how long she stood there, arms crossed, holding tight to her body as if she might break away into thousands of pieces and float away in the surf if she let go even a little. The wind tore through her clothes, icy needles against her skin, but she didn't notice. All she heard was the sound of the wind screaming, *he's gone, he's gone.*

RONAN DIDN'T KNOW HOW long he'd walked, lost in the dark haze of anger and betrayal, but he suddenly became aware, with his warrior's senses, that he wasn't alone.

He whirled and saw Ceannas standing, clothed, a few feet away. In his hands was his sealskin.

"I could have killed you," Ceannas said easily. He sauntered a few steps forward. "You had no idea I was even there. You're slipping."

Ronan scowled. "I am not in the mood for company right now, Ceannas."

"Too bad," his second Anchor said in a nonchalant tone. "Lord Prion filled me in. Her uncle, huh?" At Ronan's glare, he looked away with feigned casualty. "Seems I just missed your little get-together. I had intended to deliver his lordship's precious pearl harvest myself, but it seems you've had quite the fun-filled night without me." He sounded disappointed.

"Ceannas," Ronan growled, his hands clenching in his sealskin. The silky material bunched in his fists, reminding him of just what he'd lost. Not just his ability to protect his clan, but now his heart, as well. "Now is not the time."

She sent me away, he thought incredulously. *She really sent me away.* The thought threatened to overwhelm him. The wind seemed to scream around him, echoing his thoughts, *away away.*

"Now is *exactly* the time, my friend," Ceannas said with a small smile. "You see, Lord Prion let me know what you had planned for tonight. And at first, I was hurt." He put a hand over his heart, his expression tragic. "*How could he leave me behind?* I thought to myself. Then I thought about it. What was it about this mission that was worth more to you than our friendship, something so important that you would risk the safety of our clan with your absence? And I realized it had to be your relationship with this human."

Ronan stared at him bleakly. That was what he'd once thought, too. Now he knew differently.

"But then I had a revelation. She's not just some human, is she?" He gazed at Ronan shrewdly. Ronan stared back.

"How long have you known?" Ceannas asked in a soft voice.

"Since I met her." His voice sounded rusty, as if unused for a very long time. "I felt the True Mate bond instantly."

"What did it feel like?" Ceannas looked eager, hungry for the information.

Ronan shrugged. "Like coming home. Like donning your sealskin for the first time. Like finding a part of yourself you never knew was missing until it was suddenly there."

Ceannas's dark eyes watched him.

Ronan sighed. "But it doesn't matter now. We can go home." The emotion felt like it was draining out of him, the anger, the hurt. All that was left was a vast emptiness that seemed to swallow him like the sea, and all he wanted was to be swallowed by it.

"What do you mean, go home?" Ceannas asked incredulously. He held out a hand to indicate the way they'd come. "Your home is back there, with your mate. That's where your heart is."

"Not anymore," Ronan said wearily. "She sent me away."

"What do you mean? She can't do that."

"She already did."

Ceannas looked back, as if he could see her in the distance. He looked confused, and suddenly very young. "But... if she's your True Mate—"

"She doesn't want me!" Ronan cried. His voice cracked with the strain. He held out his arms wide to indicate the entire situation. "She sent me away! She rejected me! She doesn't want this bond. So I had to let her go."

"But... don't you love her?"

"More than my life," Ronan whispered.

"So because you love her, you're letting her go?" Ceannas asked quizzically. "That doesn't make any sense."

Ronan closed his eyes and shook his head. No, it didn't. Not in the slightest. But she had made very clear what she wanted. Instead of giving him back his skin and telling him of her love, she made her decision very clear with her actions as well as her words. She didn't want him. The thought rang in his head like a cracked bell.

"She doesn't want me," he said softly. "So I will return home. It's for the best."

Ceannas cast another doubt-filled glance behind them, then stepped forward and clasped Ronan's shoulder. "Okay then. Let's go."

"Go?"

"Go where?"

"The King and Queen want to see you." Ronan nodded wearily.

As they walked towards the water, Ronan tried to let the nearness of the water cleanse his mind of all his negative thoughts, tried to let the sound of the waves replace that sound of loss that rang in his head.

At the shoreline, they both stripped, letting their human clothes fall to the pebbled beach. Ronan stepped naked into the water, letting the icy coolness prickle his skin to numbness. "It's for the best," he whispered to himself.

He pulled his sealskin over his back, curled into the change, and disappeared into the water.

CHAPTER 25

THE NEXT MORNING PASSED in a haze. Una dimly realized she should plan how to get Harper's skin back without Ronan, but all she felt was a dazed emptiness inside that made thinking difficult.

There was a knock at the door around mid-day.

Una roused herself from the lumpy couch, wincing as her back twinged in protest. How long had she been sitting there?

She opened the door to find Lyall dressed in her festival finery, an off-the-shoulder white dress that flared in at her waist and out above her knees. She grinned at Una and dipped her sunhat in greeting before she registered Una's dismal expression.

"What's wrong?" she asked as she hurried inside and shut the door behind her.

"He's gone," Una ground out. Speaking was difficult around the lump in her throat. Tears threatened to break forth, but she blinked and held them back. She wouldn't break down. Not now.

"What do you mean? How could he leave?" Lyall cast an urgent glance around the house, as if expecting Ronan to suddenly appear.

Una explained about the fight and Ronan's reaction to getting his sealskin back. As she spoke, Lyall's jaw dropped open, and her eyes grew wider. When Una told her that Ronan had left, her face changed to a scowl.

"That scoundrel! I knew he wasn't aboveboard! How could he be slinking around my house, pretending to be my father's business partner and pretending to be in love with you—"

Her words were like a slap to the face for Una. Pretend to love her? She was positive that hadn't been the case, regardless of the fact that he'd left. What she'd felt for him had been real enough—she couldn't fathom how he could have reciprocated so much in falsehood. But Lyall was still going.

"—going to slap some sense in him next time he dares come around my father's house! How dare he treat you that way!"

"I sent him away," Una managed. The fog in her head was clearing in the wake of Lyall's tirade, and she felt lighter, more clear-headed. "It was my fault."

"Your fault? If he truly loved you, nothing should have been able to make him leave!" Lyall declared.

Her indignation made Una smile, though her face felt as if it were made of stone and might crack under the pressure of movement.

"But what are you going to do now?" Lyall asked, putting a hand to her mouth. "How are you going to get the skin back?"

"I'm going to do it myself," Una said. Her eyebrows raised in surprise as she realized she was right; there was nothing else they could do.

"Shouldn't you wait until you can get help?"

"From whom?" Una asked. "Your father? He'd let her rot, for all he's interested in helping."

"Maybe he can get another Anchor to help? He did say he was their commander...?" Lyall's voice was hesitant, and her fingers plucked and fidgeted with each other.

But Una shook her head. "I can't wait that long. He couldn't get word to them fast enough and the party's tonight." She pursed her lips and nodded. "It has to be me."

"You!" Lyall squeaked. Her face was a mask of misery. It was clear that she remembered her father's words.

Una reached out and took her fidgeting hands. "I can do this, Lyall! I have to! Don't you want me to save the town?" Lyall nodded. "I'll never get another chance like this. It's either tonight or never."

Lyall was quiet for several moments, a small V forming between her eyebrows as she thought. "Well, okay, so far this hasn't gone as planned," she said in a timid voice. "But I can help. I can distract the Mayor while you check out the statue."

"I can't ask you to do that," Una said. "Let me just think for a minute, and we can come up with another way. Maybe someone from the town can—"

"No!" Lyall exploded, slashing her hands through the air. "Nobody ever suspects that I am capable of great things!

Not Rory, not my parents, and not you. But I can do this!" She turned a beseeching expression on Una. "Let me help."

"Well," Una said slowly, thinking out loud. "Without Ronan"—the name caught in her throat—"I can get the skin instead."

Lyall scowled in silence for a moment, then her eyes lit up. "Oh! That's perfect!" she exclaimed, throwing out her arms in excitement. "I can buy you the time to look while you're there! I can keep them busy. It will be dark. You'll need a candle. And a shovel." Una regarded her skeptically. "In case you have to dig!"

Una rolled her eyes, and Lyall set her shoulders. "I am stronger than you give me credit for!" Her voice was earnest. "I can help you in a way nobody else can. And if you don't take care of it tonight, when will you? When will another opportunity like this arise?"

Una bit her lip. Lyall had an excellent point. When would the stars align like this for another opportunity?

She nodded, reluctantly. "Ok." Lyall bounced in excitement, but Una held up a warning finger. "But we do this carefully! So very carefully." She grumbled to herself, "Uncle Hugh's going to kill me if he finds out."

"He'll kill both of us," Lyall said in a cheerful tone. She didn't seem fazed in the slightest. "Now, what do we need to do?"

Una thought. "I need to change into something suitable for the party. And I'll need a candle." She glanced around her feet, as if she might find one lying on the floor.

Lyall clapped her hands together. "And a shovel!"

Una looked at her grimly. "This is a very serious thing we're doing. Your father was right, Adair may be dangerous. We'll have to be careful."

Lyall nodded with a serious expression, but her eyes sparkled with barely contained excitement. "Of course. Now let's go. Father let me take the cart."

"That'll be faster than going on foot. It should put us at the party at a reasonable time. Just give me a moment to get ready."

She dashed around the house, grabbing a small bag and a candle, then hastily snatched a nicer dress from the chest at the foot of her bed. As she shucked out of her work dress, Lyall turned her back to give Una some privacy. She pulled the nicer dress over her head and paused, hesitating with her fingers on the bustle ribbons.

Ronan had been here not even a day ago. She imagined she could still smell him in the room. She tied the ribbons into a bow, feeling the absence of him, feeling an emptiness inside her that had everything to do with the selkie-shaped hole inside her heart.

Her hand fell and caught the edge of the headboard of the bed, and she let her fingers slide over the grainy surface, feeling the grooves left by her father's axe when he'd made it. This was where they'd first slept together.

No, she caught herself. Here was when she'd first started falling in love with him.

Her heart ached. She put a fist to her stomach and curled around it, bowing under the pain inside her. How could something hurt so badly without a physical wound? There seemed to be a sea inside her, tumultuous waves of confusion and hurt and fear. What was she without him?

Half a person, half a heart. He had become to her like his sealskin was to him—vital, a necessary part of her being. Without him, what was life?

Necessary, she reminded herself. Life was necessary. She hadn't needed love before, she wouldn't need it now. She had survived without Blair, hard as it had been. This was just another kind of hurt, another obstacle in her path.

She straightened, putting her fist on the headboard and letting the rough grain of the wood ground her.

She didn't need him any more than he obviously needed her. From the start, this had only been about lifting the curse—that was what was important. That was what mattered. Love had never been part of the plan. This was always how it was going to be. She nodded her head in the dark. That was what she would focus on.

Focus on the problem, Ronan had told her. She could do that much. There would be time to lament his loss later. For now, she had work to do.

She passed a hand over her hair to smooth it and stood behind Lyall. She planted a watery smile on her face and straightened her shoulders. "How do I look?"

Lyall turned and took her in. Then she smiled and held out her hand. "Like you're ready for trouble. Partners?"

Una's smile slipped. She had thought she and Ronan were partners. *It just goes to show*, she thought bitterly. *Love isn't possible for me.*

Una clasped it and they shook. "Partners."

CHAPTER 26

A SHORT WHILE LATER, they approached the Town Hall. It was lit up from within, light shining warmly through the windows. A string of lanterns lit the sides of a large tent half-visible around the back of the stone building.

"Remember," Lyall said, "take as much time as you need at the statue. I'll keep both of them busy until you reappear. Once you get the skin, stow it in your bag, and we'll give it to her later. We don't want to risk Adair knowing what we're up to tonight. Got it?"

Una shook her head in acknowledgment. It was hard to concentrate on their job when all she could see was Ronan's bleak face when she'd told him to go. He had said her name and it held all the emotion he'd ever shown her. But it held caution, too. As if he was scared to say anything more. What had he been about to say?

"Una!" Lyall hissed. "Get your head together! This is dangerous work." Lyall slapped Una's shoulder, hard, and Una startled back to the present moment.

"I'm here," she growled. "Quit hitting me. I'm good."

"Are you?" Lyall asked softly. "Because if you're not ready..."

"I'm ready." Una's voice was grim. She put Ronan's face out her of mind—

—*this changes everything*—

—and focused on keeping her back straight as they parked their horse with the other horse carts and headed around the side of the building for the tent entrance. At the flap, they paused and looked at each other. Both took a deep breath, straightened their shoulders, and plastered identical fake smiles on their faces.

Una pushed the flap aside. Lyall's jaw dropped as they emerged, and Una felt her eyebrows lift in surprise. They'd transformed the garden behind the Town Hall into a fairy wonderland. The tall tent was pitched high enough to brush the tops of the tallest hedges and a hundred tiny lanterns hung from the ceiling, creating the effect of a starry night.

Underneath the tent, round tables and chairs ringed the space with a set of shiny waxed boards laid down in the middle for a dancing floor. At the front, a five-member band was playing with furious abandon while several couples danced in a circle to the tune. To one side of the tent, a small crowd gathered around a couple, which Una saw was Adair and his wife.

Lyall leaned close to speak in Una's ear. "I say you make for the statue now, while they're distracted." Una nodded and turned to go back through the tent entrance when a pair of bodies blocked their way.

"Una MacCallan! Oh no, it's Tod now, isn't it?" boomed a loud voice. It was the butcher, James Preas with his wife hanging on one beefy arm. His scraggly beard was braided down his chin and he was dressed in his finest collared shirt for the occasion, though his pants legs had the faintest hint of dark stains around his thighs, as if he'd wiped his hands on them at work instead of his apron.

His wife, Annis, preened at them with her small, piggish eyes. "Ladies, how lovely to see you tonight," she simpered in her girlish voice. She gave a sour once-over to Lyall, who looked radiant under the lamplight, then hugged her husband's arm tighter to her side. She flashed a false smile, which Una returned. Even under normal circumstances, she'd never been fond of the butcher's wife, who patched fishing nets for the local sea captains. Una didn't care for the way Annis spoke about Lyall, who Annis opined to anyone who would listen that Lyall was working in a job above her station.

"Have you been here long?" asked James, oblivious to the female tension around him.

Una opened her mouth, frantically fishing for a reply, but Lyall smoothly stepped in. "We just got here, but we were going—"

"Going? Nonsense!" James exclaimed, dropping his wife's arm and picking up Lyall's hand. Behind him, Annis scowled. "You have to at least visit the Mayor and his wife! They're the guests of honor."

Una refrained from mentioning that they were hardly guests at their own party, but James swept Lyall forward, weaving through the throng towards the crowd circling Adair and Harper. Lyall cast a frantic look over her shoulder as Una and a huffy Annis followed in James's wake.

The large man pushed his way through the group until he was at the front and presented Lyall to Adair with a flourish. The Mayor was deep in conversation with two other men.

"Caught this lady trying to sneak out before the party had even begun!" James laughed, patting Lyall heavily on the shoulder. Una thought Lyall's knees might buckle from the blows.

Adair frowned at the interruption, then his face became wreathed in a smile when he saw who it was. "Miss Lyall Lios. And Una Tod! It's wonderful to see you tonight. I'm so glad you could come." He nodded a dismissal to the men he'd been speaking with, then turned to grasp Lyall's and Una's hands in greeting. "My dears, I'm honored you could come tonight."

"It seems the whole town turned out for this celebration," Una demurred with a smile, pulling her hand away from his clammy touch. The truth she now knew about him repelled her, and she couldn't help but see a predatory gleam in his smile as he grinned down at them.

"Indeed they did," Adair agreed with a smug smile. "Spared no expense for my Harper's celebration." He turned and held out a hand to his wife, who was standing silently behind him.

At his gesture, she stepped forward with a warm smile. Her long hair floated down her shoulders like a cloak. "So good to see you, my dear. You look beautiful. But, Una, where's that strapping young man of yours?" Adair shot her a sharp look.

Una felt like her face was going to turn to stone and crack into pieces on the carpet. She kept her smile, hoping it looked more natural than it felt. "He couldn't make it tonight. He felt... under the weather."

"Well," Harper cooed. "I hope he feels better soon." She motioned behind her at a large table with a pristine white tablecloth. On it were dozens of variously decorated palm-sized cakes and stone glasses. "Please, let me pour you a drink. Then perhaps we can find a seat and enjoy ourselves." Harper took Una's hand and began to usher her towards the refreshment table. Una realized she would not extricate herself easily if Harper sat down with her, and she cast a wild look at Lyall behind Harper's back.

Lyall saw it and turned to Adair with a winsome smile. "Mister Mayor, I hear you are a fantastic dancer. Perhaps you would favor me with a brief dance?" She put her fingers to her lips and let out a piercing whistle.

The band and most of the conversation nearby quieted as everyone turned to look at Lyall.

Blushing, she gave Adair a roguish, sideways grin. "My father taught me how to do that." Then she turned back to the band. "A jig, please! To celebrate our Mayor and his beautiful wife!"

The crowd around them cheered and raised their glasses, toasting the couple, as Lyall darted forward and snatched a surprised-looking Harper's hand. "Come, dance with me!" Lyall called as the band kicked up a lively tune, and Lyall led the Barrons out on the dance floor.

It's now or never, Una thought, and turned to slip back through the crowd. Most people were flocking towards the dance floor to watch the festivities, and Una was glad nobody seemed to notice that she was moving in the wrong direction.

Una made her way back to the garden entrance and darted around the corner. She took a moment to collect herself, steeling her nerves for what she had to do. Then she ran back to the parked carts where the horses were standing sleepily in their traces and pulled out her bag and the small shovel she brought. She stepped forward, keeping to the dark, shadowed areas next to the buildings to keep away from any wandering eyes as she raced towards the Town Square.

She cast nervous glances over her shoulder, expecting someone to call her name or for Adair to burst out after her at any minute. *He's busy with Lyall,* she reminded herself. He had no reason to even notice she had left the party, let alone follow her to the statue. So why was she so nervous he would appear now, especially when Lyall was busy occupying his interest?

Feeling as if her heart were beating loud enough to signal her location to the entire town, she finally saw the sight of the darkened statue come into view. She ran to the base of it and crouched next to the wall of the fountain, where it nestled against the swoosh of the woman's skirt.

She clutched the shovel to her chest between her breasts and cast her eyes about for movement. There was nobody around and the only sounds to her searching ears were the gentle tambourine beats from the party.

She closed her eyes briefly and breathed a sigh of relief. Alone at last.

She pulled the candle and matches out of her bag and lit the candle. In a crouch, she eased her way around the base of the statue looking for disturbed earth or loose stones... anything to indicate where the sealskin might be. She avoided looking at the sweeping curve of the woman herself—there was no point in looking at metal.

As the heartbeats ticked past and her back began to ache from her crouch, a nagging voice whispered doubts at the back of her mind. *Twenty-four years is a long time,* the voice murmured. *What if the dirt is smooth-packed by now? What if there are no loose stones? What if we don't find it in time?* The thought stopped her in her tracks, frozen with fear. Of all the times for uncertainty to claim her!

Her fingers wriggled like spiders against the smooth bricks, and she hated the way the slightest imperfection in the stone made her heart leap with excitement at the prospect of having found a clue, anything to prove her hunch had been correct.

But the stones were firm and solid in their places.

She worked her way around the statue, feeling her back and legs begin to cramp from holding the bent-over position for so long. Her fingers began abraded from the rough surface of the bricks, and she feared she'd never find it.

It could be anywhere in here, she thought, feeling a sense of despair. There were so many stones. So many places a sealskin could be stored.

Her fingers crawled over the smooth bricks around the middle, working her way down—

—where was it? he'd asked—

—in the cave—

—and eased along the seam on the ground where the dirt met the bottom of the brick base. She shook her head, making the candlelight flicker in the dark.

Focus! she told herself furiously. Now was not the time to be distracted.

Then, as her eyes acclimated to the darkness, she noticed a small pile of stones on the ground, where the statue butted up to the fountain on the far side. The rest of the earth was smooth, unbroken, and the stones were the only anomaly.

She pinched a few between her fingers, feeling the gritty composition of them against her skin. In the thin candlelight, they appeared like small, broken bits of brick. She glanced up, squinting in the dim light, and feeling with the hand not holding the candle.

There!

At the top of the base, where the bricks sat in a thick, capped line for sitting, were two bricks that sat askew, as if they'd been pulled away and then crammed back into place hastily. And, as she leaned closer, she saw small corners of the bricks had been chipped away.

She closed her eyes and offered a prayer of thanks to the sky. Perhaps this was a sign that her mission would be successful. Luck was finally on her side.

Trembling with excitement, she set the candle on top of the fountain wall and pried at one stone. Her fingers ached at the firm contact as she struggled to pull it free, but eventually it came loose with a small scraping sound that grated on her already tense nerves. She set the brick on the fountain wall next to the candle.

Behind the stone was darkness, a small opening.

She didn't spare the time to look around to see if anyone had heard the stone pull free. She eagerly pulled at the one next to it and it came free with almost no effort, no longer moored in place by its companion. Setting the stone down on top of the first, she reached a tentative hand into the darkness behind them.

Her reaching fingers touched something soft, and she pulled back with a gasp. Then, chiding herself at her foolishness, she reached in again. Her fingers pressed gently, feeling the softness of something that felt like a pelt, then she pushed deeper and dug them into the oily texture of the fur.

This has to be it, she realized. *It just has to be.*

With a small cry of excitement, she lifted the pelt out and turned it over in her hands. She felt a jolt, like lightning, run up her arms, and her fingers clenched in the skin, bunching the material in her fists. The same thing had happened when she'd touched Ronan's skin back in the cave. This was it!

Suddenly she heard motion behind her, the scrape of a shoe on the dirt as she noticed a new light source coming into view. She spun around.

"Looking for something?"

Adair's smooth voice sounded flat and final in the silence around them. Una fought the urge to hide the sealskin behind her back, like a child caught holding something forbidden.

"What do you have there?" he asked in a silky tone. His shadow loomed over her, flickering and dancing in the light of the candle he held. She shrank back from him. He seemed massive as he stepped toward her, moving with a fluid grace that belied his age and weight.

"It's not yours," Una blurted out and winced at the way her voice trembled.

"Oh, but it is," he said. His tone hadn't changed, and she was surprised. Shouldn't he be angry? Upset that she had found it? Yelling or screaming at her to let it go? This smooth, friendly Adair wasn't what she'd expected to meet and it was even more frightening in the contrast to his usual self.

"You've had this all along?" she asked as her mind raced. Maybe she could dash around him, then back to the safety of the party before he caught up to her. Or perhaps she could convince him to let her have it, as unlikely a scenario as that was. Perhaps she could appeal to his sense of fairness and power. He had always shown himself to be a very reasonable man.

"Twenty-four years," he mused as he took another step towards her. His shadow capered across the curves of the statue at a fearsome height. "Twenty-four glorious years with my Harper. And I'll have you put that back where you got it now."

"I... I can't..." Una stammered, her fists gripping the sealskin.

"You can't?" He made a *tsk* sound with his teeth. "I think you have made a mistake, my dear. You're meddling with things outside your understanding."

"And is that what you and my father had? An understanding?" Her voice was strident with sudden anger. He dared speak to her as if she were still a child? Someone who couldn't understand the actions of adults like him and her father?

He paused on the steps, halfway down, and cocked his head to the side. "You could call it that, yes." He resumed his descent. "He's the whole reason I found my wife. If it weren't for him, I never would have made Mayor. Harper made that possible for me. And all because of your father."

"My father hated you," Una spat.

Adair cocked his head and gave her a considering look. "Well, there's no accounting for taste. I've always figured that I owed your father for the gift he gave me that day. So after he died, I made sure my good will and money bought you some very good years. And in return, I've had many good years with my wife. And I intend to have many *more* good years with her. So, you see, we all win, don't we?"

"Twenty-four years," Una ground out. "Twenty-four years that laid a curse on our town. Was it worth it, Adair? Was it worth what you've done to Selbane?"

His steps paused. "What do you mean? I've done nothing wrong."

"You set a curse on this town for your actions."

"What are you babbling about?" The first edge of anger bled into his voice. He took another step closer.

She backed up, thinking quickly. "The curse, the one Harper laid on our town. Was it worth it?"

"What curse?"

"Did you know she was a *buidseach*? A selkie witch among her clan? Because that's who you captured. And in return, she set a curse on our town. Did you never wonder about the bad times that had fallen on the town shortly after you were married? Did it never occur to you that it was more than just *lean times*? After twenty-four years of it?"

Adair's face contorted in anger as he sneered at her. "I knew nothing other than the fact that I was in love. Harper would never do what you say she could. I would have known."

"How?" Una challenged. She kept the sealskin clenched in her hands.

"Because she's my wife!" he snarled. "I own her! I know everything she does, everywhere she goes, everyone she talks to!" His free hand flexed into a fist at his side, then relaxed, flexed and relaxed. "If she laid a curse of this place, I would have known! Known and dealt with it." He raised his fist in front of him, holding it out for her to see. "Just like I'm going to deal with you, my dear. Now put the pelt down."

"No!" Una cried, thrusting the sealskin behind her. She backed up until her buttocks struck the wall of the fountain.

Adair lunged forward, grabbing at her with the hand not holding the candle. She twisted out of reach, and he lunged forward again.

The candle fell out of his holder and hit the ground. The flame went out.

For a moment, the light from her candle made him into a twisting, distorted demon from her shadow, then he was there, reaching for her throat with his hands, his face twisted in a snarl.

She ran to one side, intending to dart around him, but he sidestepped and closed his hands on her throat. She gasped, flailing at his head with the sealskin, but it cushioned her blows. He growled like an animal caught in a trap, and she screamed, once, before his fingers tightened so that no sound could crawl out anymore.

She grabbed at his fingers with her free hand, trying to twist them away from her skin. Spots began to dance in front of her vision as he squeezed, and she let go, grasping along the stone of the fountain wall instead, looking for something, anything, that she could use as a weapon.

"Adair, let her go!" a sharp voice commanded from behind them.

Adair twisted to look over his shoulder at the sound of his wife's voice, as Una's grasping fingers closed over one of the loose bricks. With her teeth pulled back from her lips, she slammed the brick into the side of his face at his temple, and he dropped like a stone. For a second, he almost pulled her down with him, but then his fingers slid from her throat, and she fell back, gasping for air.

She fell backwards into the statue, feeling the metal of the selkie woman's dress poking sharply into her shoulder blades, and clutched at her throat. She stared with bulging eyes as Harper's slim form stepped forward with a candle.

Then the light dwindled to a pinprick and went black.

CHAPTER 27

SHE OPENED HER EYES to see Lyall's concerned face hovering over her. A cool cloth was pressed against her brow. She moaned and shoved it away. She was aware of her other hand covered in a warm blanket and tried to raise it.

"You wouldn't let it go," Harper said in a dry voice and she stepped into view behind Lyall. Una twisted her head to the side and saw she was lying on a couch in the Town Hall building. The framed compass rose with the seal points hung on the wall across from her.

"Let go of what?" she ground out. Her throat burned, and each word felt like fire.

"My sealskin." Harper's voice was hard, holding none of her usual softness. "What exactly do you plan on doing with it?" Her voice turned sardonic. "Am I to be your selkie wife, too, along with your selkie husband?"

"You knew about him?" she asked. Lyall gave Harper a fearful look.

"Since that dinner. I knew he was something otherworldly, I just didn't know what. Then when he said he'd seen the plankton glow, I figured it out. Only sea creatures know about that phenomenon, and among them, only selkies hold it as a sacred event."

Una nodded wearily. Of course she had known. She was a *buidseach*, after all. "To answer your question, I intend to give your skin back to you." She held out the sealskin and waited for Harper to pounce on it.

But Harper only looked at her through wary eyes. "What do you want?" she asked in a careful voice, as if holding some strong emotion in check.

"For you to give me back my town. Release it and let us be."

Harper stared at her for several long moments. Lyall pretended to fuss with the cloth in her hands to avoid looking at her. Then slowly Harper held out her hand and reached for the sealskin, looking as if she expected it to be pulled back at any second.

"I felt it change hands," she whispered as her fingers closed around it. "I knew when he lost control of it, and it transferred to you." She closed her eyes and held the skin up to her face, inhaling deeply. "I've been looking for this for twenty-four years." Her voice held an incredulous wonder, as if she couldn't believe she was holding it again. She lowered it, and Una saw tears in her eyes.

She stared at Una for a long moment, then turned abruptly. "Leave. Now," she commanded. As she turned and left the room, she tossed over her shoulder, "A carriage awaits you outside." Then she was gone.

Una looked at Lyall, who gazed back with a shocked expression.

"Can you get up?" Lyall asked. Una nodded so fast it made her throat ache, then sat up. Lyall helped her to stand, and they quickly gathered their bags and left.

THE RIDE HOME WAS long, made longer by their exhaustion. By the time they made it to Una's house, it was still several hours before dawn.

"What will you tell your father?" Una asked wearily as she sank onto the bed, laying back to stare at the ceiling.

Lyall hovered near her feet, fidgeting with her fingers. "I'll tell him the truth: that it was a success. We found and returned Harper's sealskin to her." She look disheveled, her hair tangled in a bushy clump behind her. But she also looked proud: she stood straighter than before, with her chin lifted as she gazed at Una with a haughty expression.

Una smiled at her, then sighed. "Now I suppose the rest of it is in Harper's hands." She bent over and scrubbed her face with her palms. "I don't know what to do next," she admitted. "I've been working so hard to help break the curse that—"

"You need to talk to Ronan," Lyall said, so softly that Una almost didn't hear her.

She closed her eyes. "I'm going to pretend you didn't say that."

"No, I'm serious. You two shared something special. That True Mate bond."

Una felt tears prick her eyes at the mention of it. "That wasn't anything serious."

"It sounded serious to him."

Una opened her eyes, and a tear trickled down her cheek into the globe of her ear. "Well, it wasn't," she insisted stubbornly. "Otherwise he wouldn't have left."

"He'd just been given back the thing that meant most to him. You saw how Harper looked at her skin. Don't you imagine he had to be wondering how long he would have to wait to get it back, too?"

But Una didn't want to hear that. She just wanted to be alone with her thoughts and her pain. "I'm too tired to have this discussion right now, Lyall."

Lyall made a humph noise, then began taking off Una's shoes and tossing them haphazardly on the floor. "You may be too tired to talk, but I guarantee you'll be up the rest of the night thinking about it."

And she was right.

Long after Lyall had left to head back home and the sunlight broke through into day, Una lay on her bed unmoving except to wipe away the tears coursing down her cheeks. How could he leave? Even after all they'd been through? After everything they'd shared?

— *"Take it and be gone from here!"*—

She'd meant it, that was certain. But the way he'd looked at her. The emotion in his eyes when he looked at her, not at his sealskin. There had been a dark emotion there, something she'd once thought was love. But had that been wrong? She thought of his eyes as he held her after lovemaking, the depths of emotion in them. Surely he couldn't fake that. It had felt sincere, had felt so real. As real as her hands on his body, as real as his mouth on hers. Something she could reach out and touch if she wanted to. Just like he'd touched his sealskin.

He had said she was his True Mate, the other half to himself, the most precious thing he could find. And yet he'd left. He'd left the first chance he got... but had he really left? Or had he been sent away?

— *"Go! I was wrong about you."*—

She'd been angry and hurt and fighting back tears. Had wanted to hurt him as much as he'd hurt her. She'd lashed out the only way she knew how. And she'd attacked the one thing that bound him to her. Why should he stay when she acted as if he meant nothing to her? There was no reason to stay in the face of that kind of rejection.

Oh, goddess, what had she done?

Around midday, there was a knock at the door. Una roused herself, smoothing the tangle of her hair back from her face, and opened it, expecting Lyall or perhaps her uncle and aunt.

But it was Harper.

"May I come in?" Her voice was regal, and Una quickly plucked at her wrinkled dress to straighten it, acutely aware of the fact that she hadn't changed or bathed since the events of last night.

She stood back, and Harper glided into the room. Una cast a quick, critical eye over her home, realizing that Harper must see it as Ronan once had too, especially after living in the Mayor's manor house for so long.

But Harper merely looked around, taking it in.

"What can I do for you?" Una asked, but Harper ignored her. She stepped over to the mantel where Una's shrine to her father rested. She leaned forward, inspecting the brass sundial compass and the necklace laid over the top of it.

"There is powerful death magic here," she said, with a glance at Una, who frowned. "Some would pay dearly for it."

"Why are you here?" Una asked, her voice sharp. It was one thing to entertain visitors, but this new Harper made her feel uneasy, as if the other woman were something predatory and wild.

Harper turned her piercing gaze to Una, and the look froze any further words in her mouth.

"Last night, you asked for something in return for my skin. Something for others, but not for yourself. Why?"

"What do you mean, why? This is my home."

"But you could leave. Go somewhere else, make it your home..?" Harper's words reminded Una of when Ronan had shared the same sentiment. It made her stomach twist in remembered pain.

She scowled. "It's my heart. I love this place. I could never leave it, and I don't want to see it die."

Harper pursed her lips together and made a low hum of understanding. Or was it disappointment? Una couldn't be sure.

"Is he dead?" she blurted out. "After we left. Did you...?"

Harper raised an eyebrow. "After you left, I gathered some things in a bag... some clothes, my sealskin, some important ledgers... and visited my husband's"—her mouth twisted as she said the word—"business partners in town.

Despite the late hours, they were quite interested in learning how Adair swindled them in the past, skimming money off their payments, moving money around to suit his purposes. It was how he got so wealthy." She smiled and her eyes held a dangerous glint. "He won't last long in this town."

"So you cursed him." It wasn't a question.

Harper's smile widened. "Greed was the curse he placed on himself. I just let the consequences come due. Don't worry, your town is safe."

Una let out a breath she didn't know she was holding. "Thank you."

"Don't thank me yet. You don't know why I'm here."

Una stiffened. "Then enlighten me." She felt she was treading on fragile ground, needing to step very carefully so as not to fall into a pit.

"You gave of yourself so that others could prosper. Where I come from, such things require a reward. A boon, if you will. So ask."

"Ask what?"

"What may I grant you, in return for giving me back my skin?"

Una stared at her with wide eyes. "I don't require anything. You said my town was safe, and that's all I—"

"There is something you want. Something left unresolved. This is your chance to make it right. I won't offer it again." Harper's voice sounded as if it was coming from very far away, and Harper realized she wasn't hearing her acquaintance from town but the selkie *buidseach*, with all her power behind her.

She closed her mouth, then closed her eyes to think. Her mind brought up an image of Ronan, standing shirtless by the sea next to her house. The sun shone on his pale skin and his hair waved like banners in the salty wind. He'd looked most at peace then, and it was her favorite memory of him.

"Ronan." The word left her lips in a whispered breath.

She opened her eyes to see Harper smiling at her with narrowed eyes.

"Ronan," Una said again. "I need to... I have to tell him something. But I don't know how to get in touch with him."

Harper cocked her head, as if listening to something in the distance.

Una continued, "I know he probably doesn't want to hear from me, probably can't stand the thought of me. But I have to let him know how I feel. I must let him know—"

"That you love him," Harper finished.

"That he is my heart," Una whispered, pressing her hands to her stomach. The emotions inside her churned at the thought of speaking to him again, and she had to push them aside to focus on Harper's words.

"I can give him that message for you." Harper moved towards the door.

"Wait!" In a flash of brilliance, Una had an idea. She rushed to the mantle and removed the necklace from the compass, setting it carefully in a small pile on the mantle. She closed the box containing the sundial compass and passed it to Harper, who stowed it away in the pocket of her dress.

"Give him this and tell him... tell him..." Una's mind raced for the right words, for she felt her time was up. "Tell him to keep this, so he doesn't forget me."

"Very well," Harper said. "I leave you now." She turned and walked towards the door.

"One last thing," Una said. Harper turned with a questioning look. "Why didn't you ever fix my Uncle—Lord Prion's sealskin? When he came to you, the day you were... captured. Was it because he led them to you?"

"That was part of it, yes."

Una cocked her head. "But that wasn't the full reason?"

Harper sighed and clasped her hands together. "The kind of magic required to repair something like that is very powerful—it would take a very strong *buidseach* to attempt such a thing. Understand that the stronger the spell, the more dangerous it is. I wasn't entirely sure I could navigate that spell accurately. If I failed even a small part of it, I risked death. So I told him it couldn't be done, which was partly true. And after he brought that horrible man down on me, I certainly wasn't inclined to try."

Una nodded, and Harper turned back towards the door.

"Will I ever see you again?" Una asked, unsure what answer she actually wanted to hear.

Harper stopped, but didn't turn around. "Not if I am very lucky," she said in a dry tone. She opened the door, swept out of it, and was gone.

CHAPTER 28

RONAN SWAM THROUGH THE icy water, followed by the gray seal that was Ceannas. His ears picked up a clicking noise, followed by three short barks. He modified his course, angling next to the rocky shoreline, and then beached himself on the pebbled beach of the clan's cave.

It was a large cave, large enough to hold all several hundred of his clan members. They were sectioned off into small, cliquish groups, dominated here or there by large males who grunted and barked at each other. Mating season was coming, and all the males were getting restless.

Some Anchors lounged naked in their human forms, their eyes scanning the waterline, ever alert.

Ronan eased himself onto the beach, waddling awkwardly on his flippers as the sand slid out from beneath him. Then he reached down, unhooked his fasteners with his teeth, and stood up, gathering his sopping wet pelt to his chest as he went. Behind him, he heard Ceannas doing the same, but he didn't look back as he strode among the selkie seals.

He nodded at the Anchors he recognized, noting that there were a few more young men around than there had been before. He'd make a note to ask Ceannas about that later.

Ahead, he saw a man and woman laying naked on the rocks, and he made his way to them.

Clasping a hand to his heart, he went down on one knee. "My King Righ, Queen Mairi, well met."

They nodded their heads at him in acknowledgment. "Well met, Ronan," King Righ said. His long grey hair fell to his waist. His wife, Mairi, gazed at Ronan with dark eyes that matched her dark hair, but said nothing as she lay back against her husband's stomach.

The King and Queen commonly lounged together in human form when the clan was resting, and it was fortunate for Ronan, as he shared his news. He rose to his feet.

"My King, Lord Prion has accepted the siren necklace as a sign of peace. We have only to sign peace treaties with them and—"

"We are already ahead of you there, Ronan," King Righ said with a gentle smile. He nodded his head to indicate someone behind Ronan. "Ceannas has already brokered that date and time."

Ronan glanced behind him and saw a naked Ceannas grinning wickedly. Ronan smirked. "It seems my absence was not missed."

"I wouldn't say that," Queen Mairi spoke up. She had a small frown on her face. "I hear a human stole your skin? But obviously you have gotten it back." The statement wasn't a question.

Ronan nodded, unsure of how to proceed. The Queen could be as mercurial as her son, Prion, and he would need to speak discreetly around her.

"So there is no problem any longer." Queen Mairi's voice held a flat finality.

Ronan nodded again. "I took care of it, my Queen."

"Good. See that it doesn't happen again."

Ronan bit back the surge of irritation that rushed through him. As if he'd asked to be kidnapped? Or had enjoyed the torment of not knowing where his skin was?

But you did enjoy it, his mind whispered. He'd enjoyed many parts of it. The thought brought to him the image of Una laying on the bed, her hair spread about on the pillow below him, her mouth forming his name. He closed his eyes. This was not the image he wanted to remember. He wanted all thoughts of her banished from his mind, and he pushed aside the tide of grief that threatened to overwhelm him.

Through this, the King and Queen observed him carefully, their faces giving away nothing.

He opened his eyes again and met their gazes. "It won't."

"But you left something behind, yes?" Ceannas's voice spoke up behind him.

He turned and gave his second a warning glare. "Leave it alone, Ceannas."

"What is this?" Queen Mairi asked. "What did you leave behind?"

"His True Mate, Highness." Ceannas's voice rang out in the cave. In his peripheral vision, Ronan saw several heads turn in their direction. Inwardly, he winced.

King Righ cocked his head in surprise. "Ronan, is this true?"

He sighed. "Yes, my King." Even to his ears, his voice sounded very tired.

"Why did you leave her?"

"I didn't," he ground out between gritted teeth. Must he bare his soul to his entire clan now? "She commanded me to leave."

"And you listened." Again, the statement wasn't a question.

An image of Una flashed through his head: her standing with her back to him, arms wrapped around her ribs as if trying to hold herself together, like she might break into hundreds of pieces if she let go. Her shoulders were tense, as if waiting for a blow that never came. She had been in pain then, he could tell. And he had done nothing to ease it. What kind of True Mate was he to let her stay in pain like that?

She'd lashed out, he knew. Had tried to hurt him the same as he had hurt her with his carelessness. He'd been so surprised at seeing his skin again, at getting it back before they'd lifted the curse, that he hadn't had time to think, hadn't had time to process his feelings, complicated as they were.

But he had left her. In pain. Feeling betrayed. He didn't deserve a mate like her. Didn't deserve to call her his love if he only ran when she needed him most.

Pain wracked his body at the thought, and on the tail of it, hope. Maybe all was not lost? She couldn't have meant what she said, not if she looked like she did when she said it. Surely he could still win her back. Surely.

"At my folly, King Righ." His voice was strong when he answered this time. He knew what he had to do. "I can fix it, though. I just need a little time."

"You abandon us, then ask for more time?" Queen Mairi asked in a lofty voice. "That's bold of you."

But Ronan knew better than to rise to her bait. He watched as King Righ stroked a hand down her arm, quieting her. It was a subtle correction, and he was surprised they let him see it—they were usually a united front, and never let others see their open gestures of affection.

"It is, my Queen. But I ask it on behalf of my mate, the one I left behind. I must rectify my leaving. I left her in pain."

"Then go to her," Queen Mairi said with a small wave of her hand. She spoke in an indifferent voice, as if it mattered little to her. But behind her, King Righ smiled and nodded at him.

He clasped his hand over his heart again, bowed, and turned. He strode past Ceannas, who wore a smug smirk.

"I need to see you *now*," Ronan growled. "Back at the cave."

Startled, Ceannas turned and followed him. They donned their sealskins, changed, and plunged back into the water.

CHAPTER 29

UNA RETURNED HOME THAT afternoon tired but happy. She had done good business that day, with the tide levels having risen back to what they were years ago. The docks had flooded slightly, making the seamen grumble about the extra work, but she was glad for it. She knew good things were to come.

The real talk of the town hadn't been the rising water table, however. That had been minor compared to the gossip floating around about the Mayor. Nobody had seen him since the party. The men had convened at the local tavern to discuss future actions, and all the options put forth demanded jail time from the constable.

But nobody had found Adair. The drunken group that had stormed his house, demanding answers, had been met by his confused house servant. He told the men that Adair had returned after his wife had already left, taking the house's horse and cart himself, with nary a servant to accompany him. And after Harper had visited several of the local businessmen, telling them of Adair's treachery, she had vanished, too.

Una had heard this from several customers, who all seemed to think themselves the first ones to promote the news. She had "oh no!"ed and looked appropriately shocked, always smiling secretly once they were gone.

Then Una had concluded her day with the best business she'd had in nearly three years and found a note nailed to her door.

"Meet me tomorrow in the cave. I have to say goodbye."

The note had rocked her. She knew immediately who wrote it, despite it lacking his name at the bottom. But she knew. Her heart had twisted painfully. So he would give her a proper goodbye after all? She supposed she should be grateful. But it just gave her a headache, and she went to bed.

She woke the next day and immediately reread the note again. And again. And again. Each time, she felt like she would glean something new from it, some nuance she had missed the night before. But there were no new revelations.

Just the note and his scrawled handwriting, so obviously unused for a long time.

"I have to say goodbye."

The words hurt. Hurt her heart and hurt her head. To lose him only to get the chance to see him one more time, and then lose him again? She didn't know if she could take it.

"I have to say goodbye."

It had broken her heart—what was left of it to break, that is—and she'd spent the day vacillating between racking sobs and anger. She spent the day at her house, fretting over what to say, what to wear, what to do. Of course she would go—the thought never crossed her mind not to. She longed for him too much to turn away the chance to see him again. She was hungry for the opportunity in a way that ate at her soul, gnawed at her insides like a hungry rat.

But how to play it? She was too proud to grovel. She would not beg him to stay, regardless of how her heart cried out at the thought. But she couldn't ignore the fact that he had left her, had gone away when she needed him the most to be strong. She would have to address that. If she had time.

Time!

She looked out the window to find the day had already passed and was edging into the latter half of the day. She had spent so much time fretting over the meeting that she had almost missed it.

If he was still there.

If he would wait for her.

She gathered herself together, making sure to tightly pin up her hair so it wouldn't tangle in the wind. Going to the mantle to put on the necklace he'd given her, she found it wasn't where she'd left it. She searched the floor on her hands and knees, checking under the furniture there was no way it could have fallen under, but to no avail. It was gone.

She suddenly remembered Harper's voice, coming to her as if from very far away. *"There is powerful death magic here. Some would pay dearly for it."* But the necklace had been there after Harper had left, Una was sure of it.

It didn't matter. With a pang of sorrow at having lost the last thing she had of him, she opened her door and went down to the boat. The sun shone on the horizon, low in the sky. It wasn't yet time for colors to bleed into the horizon, but dusk wasn't far off. By the time she would reach the cave—

—if he was still there—

—it would be close to night.

— "This changes everything."—

It certainly did.

She settled herself into the boat and picked up the oars.

She was ready for battle.

CHAPTER 30

UNA MADE HER WAY down the inlet to the cave where they first met and docked her boat as she had that day she'd come searching for mussels, hiding it amid the tall clumps of sea grasses. As she had rowed, *how could this have happened?* slowly made way for *how could he do this to me?* Her anger, which flared hotter with every stroke of the oars, had pushed aside her desire to see him.

She dashed the pair of tear tracks from her cheeks with an angry swipe. *He won't get the satisfaction*, she thought. And she marched towards the mouth of the cave.

But as she approached, she saw a flickering glow coming from inside. She looked around but saw nobody waiting for her. The wind blew a steady song over her clothing, making her skirt billow in the salty breeze—*keep going*, it called. *Keep going.* Slowing, she eased her way to the entrance and peeked in.

Inside was lit with what looked like a thousand stars. Small candles sat in clusters on every boulder, clumped together in notches in the walls. Brightest of all was a group of candles that sat atop the boulder where she'd once hidden to see a selkie change his skin. It sat like a beating heart in the glow of the cave.

She felt her soul still. The anger she'd carried and fanned inside her dimmed and went out as she gazed around her in amazement. Who had done this? And when? She crept inside, closer to one of the boulders, and saw the candles had pooled wax dripping down the sides of the rock. They'd obviously been here for some time, waiting for her.

"Do you like it?" The voice came from behind her, and she closed her eyes, savoring the feel of it in her ears. She didn't know how badly she'd ached to hear him again until this moment.

Turning, she opened her mouth to speak, but nothing came out. He stood in the doorway in his white shirt and drawstring pants. The same clothes she'd seen him change into the day they'd met.

It seemed a portent, another sign that he was truly leaving her for the life she'd forced him to leave behind for a while. She felt a traitorous tear trickle down her cheek and hid her face in her shoulder to wipe it away.

"It's incredible," she breathed. And it was true. The sheer beauty of the cave, of him being in here with her, made her heart hurt.

He stepped forward, and she saw he was barefoot. It made her smile a little. Of course he was.

He gestured around the cave. "I wanted it to be beautiful for you. The way it's beautiful for me." He paused, then stared earnestly into her eyes. "The way *you* are beautiful to me."

She blushed and ducked her head. This was not what she wanted from him. She wanted a quick goodbye, something easy for him that would let him leave her life as quickly as he came into it. She didn't want tenderness and uncertainty. That wasn't him. That wasn't the Ronan she knew.

"That's not why you're here, though," she said, willing her voice to be strong. She straightened her back. "I'm glad you're safe," she added. She longed to run her fingers over his ribs. To let her hands roam over his chest and up to his face, to be sure he was really here, safe and whole.

He nodded. "Thanks to you, I am. But you're right. I didn't come to... I wanted to say goodbye." He nodded again, as if steeling himself for what was to come. "And I have."

She nodded, then paused. "So that's it? You're just going to leave now? Slip into your skin and into the ocean forever?"

He shook his head.

"What then?" she asked, feeling the anger rise in her. This was the battle she'd come ready for, and she meant to have it. "You're not even going to tell me goodbye?"

He shook his head again. "No. And I'm not going to."

"What?" She couldn't believe what she was hearing. Surely she must have heard him wrong. "What do you mean?"

"I already said my goodbyes. Here, earlier. I said goodbye to my clan and to my family. I passed along some final advice to Ceannas and gave him my blessing. I know he'll do a great job protecting the clan in my absence."

Absence. The word rang in her mind. Not his absence from her. From *them*.

"This wasn't how it was supposed to go," she whispered, staring. She felt unsteady, as if the cave were shifting beneath her feet. "You were...I thought..."

"You thought what?" He frowned at her.

"That you were saying goodbye to me!"

He shook his head. "How could I ever say goodbye to you? You mean more to me than my sealskin. You are my whole heart. Without you, I am nothing, a shell, a hole. I could say goodbye to you no more than I could part from my soul."

Una reeled, taking a step back and steadying herself with a hand on the nearest boulder. This was the last thing she'd expected to hear. And to hear him speak what was in her own heart, to hear her secret whispered back to her... It was more than she ever could have hoped for.

"You are my heart too," she whispered. She saw his eyes flicker in the light as something dark passed through them, some strong emotion she now had a name for. How could she ever have thought it to be anything else?

He took two large steps toward her, and suddenly she was in his arms. He was holding her, supporting her, as his lips crushed down on hers. He poured his passion into the kiss, his love, his feeling for her, and it rocked her to her core.

She answered, tasting his tongue and matching him ardor for ardor as she poured her sadness and fear and love back into him. His hands stopped supporting her and took on an urgency as they clenched in the fabric at her waist.

"Oh, Una," he murmured against her lips. "I can't stand it. I need you."

She made a low noise of wanting and began pawing at the hem of his shirt, pushing it over the smooth skin of his stomach, pushing it higher over his strong chest. He stepped back from her and, in one motion, shoved it over his head so that he stood bare-chested in the candlelight.

Her lips parted as she took him in. He watched her watching him, his eyes dark with need and love, and untied the drawstring of his pants. Keeping eye contact with her, as a slow smile played along his lips, he hooked his thumbs in the waistband and pushed them down over his hips. She stared at the V-shaped muscles that flexed at his abdomen as he stepped out of his pants and tossed them to the side. His erection pointed huge and dark in the dim light. Then he stepped forward and went to his knees in front of her.

She stared into his eyes as he gathered the hem of her dress in his hands and slid them up her legs. Slowly, oh so slowly, his hands glided along her skin as he rose, caressing her bare knees, thighs, and higher. His palms slid over her buttocks as he pulled the dress higher, and she closed her eyes to savor the sensation.

"No," he murmured. "Look at me. I want to watch you."

She opened her eyes and met his, trying to slow her breathing. The touch of his hands on her burned, as if he left a trail of fire up her body. The dress came higher, and she felt the cool air on her breasts as he lifted the material over her head. She reached up and took out the pin holding her hair up. She shook her head, letting her hair fall to brush against her back.

Ronan made a guttural noise of appreciation. "I love your hair when it's down," he murmured as he slid his hand up the back of her head to grip a fistful of the silky mass. He leaned forward and pressed his lips against hers again, softer this time, as he stepped forward. The roughness of the hair on his chest brushed her nipples, and she moaned into his mouth.

"Now, Ronan. I want you now."

Ronan smiled and his expression was full of dark promises. "Gladly, my lady."

He dipped his head and took one nipple into his mouth. She moaned as he suckled, kneading the other breast with his hand. "God, I love your body," he breathed. She gripped the hair at the back of his head in a gentle fist in response.

He sucked and nipped, and she made a small squeak of surprise. Grinning up at her, he straightened, and then pulled her into his arms. Her legs wrapped around his waist. He pressed her back against a boulder, and she felt the coldness of the stone seeping into her skin.

"Too cold!" she gasped, "and kinda... painful." He chuckled against her mouth. She wriggled her hips against him, feeling his hardness at the tender junction between her legs. He gripped her thighs firmly and walked her across the cave, towards a blanket that lay spread on the ground.

As he lay her carefully down, she glanced at it in surprise. "You've thought of everything," she said with an arched eyebrow.

He grinned at her in response and lay so that his body covered hers. "You have no idea how long I've been thinking about this." His voice was a growl that sent shivers into her stomach, tightening things low in her body.

He kissed her, and there was nothing gentle about it. His tongue plunged into her mouth, flicking across the roof of it, gliding across her tongue. She arched under him, feeling his hands slide down the side of her to cup her hip in his large hands.

Her fingers caressed the strong muscles of his back, feeling them ripple under her touch, and she marveled at the man she held on to. How careful he was with her and how intense.

"How long have you been thinking about it?" she teased with a grin.

Ronan leaned over to suckle on her earlobe, sending sweet shivers down her spine. "Since you showed me your father's shrine."

She pulled back in surprise. "That feels like ages ago! Before I gave you back your skin even."

He chuckled into her ear. "That's right."

She lay back and pressed his chest to stop him. "You knew? Even then?" she asked in a wondrous voice. Her eyes searched his intently.

His smile slipped from his face as he regarded her. "Even then." He leaned forward and pressed his forehead against hers, closing his eyes. "Heart of my heart," he whispered.

"Heart of my heart," she whispered back. She felt amazed and warm throughout her body, consumed by the enormity of his feelings for her.

She scrunched her shoulders from side-to-side, digging them into the sand beneath the blanket. "This is lovely," she said, indicating with her gaze the candle-lit cave around them.

"All for you, my lady." He kissed her and slid his body down hers, toward her legs. With dark eyes, he flashed a smile, then pushed her thighs open so he could slide low between them. His tongue glided along the junction of her thighs, down through the bush of hair to the sweet spot between her legs.

She gasped as his tongue flicked once, twice, three times against her, then slid in one long stroke upward. He dipped his head, using his nose to rub at the hard nub of her, making her squirm. He clamped his hands on either side of her thighs to hold her still.

"Don't run away yet," he admonished with a smile in his voice.

"Isn't that my line?" she retorted, and then gasped as he sucked hard on her clitoris. "Ah! Ok! I give."

He laughed against her and laved her with his tongue, making her writhe. One hand slid under her buttocks, gripping her, and the other hand delved two fingers deep inside her. He spread his fingers wide, making her feel full and tight, and slid the fingers slowly in and out of her. As she moaned his name, he grinned up at her, but she had her head back and her eyes closed, surrendering to the sensations.

He began thrusting faster, licking her clitoris with his tongue as he pumped his fingers inside her, matching her breathless cries as she came closer and closer. Finally she came with a cry, shuddering and shaking with the force of her climax. His fingers slowed, becoming softer and gentler, before he withdrew. He slid alongside her, careful not to lie on top of her, and pulled her head on his shoulder.

"You are a very talented man," she murmured sleepily. She kissed the pectoral muscle next to her face.

He grinned wickedly at her. "Oh, I have great and many talents. But you make it easy. I want you to be happy." He lifted so that he leaned over her. His eyes searched hers, and she saw uncertainty there for the first time. "Una. I want you to be happy, in all ways."

"You make me happy," she said, the smile sliding from her face. This was a new Ronan, one she wasn't accustomed to seeing, and she wasn't sure what he was getting at. He obviously wanted to say more, but seemed to struggle to find the words.

"I want to always make you happy. For every day, for every year you are alive. For as long as we live." She smiled at him, and he took her hand in his, pressing it to his bare chest. "Marry me, Una. For real, this time, not for pretend. I want it to be real with you."

She sat up, staring at him, feeling like her heart would burst from emotion. "Are you serious? You really want this?"

"I am married to the sea. That I cannot change—"

"And I wouldn't want you to," she began, but he shook his head to silence her.

"I can't change what I am. But I *have* changed. You have made me a new man. And I want to spend the rest of my life with you, married to you, forever."

"Forever forever?" she asked with a small smile.

He grinned down at her. "Forever forever."

She threw herself at him, wrapping her arms around his shoulders as she kissed him deeply, passionately. "Yes!" she cried. "Of course I'll give you forever!"

He wrapped his hands around her ribs, and the pressure nearly crushed her. But she didn't mind. She reveled in the feel of his body pressed to hers, knowing that he was fully hers for as long as she lived. That he would never leave her again.

His kiss became more urgent, and he pressed her back onto the blanket. Her hands fisted in his hair as he shifted to ease himself between her legs. She felt the hardness of him pressed against her and groaned as he slid up and down the length of her.

"You're so wet," he marveled as he kissed his way down her neck.

In response, she gripped his buttocks and pulled him tight against her. He responded with ardor, sliding inside her so quickly it made her cry out with pleasure. He filled her, making her feel tight and warm and beautiful. She gripped him as he slid in and out of her, slower at first, then faster as she urged him on with her cries.

They came together, their voices echoing around the cave like a chorus as they climaxed together. Ronan felt the True Mate bond tighten almost painfully inside him, and he knew she felt it, too. Suddenly he was aware of two sets of lungs gasping for air, two hearts beating in frantic rhythm as their bodies shuddered together and then slowed. He felt, rather than heard, her murmur of languid satisfaction through the bond between them.

"I can feel you inside of me," he said in wonder.

She made a happy murmur of assent. To test the feeling, he sent a wave of love through the bond and saw her shiver as she received it. He couldn't hear her thoughts, he realized, not exactly, but he could feel what she felt and receive similar feelings from her.

This was the release he'd been waiting for. This was the climax of their love.

Afterward, he remained inside her, leaning to one side so she didn't have to bear his full weight. She grinned up at him.

"That was lovely." She felt a little drunk, buzzed and sleepy in the afterglow. The bond between them was alight in punch-drunk sensation.

"I agree." He kissed the tip of her nose. "But not as lovely as you."

He sat up, sliding out of her, and she made a noise of disappointment. She rolled on her side, propping her head on one hand as she watched him walk in all his glorious nakedness over to the alcove on the wall where the candles were most clustered. Where the beating heart flickered.

He picked up a small bundle and returned to sit next to her on the blanket. She sat up, staring at his hands, as he folded open the fabric to reveal its contents. Inside was a folded, oily pelt.

"Ronan," Una gasped. "Your sealskin?"

He nodded.

"It's lovely. But I don't understand."

"I want you to have it, Una."

"I can't take this!" She looked at him with wide, shocked eyes.

"It's mine to give to whom I see fit. But I want this to be a peace treaty between us, a promise that we'll always be together, on each other's side, putting each other before ourselves, always." He looked deep into her eyes. She saw the depth of his love for her in his eyes, shining like the candlelight around them. "You took this once from me. Now I give it freely to you."

Una put her hand on the sealskin and closed her eyes. She felt Ronan's hand cover hers.

"I accept."

Ronan leaned forward so that their foreheads touched.

"Always?" he asked.

"Always."

And she meant it.

EPILOGUE

THE DOOR CHIMED AS it swung open, and Una privately thought she wasn't so sure Ronan's bell idea had been a good one. All day long her shop door had been chime-chime-chiming its way into her thoughts and it was distracting.

This time, when she looked up with a forced smile, it changed to a genuine one instead. "Lyall!" Lyall flounced into the shop, holding the hand of a blushing young man.

"And... Lucas, isn't it?"

"Y-y-yes, m-m'am," he stammered, looking as if he wanted to be anywhere but here. "L-Lucas Hew."

Una narrowed her eyes at Lyall, who grinned at her, then nodded her head. "Yes, I remember. Dr. Scott's intern, right?"

Lucas nodded. His cheeks were two bright red apples against his freckled face.

"What brings you in this afternoon, Lyall?" Una asked in an innocent voice. She had an idea, but didn't want to say it aloud.

"I just wanted to know if you'd be going to the new Mayor's swearing in this afternoon," Lyall said. She swung the hand holding Lucas's with a meaningful look at Una.

Una nodded. So it was like that, was it?

"I was thinking of closing up shop early today. If Ronan lets me. He's a task-master for work."

"Am I now?" came a smooth voice behind her. His tone sent shivers down her back, which she hoped wasn't noticeable to Lyall and her new beau. Through the True Mate bond, she felt a flash of desire that curled like a warm ember in her stomach.

Ronan stepped up close behind her, sliding one hand possessively around her waist. The other brushed back a tendril of hair so that he could kiss her neck. That time, she did shiver, and Lyall's grin widened.

"Con-congratulations," Lucas said to Ronan. At Ronan's questioning look, he added, "On your marriage?"

Ronan chuckled and squeezed Una's waist behind the counter. She shifted her weight so that her back brushed against his chest and he chuckled again. "Oh, right, that. I'd almost forgotten about it." Una scowled at him over her shoulder and elbowed him in the stomach.

It had been a quiet ceremony at Una's house, with only her Aunt Leannan and Lyall in attendance as her Uncle Hugh had performed the commitment vows. Lyall had fashioned Una's gown, a simple white shift that sat off her shoulders and flared like a mermaid's tail at the bottom. She and Ronan had barely heard her Uncle's voice as he made them repeat their statements of love and affection to each other—their eyes had remained locked on each other's the entire time.

Una shivered as she remembered the way Ronan had sent the pulses of adoration and lust through the True Mate bond while they gazed at each other. Though they had only been True Mated for a short time, she wondered how she had ever felt whole without the bond between them, showing her Ronan's feelings like an open door to his soul. It was the most intimate of unions, and she couldn't imagine ever being without it.

Ronan grinned at her, then at Lyall and Lucas. "And you two will be at the Inauguration festival too, I take it?"

Lyall smiled broadly. "We're going *together*." She wiggled her eyebrows at Una, who tried to hide an answering grin. Lucas smiled at Lyall, who smiled back at him. For a moment, the two just stared goofily at each other.

Ronan cleared his throat, and Lucas startled, facing them with another blush on his cheeks. "I hope you two have a good time. We will certainly be there."

"Who knew Constable Skene would have political aspirations?" Una mused.

"Father says he will be the best town Mayor in at least twenty years," Lyall said in a sarcastic voice. Lucas nodded, but looked slightly green at the mention of Lyall's father, Una noticed. She smiled to herself. She hoped he wouldn't be too hard on Lyall's newest suitor. Surely a doctor's apprentice should be good enough for his daughter.

"And then to have your birthday party a few days later?" Ronan said to Lyall. "This town won't know what to do for the rest of the year." Lyall blushed prettily, and he grinned at her. "Tell your father I'll be by with that fish shipment tomorrow." His hand tightened on Una's waist. "I have some other news for him as well, but it can wait until then."

Una knew that meant selkie news. Her husband may have forsworn his Anchor duties, but Ceannas still kept him abreast of current events. She knew Ronan's clan would move on soon, what they called The Migration, and that had him slightly on edge as this would be the first time in fifty years he wasn't present for the trip.

Lyall and Lucas said their farewells and stepped out of the shop, with the bell tinkling merrily behind them.

"Do you miss it?" Una asked softly, staring at the closed door.

Behind her, she felt Ronan's chest rise in a sigh that tickled her ear. "Sometimes," he admitted, "when I change and swim with Ceannas. It's a bit lonely not being Anchor any longer, not living with them anymore. I'll miss seeing them every day." His arms snaked around her ribs to hug her tightly from behind. He buried his face in her neck and inhaled the scent of her. "But I know where I belong."

She smiled and looked down at his large hands placed over her stomach. She knew right where she belonged, too, and it was in his arms.

She turned into his embrace and pulled his head down to hers.

They were exactly where they both needed to be.

Please feel free to leave a review for this book on Amazon and Goodreads!

Head to the next page for a free preview of *Saving the Selkie's Heart*, available December 2022!

FREE PREVIEW OF SAVING THE SELKIE'S HEART

LYALL PULLED THE SEALSKIN from the bag, marveling at the weight of it, even dry. She held it up in front of her, inspecting. It was small, the size of her torso, and she had no idea how something so small would fit her body. The pelt was a dark gray with small black spots dotting the area above what seemed to be the tail flippers. The fur was glossy, silky underneath her hands, and the dark gray blubber underneath was dried and stiff.

How did this work?

She shook the skin, then draped it over her front like an apron and waited for the magic to happen.

Nothing.

She held out her arm and draped it over. It covered her from shoulder to wrist, and the flippers hung limply down either side.

Nothing.

Knowing it would be useless, she tried the same motion on the other arm, but again, nothing happened.

She growled in frustration. She'd never been allowed to see the selkie Anchors change when they visited, though she'd tried peeking from the house windows. But the shoreline was hidden from view by the bluff, and she'd never seen anything.

Maybe she was wearing it wrong?

In a flash of inspiration, she swung it around the back of her like a cloak and draped it over her shoulders so that the side flippers lay across her collarbones. As her hand lowered, she felt something sharp scrape across her palm. When she looked at it, she realized small hooks made of something white, like bone, ran down the length of the sealskin. After inspecting the other side, she saw small fasteners running parallel to the hooks.

Maybe she had to fasten the two together?

The waves whispered as they slid over her skin as she forced her chilled fingers to fasten the tiny hooks, what felt like dozens of them, to get the skin to close around her like a coat. Then she held it in place and reached up to pull the flattened head over her own blonde curls.

She waited, feeling the water lap at her ankles with icy teeth.

A tingling sensation crept over the back of her neck, like ants crawling over her skin. She twisted her head, trying to get rid of the feeling, but it intensified. It spread across her shoulders, everywhere the pelt touched, then continued down her arms and spine.

This is it! she thought with a feral grin.

She closed her eyes, surrendering to the change.

But as the tingling encompassed her body, it started to change, becoming more intense, sharper. It felt like bees were stinging her and she cried out as the sharp sensations pierced her skin.

She curled forward, falling to her knees as the stinging intensified. Then she realized, something strange was happening to her arms. They felt shorter, stronger as she lurched onto her hands so that they bore the weight of her upper body. Behind her, her legs involuntarily stretched out and she began to cry. Her legs burned as they fused together, turning into one strong tail with two flippers on the end.

She was being consumed by fire and her mind raced to figure out how to end it. Pain was everywhere, turning her brain into a single alarm of terror. She had one single thought—*what's happening to me?*—before the change crashed over her and everything went black.

IT WAS DARK WHEN she became aware of herself again. Her mind felt sluggish and slow as she tried to figure out where she was. The pebbles of the beach underneath her were like small, hot balls and she longed to cool her skin in the water that lapped at her head.

She tried to raise herself up, intending to crawl into the water to relieve the pressure, but her body wouldn't respond. Her entire being felt like it belonged to someone else as she tried to move her legs to push herself forward. But instead, she only managed to roll herself on one side, tipping over like a barrel.

She let out a startled cry as she rolled and was startled to hear a strange hoarseness to her voice. The sound she'd let out sounded like a bark rather than a human's cry. She tried to lift her legs again and she rolled over on her back, half submerging herself in the sea. She squinched her eyes shut against the brine of it and wriggled harder.

Immediately she felt lighter, more in control of herself. She wriggled her body again, trying to use her hips to lurch herself further into the water, and it worked. She slipped fully under as a wave crashed over her, carrying her forward into the dark coolness of the water.

It was like another world. She wriggled her body again and felt the pressure of the water change as she swam forward blindly. Angling upward, where she knew the surface to be, she tried to stand, knowing she was in shallow water still. But her legs couldn't find the sandy bottom.

Still, she managed to work her head above the churning water. Only then did she take a deep breath she hadn't realized she'd been holding and opened her eyes. She realized she was further away from shore than she'd been moments before and felt a moment of panic. Her parents had often warned her of the danger of rip currents that would carry her out to sea farther than she could swim, and she fought to keep herself from flailing in panic.

But her arms didn't feel right as she moved them, and she found herself slipping under the surface of the water again as another wave crashed over her. She scrunched her eyes shut at the last moment as her head submerged below water.

She fought to kick her legs to breech the surface again, but her body didn't work the way it was supposed to. In a panic, she thrashed, kicking and moving her arms as hard as she could, certain she'd been caught in a rip current that would pull her under forever.

In desperation, she opened her eyes, intending to kick her way to the surface with her dying breaths, if need be. But instead, she froze as she took in the sight of the sea floor below her.

Several feet down, she saw a clump of brain coral surrounded by an assortment of fish so brightly colored it was as if they had sunlight filtering down on them. She looked around, her panic momentarily forgotten, as she saw the strange world of life that had been hidden just below the surface.

It was like nothing she'd ever seen before and she hung, motionless in the water, letting the current push and pull her in whatever direction it wished as she took in the tableau in front of her.

How could she see under the water? And how was she able to hold her breath longer than she'd ever been able to before? She glanced around her and saw the darkness of the rest of the ocean stretching out before her. What else lay under the water? What exotic things could she find if she went a little further?

Motion caught her peripheral vision and she turned, sensing something moving close to her body. But as she turned, it turned with her, staying just out of sight. She cocked her head. It had looked like the tail of some great seal, the kind her father had taken her to look at from the cliffs south of Selbane. They had been lumbering and clumsy out of the water, but once in, they'd moved like bullets, darting and leaping in and out of the water as if they'd been born to it.

She craned her neck, bending her body nearly in half, impossibly limber, and saw the rest of her body. It was covered in glossy dark fur. Where her legs had previously been, now was a long body that tapered to two flippers clenched together as a tail.

She had done it! She had changed!

Then she remembered: she had to get to the surface. Instinctively she flicked her tail in a single, strong stroke, and she shot upward until her head broke the surface of the water.

She let out an explosive breath and hung there, unconsciously moving her arm flippers from side to side to keep herself afloat as her tail lazily moved in gentle motions.

Ducking her head below the water again, she consciously kept her eyes open. Immediately she saw, as if looking through clear glass, the life teeming under the surface of the water. Then she raised her head out again. Her sight changed, blurring.

Interesting. Obviously, her seal eyes were more accustomed to water vision than above-air vision. Gathering her breath, she dove beneath the surface again.

Now that she realized her body was a single, long muscle, moving through the water was easier. She tested her abilities, turning left, then right, aware of the movement of her flippers on either side as she torpedoed through the water with ease.

Turning wasn't so hard, she found, and neither was pausing to hang suspended in one place in the water—she held her position easily once she stopped trying to move forward. It was as if her body was made for motion, like it wanted to be moving as much as possible. The slightest effort propelled her forward at a surprising speed.

She became aware of the noises around her, the slight gurgling of the water as it rushed past her ears, the whoosh of the waves as they crashed above her head. And further out, just beyond what she could make out, small squeaks and barks.

That sounded like the noise she'd made on the beach. Maybe that meant she was close to others of her kind!

She swam to the surface, took a deep breath, and dove beneath the water, delighting in the effortless way she moved through the water. As she swam, she tried not to focus on the things she saw: the fish darting in and out of the coral reef below her, the large stones that sat like humped sentinels here and there, the thick chunks of driftwood that lay like discarded limbs.

Focus! she reminded herself. *You're trying to find others like you.*

The barks got louder as she followed them, twisting and turning through the water for the sheer joy of the movement. Then finally she saw them, slim shapes darting through the water in a large school.

She blinked and paused, hiding behind a half-submerged boulder to keep out of sight. How did she know whether those were seals or selkies? Then one darted close by her and she saw a small satchel tied around its neck, the fabric bottom bulging with its contents.

That had to be selkies, she thought. Seals had no trinkets or valuables to carry with them. She watched, feeling suffused with excitement, as the large group passed her. Then, as the throng began to thin, she swam forward and joined the end of the train.

She swam behind them, hearing the clicks and barks as they spoke to each other in the water. She'd keep quiet, observe everything about them, and hope they didn't realize she was a stranger among them. There was no telling what the Anchors would do if they found out she was the daughter of the prince.

Guilt twisted in her belly. Her father would be worried sick about her by now, after she didn't come home that night. An inquiry into town would reveal that she hadn't shown up for work at Madam Ruadh's shop either. But she steeled herself. She was doing all of this for him. He would come to see that later. And once she got the Great Elder to restore his sealskin, he would be so overjoyed, he wouldn't be nearly so angry that she'd risked herself to do it.

He will be grateful, she told herself firmly. He would be too busy changing back into a seal for the first time in over two decades to bother with punishing her.

Content with this knowledge, she swam on.

Continue reading *Saving the Selkie's Heart*, Book 2 in The Selkie Seas series, available December 2022!

FIERCE SELKIE ANCHOR CEANNAS must protect his clan during the Migration, a rite of passage that occurs every 50 years. When he discovers a runaway selkie, the daughter of his prince, he must figure out a way to divide his duties, especially when keeping her alive demands all his attention.

Lyall wants desperately to find out where she belongs. When the opportunity comes to visit the Great Elder and save her father's damaged sealskin, she sneaks away to join the clan in their Migration. The only problem? Being born a human, she hasn't the first clue how to survive on her own as a selkie!

The last thing Ceannas needs is babysitting duties, and Lyall only has eyes on her mission. But as Ceannas teaches Lyall how to exist in her new element, the attraction between them grows stronger. Can their love withstand their honor-bound duties? And what will it cost each of them to do so?

Saving the Selkie's Heart, available in ebook and print
December 2022

For info about new releases, please join my email list
(www.EllaRoseBooks.com/newsletter).

Afterword

Thanks so much for reading *Stealing the Selkie's Heart*! I fell in love with Ronan and Una from the moment I met them, and writing this story was the hardest one I've ever written. I really hope you enjoyed reading it, and if you want to start a discussion about it, feel free to email me at ellarose@ellarosebooks.com. Also, don't forget to leave a review on Amazon or Goodreads!

If you'd like to read more about this world, you should DEFINITELY sign up for my newsletter (http://www.EllaRoseBooks.com/newsletter) to get a free novella, *Losing the Selkie's Skin* (Prion and Leannán's story), and to stay up-to-date on all new and upcoming releases. I've got a few short stories set in The Selkie Seas world, and you can find out more about them on my website, www.EllaRoseBooks.com/Books.

Of all the social media channels, I'm most active on Facebook (http://www.facebook.com/EllaRoseBooks) and TikTok (@EllaRoseWrites), though I'm also on Goodreads (@EllaRoseWrites), Instagram (@EllaRoseWrites), and Pinterest (@EllaRoseWriter). My website is www.EllaRoseBooks.com. I look forward to seeing you around teh interwebz!

Acknowledgments

I am ever grateful for a God that answers promises.

This book would not have been possible without Cathy Yardley and her Rock Your Writing instruction (http://www.RockYourWriting.com)—you are worth your weight in cheese, my friend, and I can't wait to work on the next adventure with you!

Further thanks to my editor, Tiffany Tyer (http://reedsy.com/Tiffany-Tyer), whose encouragement and hard work made this book what it is. Any gaffs that you find, dear reader, is fully on me and not her.

And finally, to my friends and family who never gave up on me, even when I wanted to give up on myself. Know that I'm raising a toast in your honor now. And let us never be too old for fairy tales!

About the Author

Ella Rose is a paranormal romance author who loves kink, ink, and cake, and hopes you do too. She is a bi-sexual author writing through a Bi-Polar Disorder lens and thinks representation and mental health matter. Her first book, *Losing the Selkie's Skin* (A Selkie Seas prequel novella), is available in ebook on most retailers (http://books2read.com/losingtheselkiesskin). Her latest selkie short stories will appear in Dark Rose Press's *Worlds Apart* and Dragon Soul Press's *Beyond Atlantis* anthologies. She is a member of Romance Writers of America and the Paranormal Romance Guild.

You can follow her on:

- Facebook (http://www.facebook.com/EllaRoseBooks)

- TikTok (@ellarosewrites)

- Goodreads (@EllaRoseWrites)

- Instagram (@EllaRoseWrites)

- Pinterest (@EllaRoseWriter)

And find out more about her at www.EllaRoseBooks.com. To stay up-to-date on all things Selkie Seas, sign up for her newsletter (www.EllaRoseBooks.com/newsletter).